ALSO BY CORINNE MICHAELS

The Salvation Series
Beloved
Beholden
Consolation
Conviction
Defenseless
Evermore: A 1001 Dark Night Novella
Indefinite
Infinite

The Hennington Brothers
Say You'll Stay
Say You Want Me
Say I'm Yours
Say You Won't Let Go: A Return to Me/
Masters and Mercenaries Novella

Second Time Around Series
We Own Tonight
One Last Time
Not Until You
If I Only Knew

The Arrowood Brothers
Come Back for Me
Fight for Me
The One for Me
Stay for Me
Destined for Me: Arrowood/Hennington Crossover Novella

Willow Creek Valley Series
Return to Us
Could Have Been Us
A Moment for Us
A Chance for Us

Rose Canyon Series
Help Me Remember
Give Me Love
Keep This Promise

Whitlock Family Series
Forbidden Hearts
Broken Dreams
Tempting Promises
Forgotten Desires

Ember Falls Series
All Too Well
Here and Now
Against All Odds
Come What May
Won't You Stay

Co-Written with Melanie Harlow
Hold You Close
Imperfect Match

Standalone Novels
You Loved Me Once

against all odds

CORINNE MICHAELS

sourcebooks
casablanca

Copyright © 2025 Corinne Michaels
Cover and internal design © 2025 by Sourcebooks.
Cover design by Antoaneta Georgieva/Sourcebooks
Cover images © Nottomanv1/Getty Images, anand purohit/Getty Images, serkan6/Getty Images, Khaneeros/Getty Images, vector_ann/Getty Images, YOTUYA/Getty Images, photography by Linda Lyon/Getty Images

Sourcebooks and the colophon are registered trademarks of Sourcebooks.

All rights reserved. No part of this book may be reproduced in any form or by any electronic or mechanical means including information storage and retrieval systems—except in the case of brief quotations embodied in critical articles or reviews—without permission in writing from its publisher, Sourcebooks.

No part of this book may be used or reproduced in any manner for the purpose of training artificial intelligence technologies or systems.

The characters and events portrayed in this book are fictitious or are used fictitiously. Any similarity to real persons, living or dead, is purely coincidental and not intended by the author.

Published by Sourcebooks Casablanca, an imprint of Sourcebooks.
1935 Brookdale RD, Naperville, IL 60563-2773
(630) 961-3900
sourcebooks.com

Originally published by Corinne Michaels in 2025.

Cataloging-in-Publication data is on file with the Library of Congress.

Printed and bound in the United States of America.
LSC 10 9 8 7 6 5 4 3 2 1

*To the girls who made themselves small
to fit in spaces they didn't think they deserved to be in.
Take up space. Use your voice.
Be heard. You deserve it and more.*

CONTENT WARNING

Dear Reader,

It is always my goal to write a beautiful love story that will capture your heart and leave a lasting impression. However, I want all readers to be comfortable. Therefore, if you want to be aware of any possible CW, please scan the QR code below to take you to the book page where there is a link that will drop down. If you do not need this, please go forth and I hope you love this book filled with all the pieces of my heart.

CHAPTER 1
VIOLET

"So how was your trip?" Eleanor, my personal assistant, asks.

"It was...fine. Good, even," I manage, struggling to get that last part out.

Three weeks ago my husband came home and told me to pack my bags, that we were going away. He needed a break from the rigors of Hollywood and filming. Since his last movie had just wrapped, I was all too happy to spend three weeks away from it all.

The last four years have been a whirlwind for us. We went from Dylan being an out-of-work actor to him getting huge roles. But the money, fame, and constant hounding from the paparazzi were not something I was prepared for.

I hoped—for him—his break would come, but this has been out of my wildest dreams.

"That's good," she says as she grabs her tablet. "Do you want anything else from the store?"

"I would just prefer to go to the store, Eleanor. You don't need to run errands like that."

This is the part of it that I hate. The feeling of being trapped. When my husband and I were in the islands, it was like the world didn't exist. For the last three weeks, we could go out, have dinner, and not be bothered. It was truly amazing in that regard.

What wasn't amazing was that Dylan ignored me half the time.

He was always on his phone, always talking to his agent or publicist. I get it—he's important—but I miss having a husband.

I miss…him, or at least the man he used to be.

"I know you *can*, Mrs. Leone, but this is my job. I'll get the stuff for dinner. I know Mr. Leone requested chicken from that spot near where you used to live. I'll make that drive and then get whatever else you need."

I internally roll my eyes. Of course he wants her to drive an hour to get chicken. "You don't have to go near the pier—he can deal with whatever chicken you find from here," I say, sitting on the bed with a smile. "Truly, he'll never realize."

I wish people got to know the Dylan I knew. The one who would laugh as we made late-night fast-food runs. The guy who never cared about the name on a label and just bought what was on sale. The idea of a personal assistant was comical to him. Now he has a whole staff and has decided that I, at least, need Eleanor.

"It's not a problem. His assistant is busy, and we're a team."

Right. We're a team.

Too bad it doesn't feel like I'm part of that team.

I'm on the outside. The wife who isn't in the industry. The wife who doesn't want to put on a full face of makeup to run to the store. Who doesn't stand the right way so that they get the good angles. The wife who gets shredded online by people she's never met and is told she's not good enough for him.

I hoped when we were on our trip, I'd find that man I married seven years ago, the one who didn't care about any of that, who just loved me.

And he was in there at times.

Even the one night we had sex, it was perfunctory and distant. There was no connection between us, and as soon as we were done, he was back on his phone and ignoring me. I rolled over and cried silently until I fell asleep.

I sigh heavily and smile at Eleanor, knowing this isn't a battle I'll win. "Okay, he should be home in a few hours, so just let me know when you're heading out."

"Do you need me to unpack for you?"

"Thank you, Eleanor. Truly I appreciate it, but you don't have to do that." I'm perfectly capable of unpacking and doing things around the house, regardless of how much money we have.

"I don't mind."

I smile warmly at her. "I know, but if you have to go get him his special chicken, it's going to take you at least an hour. You can go, and I'll do whatever I need to here."

She nods. "I'll be back as soon as I can."

"Drive safe."

Eleanor leaves and I head upstairs. I unpack and put a load of laundry in—which I know will cause a stir, because the housekeeper keeps telling me I don't need to do it. Then I make the bed because, I swear, it feels better at night when you get in a made-up bed.

There's nothing else to do, so I make a bag of popcorn and plop my ass on the couch. I turn on the television and then hear the vibration of my cell phone, which I apparently left upstairs.

Crap.

I leap off the couch and run up the ridiculously polished staircase, focusing on not cracking my head open as I rush in case it's my parents, who are out of the country. But I miss the call anyway.

It was my best friend, Analeigh.

I get back downstairs, and before I can press the button to return her call, I freeze.

The phone begins to ring again.

But, I swear, I can't even register it.

My eyes are glued to the television as one photo slides to another.

"It can't be," I whisper, my throat growing tight.

The first photo comes back again, and the headline crawling across the bottom makes my bile rise.

Dylan Leone and Whitney Reisinger—a real-life couple after their movie? It seems so!

The phone begins to vibrate in my hand, and I answer: "Hello?"

"Violet! Are you okay? I just saw..." Analeigh is talking quickly.

"It's a lie, Ana. It's not...true. It can't be. True? Can it? I mean, this is photoshopped, right?"

I keep seeing Dylan's hand on her hip as he kisses her. It's probably an on-set photo. But...that's not the set. That's a beach.

They filmed the movie in the mountains a few weeks ago.

Another photo of Whitney and him, lying together, holding hands as she is taking the selfie, rolls onto the screen.

Another—this time he's wearing only a towel, and he's winking.

"I'm not sure," Ana says, but the tone tells me she's sure.

A tear trails down my cheek as my heart and my head get on the same page.

It's all true.

The gossip reporter appears on the screen and talks to the host. I turn the volume up.

"I mean, I'm not surprised, are you?" the reporter asks.

"I am a little. Wasn't he just on vacation with his wife?"

The first girl nods. "He was, which is why I bet these got leaked now. I'm sure Whitney was none too happy finding out her man was on the beach with his wife."

"Say that aloud one more time," the other host says with a laugh. "Her man? I mean, I feel bad for his wife."

"Look, Dylan Leone is the hottest thing in Hollywood right now. I'm not saying she should've expected this, but I'm *not* not saying she should've seen it coming."

I sink down on the floor, holding the remote, not even knowing whether Ana is still on the phone as I cry.

I didn't see it coming.

I didn't know he was cheating on me. For how long? Why? What did I do other than support him?

I gave him everything. I left my job. My life. My family. All to come here for him.

Everything was about him, and then *this is what I get?*

My phone rings again, and I glance down. The photo of us just three days ago pops up. Dylan is calling.

How nice of him? Dickhead.

I throw the phone as hard as I can, watching as it shatters, pieces of glass sliding against the hard floor. The shards mimicking my heart.

Broken.

There's nothing that man can say that I want to hear. Nothing that could make any of this okay.

He used me. We had sex just a few days ago, and he was sleeping with another woman.

The sick feeling in my stomach gets heavier, and I rush to the bathroom, where I empty my stomach.

I hate him.

I hate that I ever loved him and trusted him.

I don't know how long I sit on the floor in the bathroom. The tears keep falling as my entire life slips away in front of me.

"Violet!" I hear Analeigh calling. "Violet? Where are you?"

I stand, forcing myself out of the bathroom and moving toward my best friend, who's standing in my entryway. When we see each other, we stop.

Tears are filling my vision, making it hard to see, but it doesn't matter, because she rushes toward me a moment later. Analeigh's arms are around me, holding me as I sob. "How could he do this?" I ask.

"I don't know."

"I'm stupid. I'm so stupid."

She pulls back. "Listen to me right now. You are *not* stupid. You did *nothing* wrong. Nothing! This is all his fault, and I swear to God, you say the word and we'll find a spot in the desert to let his body be eaten by the vultures. Remember, that country girl band left us instructions in that song about Earl or whatever."

Ana manages to pull a smile from me, which I didn't think was possible. "What do I do now?"

She brushes my tears away and takes my hands. "Do you want to stay here tonight or somewhere else?"

"I don't want to be here. I can't see him."

"Okay, then let's go pack a bag, and you'll come stay with me and Nick. He's in surgery tomorrow, so we will have the house to ourselves and we can figure out a plan."

With blurry vision, I nod and turn to head back to the bedroom. With each step I take up the stairs, I feel the sadness leaving me and being replaced with anger. After everything I did for him, after staying with him even when I wanted to leave.

For putting up with his neglect, his selfish habits, and the way he let me wither into the background for his gain.

I stand in the bedroom, feeling so many emotions and at a loss for what to do now. What do I take? Everything here feels—tainted.

"Vi?"

I inhale a shaky breath. "I don't need anything. Please, just get me out of here."

Analeigh pulls me to her side and walks me back down the stairs. "Where is your phone?" she asks.

"In pieces, just like my life."

"Okay, then. I'll text Eleanor so she knows you're okay. I'm sure she's tried to call."

Yes, I'm sure she has. I can only imagine she's freaking out on her way back to me.

Analeigh grabs my purse, and then she ushers me out the door. Just as we get to her car, Dylan's car pulls up, blocking her in.

Oh God, I…no.

"Get in the car, Vi," she says, squeezing my shoulder.

"Violet! Wait, let me explain!" Dylan says as Ana gets me to the passenger door. "Violet, please."

"Explain? What are you going to say? Is it true?" I ask, whipping around to confront him. His face falls, and I realize what a shitty actor he is. "You can't even pretend."

"I don't want to lie to you."

I laugh once. "Fuck you. You've been lying for God only knows how long."

"It wasn't like that," he says, and I don't even know what that means, but I've had enough. I glance at Ana, and she wordlessly hears my plea to get me out of here and away from him.

"No one wants to hear a fucking word you have to say, Dylan. You've made your bed, so go find your mistress and lie in it."

Ana gets me inside her car, closing the door, and then turns on him. "Move your car."

"Not until I know what she wants."

"What she wants?" Ana screams. "She wanted a husband who didn't break her fucking heart. She wanted a husband who didn't take her away to the islands, all the while preparing to ruin everything she thought she knew. She wanted a good man, which you're clearly not. She wanted fidelity, which you didn't give her. So now what she wants is for you to move your fucking car so she doesn't have to see your lying ass."

If I wasn't so numb, I would be clapping for her. Every girl needs a friend like Analeigh.

He turns away from her, coming to my window. "I didn't want you to find out this way."

I look down at my hands, refusing to give him any more of my time. He's wasted enough of it already.

Ana opens her door. "You know what, Dylan? I've warned you."

Then my best friend gets in the car and calls her husband. "Nick? How much do you love me?"

He hesitates. "More than you know, why?"

"I'm about to fuck some shit up, and it's going to cost us some money."

Nick chuckles. "Do you have Violet?"

"I do."

"Will this costly thing piss Dylan off and make Violet happy?" She grins and starts the car. "It will."

"Then have at it, my love."

Ana has the widest smile I've seen on her. "Thanks, babe." Her eyes meet mine. "Fuck him." Then she maneuvers the car around Dylan's, driving over the landscaping he paid a fortune for. She stops and looks back at the tread marks, then shrugs, puts the car in reverse, and slams into his before going back into drive and flipping him off out the window as she leaves.

"Fuck him," I say as I watch what once was my sanctuary fade away behind me, knowing where I want to go to feel safe again.

Even if returning to Ember Falls means I have to face my past.

CHAPTER 2
EVERETT

Oh look, another day in paradise.

And by paradise, I mean—purgatory.

Today is the same fucking thing, just wash, lather, repeat. Also, why the hell do we repeat? Like, shouldn't it work the first time?

Whatever.

"Oh, look who's here for free coffee!" My best friend Hazel says as I enter the door of Prose & Perk.

Like I do every morning.

Why? Because my life is literally the same shit on a different day. So, here I am again, world, doing the same thing.

Wake up at five a.m., like clockwork, go see my mother and get her set for the day, get coffee and see the same patrons who come at the same time, before I leave to spend the day with animals.

"Jesus, you're hostile today," I say with a sigh, leaning against the counter.

"Sorry, I'm just exhausted. I went on another date last night that ended with me getting fast food on the way home because he told me that I should eat salad only."

"Fuck him," I say quickly. "No one should ever tell you what to eat. What's his number? The guys and I will pay him a visit."

Hazel and I have been best friends since we were kids. She's like a sister to me, and I'll kick anyone's ass who hurts her.

"That's very sweet, but I handled it." She grins.

I'm a little afraid for him then. Hazel's fucking vicious when she wants to be. One of my teammates on my Frisbee league, Miles, pissed her off once, and she put a laxative in his breakfast. Poor guy was running to the shitter all day.

I'll be honest, I really didn't feel bad for him, but I pretended.

"I'm glad you're so mean sometimes, just not when you're mean to me. Now, can I please have some coffee? I have to get up to the Joneses' farm and check on the foal that was born. The mom is a little lethargic, and I want to make sure everything is fine."

Being the town veterinarian is honestly more than I could've ever dreamed of. When I chose to walk away from baseball, there really was only one other option for me, and it was this.

"Aww," Hazel says in a singsong voice. "She had the baby? Didn't she lose her foal two years ago?"

"Yes, and I promised I'd be there early."

We both look at the wall clock. "This is early?"

I let out a long sigh. "Mom had a rough start to the morning, so…"

She gives me a soft smile. "I'm sure they'll understand and have no fear—I have coffee."

The owners do understand and thank God for the coffee.

"I called, explained, and they said both animals appear to be okay, but both the mare and the foal need to be examined to ease their minds, I think."

"But you don't think they're okay, though?"

I shrug, not sure what I think until I get there. "Jones said the foal was still a bit sluggish but had improved, so I didn't need to rush. I also think after the way they lost the last one, they're a bit shaken up." Understandably so. It was traumatic for everyone.

She turns and starts pouring coffee into a cup. "Well, it's a happy day for the Jones farm and you, since I'm going to give you this cup"—she holds the cup in her hand and her voice becomes stern—"and *only* this cup, for free, because you had a bad morning *and* I'm a wonderful friend."

I know better than to make my normal sarcastic remark about her friendship since she cut me off from my daily coffee the last time I did it. Plus, she's being kind, so I'll just wait until she's back to being her ungiving self.

"Thank you. I appreciate it. Truly." And I do. Hazel always is there for me.

"You're welcome. What's going on with your mom?"

Hazel knows all about my mom's condition, but I don't want to get into it. It's hard being the sole caretaker, and today was just one of those days. Couple that with the monotonous tone of my life and I'm grumpy.

"It's nothing I haven't dealt with before," I say, pushing it off. There's nothing anyone can say or change about it. I just had to accept my life and make the best of it.

"Everett," she says softly. "Talk to me. You can't keep all this built up. You need someone to lean on as well."

I shrug. "Then I better go find that someone."

She rolls her eyes, knowing my tactics all too well. "Yes, what a lucky human they will be. I'll be sure to provide *them* with free coffee. She'll need it after one day with you."

"You wouldn't."

One brow lifts. "Wouldn't I?"

Yeah, she totally would.

I start to make a remark back to her but opt to take a sip of the coffee instead, and the door chimes.

And on cue will be Ainsley, who is engaged to my Frisbee teammate, Lachlan West.

Because…it's Ember Falls where life is on repeat.

I turn to see my buddy, but when I see the person entering, my heart stops.

It's like one of those movie scenes where the camera zooms in on the guy who is completely dumbfounded as he sees the girl.

That girl.

The girl who wrecked your fucking life and you never thought you'd see her again.

Only that damn girl is standing in the coffee shop, looking back at you.

Yeah, that fucking moment.

The world around me is fuzzy, and I'm staring into the rich, amber-colored eyes of Violet Stewart.

She blinks a few times, her eyes widening, and then there's a shriek behind me, breaking the moment completely.

"Violet! Oh my God! Violet!" Hazel yells and rushes around, bumping my shoulder as she goes past me.

Violet's gaze snaps to hers, and she smiles. "Hazel!"

They hug and Hazel rocks her back and forth, over and over like she's a long-lost friend, which I guess she is.

However, she's more than that to me. She's the only girl I've ever loved. She's the one I was going to marry.

Until I wasn't.

"My God, how are you? You're in Ember Falls? When did you get here?" Hazel fires off the questions and then turns to me. "Did you know she was back? Why didn't you tell me?"

I'm still standing here, like an idiot, unable to form words.

Dear Universe, when I said that life was the same and I was bored, I didn't mean you should throw the one person in my life who could upend it all.

Violet glances at me and then back to Hazel. "I just got in late last night, actually. I…I haven't seen anyone, well, until now."

Hazel grips both of her wrists, shaking her head in amazement. "I can't believe you're here. I've missed you! I haven't heard from you in so long. How are you?"

Violet tenses a little. "I'm okay." Only it doesn't look like she's okay. Finally her eyes come to stay on mine. "Hey, Everett."

Her voice is exactly like I remember, like silk against the skin. The way she said my name used to be my favorite thing, and hearing it again, after so long, fucking hurts in a place I thought had died.

"Violet, hi," I say. My throat feels as though it's closing, but I play it cool and manage to walk to her. I rest my hand on her arm and kiss her cheek. "It's good to see you. It's been a long time."

She pulls her lips between her teeth and then pushes out a deep breath. "It has. How have you been?"

Bored as fuck, but it seems that's done now.

"He's the same, as always, other than the fact that he's a veterinarian and a mooch." Hazel slaps my chest. "But I can't seem to get rid of him, not for lack of trying."

I roll my eyes. "And she's still as annoying as ever."

Violet laughs softly. "That's so great that you guys are all still friends."

I clear my throat, trying to get the lump out. "What brings you back to town?"

I thought for sure, nine years ago, that Violet would come back and we'd find a way to work through all the obstacles. When that didn't happen, I waited, thinking she would sell her grandmother's house after it was left to her. That was the opening I was desperate for. However, Violet didn't come back. Instead, she hired a property manager who comes and checks on things, and that was that.

Violet Stewart was never coming back to Ember Falls.

"I'm here for a year, actually."

"For just a year?"

She nods. "I just took a job in town."

Hazel squeals. "That's amazing! God, it's like the band just got back together!"

A whole year of being near her while she's married to that douchebag actor in Los Angeles. A whole year of having to pretend I don't dream about her still and imagine the life we could've had.

Yeah, this is going to be so amazing. I internally groan and…wait, she took a job?

"What job did you take?" I ask. I'm not sure what the hell she could be doing here.

"I'm going to be teaching at the high school."

"Ember Falls High School?" I ask, because surely she wouldn't be coming here to teach, not without me knowing, since my best fucking friend is the principal and would know this as well.

She nods. "Yes, I interviewed a week ago. I wanted to come say hi, but I had to get back to LA for a meeting with my lawyer, and anyway, I didn't have the job for sure, at least I didn't have a contract from Miles yet."

"Miles? As in Miles Anderson?" I ask for a little clarification. I'd like to know who I need to murder and in what order.

"Yeah, I saw him for the interview. Obviously, he was surprised when I walked in, but then he offered me the job and sent the contract a day later. I packed my shit and here I am," she says with a smile. "Are you guys still friends?"

We were—until now.

Hazel jumps in. "Yes, we're all still friends. And wow! A year! God, we have so much to catch up on! Hey, Ev?"

I turn to look at Hazel. "Yes?"

"Don't you have to get to the farm? Check on the foal?" Hazel asks, giving me the out I so desperately need.

"Yes. It was great seeing you, Violet. I'll…see you around."

I wonder whether she's staying at her grandmother's place, because it's literally next door to me.

Hazel's eyes are warm, and there's a level of understanding filtering behind them. I give her a wink and then get out the door. I manage to keep myself together until I'm out of view, and then I lean against my truck, feeling the weight of what just happened settle around me.

Violet is back.

Violet is here for an entire year.

I can't let Violet derail me after I've worked so hard to close that chapter of my life.

The foal is doing great, which means I can now take care of my rising anger and frustration at the turn my life has made.

I drive up to Ember Falls High School, and Mrs. Hendrix buzzes me in. "Good morning, Dr. Finnegan."

I smile at the wonderful woman who has been working at this school since I went here. "Good morning, Mrs. H. Is he in there?"

She nods. "Yes, but he's in the middle of something."

I smile. "Perfect."

I push the door open, finding Miles sitting at his desk. His eyes widen, and I go right into it. "You hired Violet? To be a teacher *here*?"

Miles sighs heavily, leaning back in his chair. "Hello, Everett. Please, sit down, inform me of your complaint. It's not like I haven't had sixteen phone calls this week from parents and teachers. I've been dying to hear one from someone who has nothing to do with this school."

I sit, ignoring his bad day since I really don't give a shit. So far my day hasn't gone much better, and this little piece of news just added to the crap-ass morning. "You didn't tell me she was back."

"I didn't have to."

He didn't—have to? Is he fucking out of his mind? Of course he had to. Doesn't he know shit about bro code? "She's Violet. You know...about us."

"I know, but she asked me not to say anything, and I really wasn't sure what to say. Her situation is unique, and I figured you'd find out. Besides, it was like...forever ago. You've clearly moved on, and so has she."

He knows I haven't moved on. I mean, I had to. She was married, for fuck's sake. Not that she's going to be for much longer, but I really don't need to consider any of that, since she seems to have absolutely no intention of staying in Ember Falls.

After I left the farm, I spent about ten minutes looking her up, which is something I've worked really hard not to do.

There it all was, her husband's affair, the fact that she left him and filed for divorce, the photos of him and that new girl, who Violet is a million times more beautiful than.

I glare at my former friend. "Do you know how I found out she's back?"

"I'm sure you'll tell me."

"Damn right I will. I was in Prose & Perk, just giving Hazel my normal daily dose of shit, and then the door chimes. I think, oh, Ainsley is here. She usually comes in now to write or do research. Only it wasn't Ainsley."

He jumps in as if he can't help himself, his voice animated. "It was someone else?"

I give him the bird. *Asshole.* "It was Violet. All grown up and absolutely fucking breathtaking."

For the first time since I walked in here, Miles looks genuinely apologetic. "I honestly couldn't tell you."

"You should've."

"Maybe, but she asked me not to, and I was respecting her wishes."

I want to be mad at him—at this—but if she asked him not to, I don't blame him. That's a lie. I blame him, but I'm not as pissed about it.

My voice softens. "She's married to that cheating bastard Dylan Leone. I knew that, I mean, we all knew since it was so fucking public."

"I didn't know," Miles confesses.

"Seriously, you are supposed to be up on all the things because you're around the kids all the time, and you didn't put that together?"

"I don't follow celebrity gossip."

That's some bullshit. "You know about music," I remind him. Last year, thanks to Miles and his musical knowledge, we all dressed up when we played a team named the Swift-bees in Ultimate Frisbee. I did enjoy tormenting Lachlan by making him wear one of the Eras shirts.

Miles shrugs. "Well, I dare you to work in a high school and not know about the world's most famous pop star. So did you guys talk?"

There's no point in lying or trying to keep it from him. Hazel will tell Penelope, his girlfriend, and she'll tell him. "A little. She said hi. I said hi. Hazel went absolutely nuts and hugged her like she was her long-lost sister."

"She kind of is." He echoes my thoughts from earlier.

"Yeah, yeah, but then I stood there, pissed and hurt and shit that I shouldn't feel. It's been like fifteen years since we spoke. I don't know why I care. Did you look online to see what has her living back here?" I ask, jumping from topic to topic, and Miles shakes his head. "I'd like to beat her asshole soon-to-be ex-husband with his own arms."

He laughs at that. "I'm going to assume it's bad."

I stand, no longer able to keep my frustration in check. "Dude, they made the internet for a reason."

"Dude, I don't look up my employees' personal lives. She promised she'd give me one full school year. She's incredibly qualified, and we've known her since we were kids. Giving her the job was a no-brainer, and giving her her privacy was also one. If she wants to tell me, she will."

Well, isn't that nice for him? I would've liked to have gotten a fucking heads-up. I would've liked my best friend to do right by me too. "You should've told me she was back. Her grandmother's house is fucking next door. I can't avoid her."

"Well, I'm sorry you think that. It's been, as you said, many years. I didn't realize it would set you off." He gets to his feet. "Now I need to do principal things, and that doesn't include standing here, listening to you." He walks beside me, placing his hand on my shoulder. "I'm truly sorry, Everett. I didn't know it would upset you this much. Come on, I'll walk you out."

I really didn't either. He's right. It has been years. I shouldn't care, but the last six years of my life has changed so many things. I work, I come home, I take care of my mother, and I do it again the next day. There's no time for dating, which would help me forget about her. Besides, who would I date in Ember Falls? Hazel is the only woman in the town who's single and I could find attractive, but she's Hazel.

She's smart, beautiful, wonderful, and yet I've never felt an ounce of desire around her, and I'm one hundred percent sure she's never thought of me that way. We're like siblings and...just no.

The pool is shallow here, and dating honestly hasn't even been on my mind.

"I forgive you—well, I will after I kick your ass at practice," I say.

"You can try."

I'll do more than that. Shit-talking is great and all, but I'd rather prove it.

"Look, all kidding aside, I wish you'd told me. It would've been nice to have been prepared."

Miles lets out a long breath. "I should've and I'm sorry."

"See you at practice?" I ask.

He nods. "See you then."

I should feel better, but I don't, because the reality is, Violet returning to Ember Falls is going to change everything. Seeing her always does.

CHAPTER 3
VIOLET

"Are you all settled in Chamber Falls?" Analeigh asks on the video call as I move around, putting the remainder of my clothes in the drawers. I've been here three days, and I've just finally gotten around to unpacking another suitcase.

"*Ember* Falls," I clarify with a laugh. "And I'm settling. The house has been closed off for so long that I've had a hard time getting things turned back on."

"Like what?"

"Well, today I tried to figure out where to turn the pump on to get hot water. That was super fun."

It really wasn't fun, because I really don't know how to do any of this stuff, but I'm learning in my newfound independence. Life is an adventure and all that.

Only it didn't work, so I'm not sure what to do.

"You know you can come back here and stay with me."

I appreciate her offer, I really do, but I can't. Hollywood is suffocating, and as much as people may think it's this big city, it's incredibly small. In the five days I was back there to collect my things, I was hounded. The press, people who claimed to be friends, old coworkers of Dylan's who don't like him and wanted to let me know more truths they saw.

I could feel myself dying inside as I stayed there.

Analeigh and Nick would've let me stay there forever, but I need to find my footing. I already took care of the biggest thing, getting a job and filing for divorce.

The rest, I figure, will work itself out in the next year.

"This is for the best," I say, putting a shirt in the drawer.

"If you say so."

Ana made it abundantly clear that she thought I should stay, but we're not the same. She likes to fight, hence the fact she backed into my husband's car after running over the lawn. There's a part of her that is unwavering in revenge. I'm much different.

I could fight, but what for? I don't want to be married to him. I have no doubt that it either wasn't the first time he's cheated or it won't be the last. We don't have children, and my lawyer said it should all be pretty simple as long as I'm not out for blood.

"I do say so. Things here are much easier, and I got a job in a good school."

"They have teaching jobs in California, you know?"

I sigh and close the drawer. "Yes, and I have a free house here in Virginia. It's a quiet town with no fucking paparazzi. No stupid cheating husbands and their mistresses who are intent on making my life unbearable."

Her eyes soften. "I get it, I just wish it was closer."

"I do too. I'll miss you, but you can come visit."

Trying to picture my bougie best friend in Ember Falls is kind of hilarious. She would've run out of here screaming if she saw this place.

Analeigh is the daughter of a famous musician and is married to the top plastic surgeon in Hollywood. She's only ever known luxury, and even living her whole life with a silver spoon in her mouth, she's the most generous and kindest person I've ever met.

However, she likes her nice things.

"I can't believe you went back to Virginia, though."

"Well, where else was I going to go? My parents are in Peru or somewhere that they can't talk to me. Ember Falls made the most sense. Besides, if my granny were alive, she'd be where I would've run to anyway. I wasn't staying in Hollywood. I don't need to watch Dylan and Whitney hook up and be the new celebrity 'it' couple."

Of course the press is spinning it to his favor. He has a very, very good publicist, who clearly is earning her job. According to the magazines today, I was the problem and Whitney is everything he needed. It didn't matter that we've been together since our senior year of college. That he had a great job as an accountant and then quit one day, letting me know he was pursuing acting school. Thanks to that, my job helped put him through the program, his copious amounts of expensive headshots, and auditions that he had to travel to get to. But apparently I'm cold and indifferent. My jealousy of his success was the failure of our marriage, and he should've left me years ago.

News to me.

Also, what kind of idiots are they when just two weeks ago they were posting photos of us on vacation? It didn't look over then, even though, if they could've seen us in private, they would've seen the signs I was pretending weren't there.

My stomach churns as I think about how stupid I was. How I excused everything away because I didn't want to have a failed marriage. Little did I know I didn't have a marriage to begin with.

"He's so gross," Ana says as she makes a gagging noise.

"Yes, he really is."

"And he's driving around in the car with the dent still. I called around all the local shops and offered them a bonus if they refused to get him in for a week."

"Truly, your mind is a scary place," I say with a laugh.

She grins. "It really is. The only good thing about this is that you were both poor when you got married, and there's no prenup, so you get half."

I snort. "Yes, such a good thing."

Analeigh sits up, pulling the camera close. "I'm sorry, Violet. I didn't mean it that way."

I put the pile of jeans down on top of the dresser and flop on the world's most uncomfortable bed with the phone in my hand. "I know that. Trust me, as vicious as you are, you don't have a mean bone in your body for the people you love."

"Has he called at all?"

"He left three messages the day I found out, as you know." I made Ana listen to them and tell me the CliffsNotes. Once I knew what he said, I listened to it at 4:00 a.m. that night and cried myself to sleep. "Since then, he called once more, to tell me he got the papers and hopes I can be civil and mature."

She snorts. "Oh, that's rich."

"Right? I swear, he's not the same man I married. Like, where is the future accountant I married who couldn't be bothered to make sure his shoes matched his outfit? I never thought he'd be the one to break my heart."

Ana pulls her lips into a thin line. "Money and fame do crazy things to people. I've seen it so many times I've lost count. Look, take this time and just focus on yourself. You can't fix Dylan. I'm not sure anything can. Do what makes *you* happy."

"I don't even know what that is."

She smiles warmly. "That's what this next year is for."

"You're right. Already, since being here, I feel lighter. I have always loved this town."

"And the boy in it," she says with a grin.

Yes, I loved the boy who lives next door. I didn't know if he'd still be here and I didn't want to bring it up to Miles when I was here for my interview, so I just asked him not to tell anyone about my possible return. Everett was destined for a great life. He's smart and funny, and his baseball career was promising. We used to sit at the field, lying on the mound under the stars, and create a fictitious life of what team he'd play for and where we'd live.

I honestly assumed he would leave Ember Falls.

Seems it was only me who did that.

Ember Falls holds some of my favorite memories. When my parents would bring me here each summer, my grandma and I would bake cookies. I'd learn a craft and spend time with Everett, Hazel, and Miles. It was fun.

It wasn't another archaeological site where I was doing my schoolwork as my parents dug holes in some ruins. Not that I hated my childhood, because it was really cool to get to go where we did, but I had no friends.

I didn't get to go to school or even be around other kids. It was only when I was here that I felt like I fit in.

A part of me just wants that again, because I never fit in with Dylan's crowd.

I smile at Ana. "I hurt him."

"You were kids. Surely he isn't still harboring anger about it."

I shrug. "Maybe, but I left and completely threw Everett away because I was so afraid of him realizing that I wasn't good enough and being with me was too much work. That he'd be in the spotlight and I would be in the shadows because he was meant to shine."

Just like my parents did.

"The irony is not lost on me."

"Me either. I didn't even call to end things, I just stopped calling."

Ana releases a long breath through her nose. "Again, you were like seventeen, and he didn't exactly come chasing after you either."

"Maybe not, but it wasn't him who made the promises. It was me. I said I'd come to where he was, and then I got into USC and I didn't think twice."

I didn't even talk to him about it. I committed to my school and wrote him a letter, because I was that much of a chickenshit.

"Have you seen him?"

I nod.

She perks up. "Well, is he still hot or did he age like shit?"

My mind recalls the way he looked in the coffee shop. His dark-brown hair that was pushed back, deep-brown eyes, and the dimple on his left cheek that I used to love to kiss. His body is lean now, but still muscular from what I could tell, and he's tall, so much taller than I remembered.

"Yeah, he's still hot."

"Are you going to bang him?"

My eyes widen. "What?"

"Don't look at me like that," she scoffs. "Your husband has been sleeping with his mistress. You should hook up with someone. When's the last time you had good sex?"

I ignore the question. "I'm not sleeping with Everett."

"Why not? Is he married?"

"I don't know."

"If he's not..."

I love Analeigh, but dear God she needs an intervention. "I'm not sleeping with him or anyone. I'm here to...find myself, or at least find some peace away from Dylan."

"Violet, I love you, you know this. I'm team Vi for life, but Dylan...is a piece of shit. He somehow got a big break, considering he's a mediocre actor, but he has a nice face, so he gets roles where people can look at him. You wanted to leave him three years ago, but you stayed because he convinced you that you'd be lost without him. Then the dickface cheated, and, like, for three years you've been in misery. Go find some joy."

"I stayed because I didn't want my marriage to be over. I stayed because I thought I could fix it, make him happy. I don't know, I was stupid."

My parents had the most amazing marriage ever. They were happy, traveled the world, were explorers, and found joy in everything. My dad told me that he and Mom agreed they weren't going to have kids, because of their careers, but then I came along and it was the best accident ever.

They loved me, found a way to have it all, and that is what they say a marriage is—sacrifice and understanding. Together, it was about balance and finding compromise to have their family.

I spent my entire life idolizing that kind of relationship. Where it's not a sacrifice but a compromise to give each other what they need to be content.

Ana's lip quirks into a sad smile. "He didn't deserve you."

"No, and I should've left years ago." I wipe away a tear.

"Are you upset because you love him still or because of how it ended?"

I think about that for a moment. Do I love Dylan? I don't. I wanted to love him. Lord knows I tried to make things work. I kept giving and giving, hoping he'd see the real me, but he never did. Not when all he could see was himself.

"It's more that I'm mortified. I found out that not only was my marriage over, but he cheated on national television. This will forever be on the internet and in magazines. People will always look at me and make their assumptions about who I am, because of him. The comments on social media are scathing."

Ana smiles warmly. "Look, people are fucking assholes. Let them be little keyboard warriors, blaming you, but remember that he'll also be immortalized as a cheating prick. You know that, right? He'll be judged as well, and I'm going to do everything I can to remind the world of exactly the type of man he is. It's going on my next podcast."

Oh, that's going to go over well. "I wish you wouldn't."

There's a gleam in her eye that I'm all too familiar with. "Wish away, bestie."

"It doesn't matter what type of things you say, Ana. At the end of the day, I married him and I put up with his shit and now I'm going to be divorced."

"And I'm going to throw you the biggest party when it's over."

I laugh. "I can't wait."

"Now tell me more about your hot neighbor."

I roll my eyes but tell her everything about when we saw each other again.

I forgot all the bad things about this house.

For instance, my house with Dylan was huge, and it came with all the modern amenities. A walk-in shower, butler's pantry, big open floor plan with beautifully designed touches, and all top-of-the-line appliances.

In Ember Falls, this house is ancient, creaks when the wind blows, doesn't have central heat or air, and has the hot water go out after three minutes.

I'm frantically rushing to rinse the conditioner out of my hair as my teeth are chattering.

I try counting to stop the numbness from the frozen ice shower I'm currently taking, but nothing is keeping my mind off it.

This is going to be the first thing I fix. Well, that's not true. I need to get the heat on first.

"Fuck it," I say, turning the water off. I let whatever product didn't rinse out just stay there and grab my towel.

I shiver and climb out of the bathtub, wrapping it around me and rushing into the bedroom, where the fireplace is blazing. I stand, dripping wet, in front of it, letting the heat start to thaw my limbs.

After a few minutes, my teeth stop chattering and I run to my bed, grab my clothes, throw them on as fast as I can, and go back to the fire.

I need to get the radiators to work again. I just don't know how. I tried turning the valves, but it was so late, already freezing, and I heard a howling noise that made me not want to be outside if it found its way to where I was.

I forgot just how cold it gets in the mountains at night. At work, someone said they thought it'll snow by the end of September.

Southern California weather is far superior to this.

Thankfully, there was a pile of firewood against the house that Grandma always kept in case the heat went out, which it did often, apparently, and I set a fire in the wood-burning stove downstairs and one in the fireplace up in my room.

Knowing that I can't just keep burning the pile of wood since it goes fast, I'm going to have to bite the bullet and ask for help.

I get in my car and ride the half mile over to what I hope is still Everett's house. I make the right down the drive, feeling like I'm fifteen all over again, only not on a bike this time.

Time feels as though it stood still in Ember Falls. His home is the same, burnt-orange siding with brick on the lower half. The rocking chairs still stand on the left of the small porch. God, so many nights Everett and I would sit there together.

My smile is automatic as the memories come forward.

As I park and get out of the car, the front door opens and he exits.

Our eyes meet and there's a familiar flutter in my stomach, the one I always got when he looked at me. My hands rest on the top of the car door, and I lift my hand to wave. "Hey."

"Hi," he says and then clears his throat.

"I was hoping you still lived here."

He pulls the front door closed. "I'm pretty sure I'll be buried on the land here."

"Oh. Do they do that? I mean, I didn't think that you could just bury someone on their land. Although I'm not a lawyer, so maybe you can. I'm going to look that up."

I really wish my brain would work right and I didn't babble around him. My chest is tight as I look at the boy I once loved and could talk to so easily. Now there's a strange tension between us.

"Are you okay?" he asks as he steps down off the porch.

I feel so stupid, but it's either I swallow my pride and ask for help or freeze to death. "Actually...I was kind of hoping you could help me? I hate to come here and ask. Trust me, if it wasn't dire...I wouldn't."

"What's wrong?"

Everett steps closer, now just in front of me, and I do my best to slow my heart rate.

You're too close, you're still hot, you're not supposed to still make me weak in the knees.

I don't say any of that, though. "I can't get the heat to work."

His brow lifts. "And you thought I could help? I'm one of the least handy people here."

I give him an awkward smile, one that's more teeth than anything. Great, now I look like an idiot as well as sound like one.

"It's the propane tank. I couldn't get the lever to turn, or maybe it's something else. I don't know, but it's freezing and I don't have enough firewood for another night."

"You used firewood?" Everett asks in surprise.

"It was that or become an icicle."

He laughs once. "You can't be using the fireplaces when you have no idea the last time they were cleaned. Let me go take care of something first, and I'll be there in ten, okay?"

I nod. "Thank you, Everett. I appreciate it."

"Of course."

I get back in the warm car and head to my house. The fire has dwindled to almost nothing, so I walk to the side porch, grab a couple more logs, and get it going again. The last thing I need are frozen pipes.

A few minutes later, I hear the familiar sound of tires on gravel. Everett gets out of the car and heads toward me. "Where's the propane tank?"

"Behind the shed on the left."

He nods and I follow him out. He's wearing a pair of tight jeans, boots, and what looks like a brown bomber jacket. He has that effortless, I'm-so-hot-I-can't-help-myself kind of vibe. It's just natural and the way his ass fills out those jeans—yeah, still hot.

Why couldn't he be ugly?

Why couldn't I roll back into town and find that he wasn't here or he wasn't still completely delicious?

It would've made this return just a little easier. Then I wouldn't have to think about the stupid mistakes I made when I walked away from him.

That's just not the way my cookie crumbles, though. I'm the girl who gets to see every error of my ways, sometimes even on television thanks to my soon-to-be ex-husband.

"Back here?" Everett asks, snapping me out of my maudlin thoughts.

"Yeah, right there."

He goes around the left, finds the buried propane tank, and lifts the lid. "The line isn't open."

"Are you sure? I turned it." I come around to look.

The wind whips my hair into my face, obstructing my view. I grab handfuls and peer at the tank.

"To open the line, it should be parallel like this." Everett turns it. "Do you have one against the house?"

"Should I know this?" I ask.

He snorts. "Probably. We're off the grid here, for the most part, so knowing your propane and septic would be a good thing."

He's probably right. "I had someone come here and keep up the property, but I don't really know the details."

"I know, or at least I figured when the house didn't crumble after a decade."

Our eyes meet, and for a second the guilt hits me. "I'm sorry, Everett."

"For what?"

For leaving you. For never coming back. For not giving you the chance to decide. For all of it.

"Everything," I say, hoping he hears it all in that single word.

Everett gives me a lopsided grin. "You have nothing to be sorry for, Vi. We were kids. Trust me, it worked out fine."

That stings. "I really hope for you it did."

"What about for you? You're married, right? Any kids?"

The way he says it, the almost tightness in his voice, makes me wonder whether he knows about me and Dylan. "No kids, and I *was* married, but I'm in the middle of a divorce."

Thank God we don't have kids. In the beginning of our marriage, I wanted to wait until we were in a better financial situation. Then, when we had money, I just couldn't...get myself to want to try.

I kept imagining the life they'd have with him always gone and in the public light. Not to mention, I'm not sure I'd be a good mom. My parents loved me, sure, but they weren't kind and loving. They were distant and work focused. The only real affection was when I came to visit my grandma. She was the warm and sweet one.

Now I'm grateful I don't have any kids who would be subject to this absolute shit show I'm living.

He nods slowly and then extends his hand toward the house. As we both start to walk, I hold my hair against my neck.

"I'm sorry to hear about your divorce," he says.

"Don't be. It's for the best."

"He's an actor, right?"

I nod. "He definitely is. He was so good at acting like he was married, he forgot he actually was," I say, hating I opened my big mouth about Dylan.

"He's an idiot to let you go."

"I think he's just an idiot." I lift my eyes to his, and we both smile. "But, right now, I sort of look like one, huh?"

"Never. You just look cold."

I laugh. "I was freezing last night."

"Come on then, let's get heat in your house so you can warm up."

I follow him back inside even though, right now, cold is the last thing I feel.

CHAPTER 4
EVERETT

I open the door to my house and pause, waiting to see if my ridiculously gorgeous former love of my life is in the driveway again.

She's not.

Relief—or at least that's the word I'm going with—washes over me. Not that I don't want to see her.

No, that's actually the damn problem. I want to see her all the time. I want to touch her, remember the way her lips fit against mine, and make her smile.

Which I do not have the time or should not even consider in the first place.

So best to avoid Violet Stewart—Leone—as much as possible.

Back to the mundane, that's what I always say.

And by always, I mean never, but that's my new catchphrase because since she returned, everything is backwards. I need forward facing.

I remote start my truck, toss my lunch in the passenger seat, and see a note sitting underneath my windshield wiper.

That's odd.

I open it, wondering when the hell someone put this here.

Everett,

You didn't give me your number and I didn't want to be that girl who was waiting outside your door at seven in the morning again, so I just left a note. I'd like to have you over for dinner tonight as a way to thank you for helping me. Here's my number, if you can text me and let me know what time works or just to say you'd rather not.

Thanks again,

Vi

My point is made, but instead of getting irritated, I find myself smiling and then plug her number into my phone and shoot off a message.

Me: You know, stalking is illegal in Virginia. Also, it's Everett.
Violet: Is it stalking if I leave a note?
Me: Pretty sure showing up outside someone's house two days in a row would establish a pattern, even if the person knows.
Violet: I'll be sure to ask my lawyer to add these charges to my tab.
Me: I didn't say I didn't like the stalking...
Violet: Some things never change.

I laugh as I start to walk back to the barndominium.

Me: So you want to make me dinner?
Violet: I'd love to have you over if you're open to it. I was going to make a pie too.
Me: Is it Granny's recipe?
Violet: Of course.
Me: I'll be there.

This is a bad idea. I know it even as I say it. Spending time with Violet isn't going to be good for me. I'm busy, living my very structured, very meticulously planned life. I don't have time for any woman other than the one who lives on the other side of this door.

I push the front door open, putting any thoughts of Violet behind me, and Brutus, *my* bulldog, lifts his head. He sees it's me, and if a dog could roll his eyes, he would. "Hello to you too, Brutus."

He does huff this time before he lays his pudgy face on his paw and returns to his nap.

Dismissed, like usual.

I scratch the top of his head and then kiss my mother on the cheek. "Good morning, beautiful."

She sits in her recliner that she's had since I was a kid, staring at the television. Our routine is practically the same. Before I leave for work, I come over and make sure everything is exactly as it needs to be for her day.

"Everett, be a dear and help me find the remote. I might have thrown it out."

"It's in the pouch right next to you." Where it stays tethered so she can always find it.

She looks down and her eyes widen. "Oh, I didn't see it. I thought I knew it was here, but I can't remember."

I smile, knowing the cadence of her life, and sit in the chair opposite her. She puts on her favorite game show, the familiar voice of my childhood filling the room.

There are times Mom is perfectly lucid and it's as though the accident never happened. Those are the good days. Where I have my mother back, even if I know it's fleeting. Then there are the days when she's belligerent, angry, and hateful because her mind won't work correctly and she misses my dad.

Most of the time, this is the mother I have, though. The one who is partially still her, warm, loving, and understanding, only she can't function fully.

I walk over to the calendar in the living room, writing today's agenda so she can see it easily. I put the approximate hours that I'll be at work, when I'll stop in for lunch to check on things, and that I'll be out for dinner, but I'll come by after.

"Mom, can you pay attention to me for a minute?"

Her blue eyes meet mine, and she puts the remote down. "What is it? What's wrong?"

I squat in front of her, taking her hand in mine. "Nothing is wrong. I just wanted to go over your day with you again."

Every day, for the last six years, is identical to the last. I say the same things, show her the same routine, keep everything exactly in the same place, and prepare for the next day.

"Are you leaving? You're not driving, are you?"

I give her a reassuring smile. "I'm going to be fine. I drive every day."

Her breathing accelerates. "I can't go."

"I know, you're not going anywhere," I say, doing my best to reassure her.

She releases a shaky sigh, and I watch the panic recede from her eyes. "I can't go in the car, Everett."

"Mom, you're not going anywhere."

Six years ago, my parents were driving home from a school charity event when my father went off the road. The car tumbled, end over end, until finally coming to a stop in a ditch. We aren't sure how long the car sat like that, my mother going in and out of consciousness as she screamed her throat raw for my father.

Since the accident, I've done everything I can to give her the best life possible. We've gone to every specialist that handles traumatic brain injuries, hoping there's an answer or a glimmer of hope she'll return to the way she was, but there's no guidebook for this type of injury.

We just have to wait and hope.

"Okay, because I can't. I can't go in a car. I can't die. I can't." Her voice trembles and I move forward, squeezing her hand.

"Look at me," I say sternly. Her eyes meet mine. "You are okay. You aren't going in the car. Do you see what it says on the calendar?"

Mom stares at it—it sits in her line of sight—but she often forgets it's there or why it's there.

"You have work?" she asks.

I nod.

"Then you'll come here for lunch, and then you're going to dinner with a friend."

"See? I'll come by a few times."

"Are you going out with Hazel?"

This is the worst part of her injury. She will probably forget what I tell her in an hour, or maybe she won't even recall it at all. "Yes."

"Oh, good, she's a very good friend."

I smile. "Yes, she is."

Mom taps the top of my hand. "Did you come here yesterday?"

"I did. I was a little late because I had to help a friend. Do you remember Violet?"

My mother's eyes soften and her smile grows. "Doreen's granddaughter? Oh, is she here? Did she come to visit?"

Doreen passed away after the accident. There are times my mother can recall it, but it's almost as though there is a before and an after. Anything before and even during the accident, she remembers, but after is harder for her.

"She's visiting, yes."

"Is she going to come say hello?"

"I'm not sure," I say, even though I know there's no way I'll allow that. New people, new things, set her off into a possible bad day.

I work to avoid that.

She pats my cheek. "You should tell her you love her. You always have, and everyone knows it. Do it before she gets away. Trust me, Everett Finnegan, life is short."

I know that all too well. "I agree."

"I miss him every day," Mom says wistfully.

She loved my father more than I ever could grasp. Even though all the cards were stacked against them—she was sixteen, he was in trade school, and they had no help from their parents—they had love. Dad became an electrician and worked hard, and Mom was a librarian. They longed for a family but weren't able to have children. When someone left me with a note on the steps of the police station, my parents didn't hesitate.

They took me in, loving me in every way possible.

When I was officially adopted, my mother says it was the single-most-beautiful day of their lives. I like to joke that it was when their luck turned around, but the current state of her life would suggest otherwise.

The accident took everything from her. Losing her short-term memory was hard, but losing my father was unbearable. I almost wish it went the other way. That she could forget the accident, my childhood, her life, her family, because then she wouldn't feel his loss so deeply.

Instead she relives the pain.

"I do too, Mom."

She shakes her head. "Where's the remote?"

I close my eyes, doing my best to hide the devastation that washes over me. "It's right next to you."

She glances down. "That's right. I have it here."

I smile. "Good."

I kiss her forehead and get up to head into the kitchen and then to the other rooms. I update the calendars that we've placed throughout the home so everything is the same, check that all the doors are closed and the locks are in place for the things that are unsafe, and grab the knobs to place them back on the stove.

My phone pings with a message from one of the techs in the office, and I see that she's added two emergencies to my schedule, so I head back into the living room.

"I need to head to the office now. Justine will be here in a few minutes."

Justine was a nurse for fifteen years, and when her mother was sick, she quit her job to take care of her. Instead of returning to the hospital after her mother passed, I hired her to care for Mom.

"Will you be home for dinner?" she asks, even though we went over all of that earlier.

"Not tonight, Mom. I'm going to dinner with a friend."

Her eyes narrow just slightly, and she looks at the calendar. "I know you told me." She takes my hand in hers. "I'm sorry. My brain is just tired, that's all."

I shake my head, giving her my most charming smile. "You have nothing to be sorry for. The calendar is on the wall, and you can always read it to know where I am."

"Bye, sweetheart."

"Bye, Mom. Be good and don't do anything I wouldn't do."

She huffs a laugh. "Since you're a hellion, that doesn't bode well for me."

I give her a wink and head into the office, hoping my day is calm so I can mentally prepare for dinner tonight.

"Dinner? Just the two of you?" Miles asks as we're sitting at Prose & Perk.

"Yup. She wanted to thank me."

"Because you opened her pipes so she could get hot?"

I roll my eyes. "Fuck off."

"Oh, sure, you are the one who gave all of us the most shit when we met the women we wanted to date, but you think I should fuck off? Not a chance, buddy. I'm riding this train until the wheels come off."

"I did it because I'm not nearly as annoying as you are."

Miles laughs once. "Sure you're not."

Whatever.

"Anyway, this is a bad idea, right?"

He shakes his head. "Nope, not even a little. I think it's a great idea."

I raise one brow, not believing him. There's a mischievous gleam in his eye, one I know myself.

"You think this is a good thing?" I ask in a different way.

"It could be."

"Right."

He grins. "You're not going to back out, I know you better than that. Do *you* think it's a good idea?"

Nope. I actually think I'm the stupidest man who's ever lived. One look at that woman and I was like a teenager making heartsick eyes at her. Hell, this morning I jacked off in the shower thinking of her. So, no, it's absolutely not a good idea to spend any more time around her.

I need to avoid Violet and her beautiful cognac-colored eyes.

"Probably not," I finally answer. "Actually, I know it's not."

"But you're going to go?"

I shrug. "I already said yes and she lives next door. It's not like there's a mystery to finding me. I'll go to dinner, get it over with, go home, and move on with my life."

Miles chuckles. "That's a good plan. Absolutely nothing can go wrong there. It's not like there's underlying feelings or emotions. I mean, go have dinner with an old friend."

I flip him off. "So, do I bring flowers or something?"

Of my group of friends, Miles is the least of a dick, and he is willing to look like an idiot for a woman he cares about. Lord knows he's made himself a fool for Penelope more times than not. It worked, though, because now they're living together and are secretly engaged. After all that's happened, they wanted to make sure her son was comfortable before springing more changes on him.

"I always brought flowers on a date—or a shovel."

I'm not even going to touch that one. "Yes, but you're stupid and this isn't a date."

"And yet here you are, asking for my advice." He grins.

I should've just searched the internet and let it tell me. "That's a mistake I won't make again."

"Honestly, don't bring flowers, go there empty-handed, show her what a douchebag you are. I think it'll just solidify that she made the right choice all those years ago when she ghosted you."

I really wonder why I'm friends with him or anyone in this town, honestly.

"She didn't ghost me."

"Then what do you call it? Disappearing by choice?"

"We grew up and moved on. That's what I call it."

Miles spins his coffee cup. "Look, from what Hazel said, it's very clear that you two are due for a conversation, where you actually lay that part of your past to rest. So let's just say that it's a friendly dinner—bring a bottle of wine so the two of you can be relaxed. Skip the flowers, since it's not a date. Wine is a friendly gesture."

I sigh, get up, and push in the chair. "Thanks for the advice."

"Everett, in all seriousness, I was there when things fell apart. I remember how fucked up for you her disappearing was. She's not planning to stay, so just...you know, remember that."

I nod once. "I know."

I hear him loud and clear: Be careful because she'll break your heart all over again.

"Well, no matter what, we're all here for you."

I huff out a breath. "Look, I'm not stupid, I have both eyes open. She's getting divorced, here for a year, and I have a sick mother, a veterinarian clinic, an Ultimate Frisbee league, and did I mention my mother? I'm not going to get sucked into some already doomed relationship."

Miles chuckles. "Famous last words."

CHAPTER 5
VIOLET

I stare at the screen of the phone, debating what to do. Dylan and I have only communicated through our lawyers and a couple of his text messages, which I ignored. This week I've been so busy with getting my lesson plans sorted, meeting all the students, and trying to get my house set up that I haven't had time to even think about my cheating soon-to-be ex-asshat.

I'm not sure talking to him is the best idea, but I also have a feeling if he's calling, there's something I need to know.

Hell, it could be that he isn't going to sign the papers and I'm going to have to allow Ana to kill him.

Tonight Everett is coming over, and I don't want to be sitting at dinner thinking about Dylan.

I'd rather not ever think of him again, but that's probably not going to happen.

"Hello, Dylan," I say, answering on impulse.

"Violet." I stay quiet, waiting for him to speak. "Right. How are you?"

I laugh once. "I'm great."

"Good. I'm...glad. Truly."

"What are you calling for?" I ask.

I'm fresh out of pleasantries. I don't care how he is. I don't care if he's great. In fact, I'm just petty enough to hope that he's miserable.

"I wanted to check on you."

"Why?" I don't believe him for a second.

"You are still my wife."

Oh, that's rich. "I have a lot of things I could say right now about me being your wife, but let's not go there. I'm fine. Thanks for checking in. I have to go."

"Wait!" he says quickly. "I called for another reason."

I knew better.

"I have plans tonight so it would really be helpful if you could just tell me why you're calling," I say, glancing at the clock.

Everett will be here soon for dinner, and I want to double-check everything.

"You have plans?"

I sigh. "Yes, I have plans. I have a life here, or at least I'm building one. Dylan, just…"

"Fine. Sorry. Listen, my new publicist thinks that I need to address the press."

"New publicist?" He's been with Catherine Cole for years. "When did you get a new one?"

"I fired Catherine after she lectured me and wasn't helping. Things are really out of hand here, and we need to make a statement jointly and maybe some photos."

I pull the phone down, staring at the screen, wondering…is he serious? Did he just ask me to do a joint press conference with him?

"Why would I do that?" My voice rises in confusion.

"Because…we should try to mitigate the press frenzy."

"I don't have a press-frenzy issue. You do."

He sighs heavily. "Vi, I need you to help. If it keeps up like this, I could lose the role of a lifetime."

"I'm not sure what you want me to say. You cheated on me, Dylan. For I don't even know how long. You took me away for weeks, claiming you wanted us to reconnect, but you ignored me, and then I get back and find out all of it was a lie. If you have a press or image issue, I suggest you ask your girlfriend for help. Now, if there's—"

"I'm going to release a statement."

"Then release a statement."

"It's going to paint you poorly unless you come back for a few days and we can salvage this mess."

I laugh once. "Dylan, I don't have a mess. I don't have a press issue. I don't have a job issue. If you want to make some big statement, making me the problem, go ahead. It's not like you haven't detonated my life already."

"You left."

"You're kidding me, right?"

"I'm just saying that you ran off, making it look bad for both of us."

He keeps saying that and I'm not even sure what I could do to get into his thick head that I don't care about his publicity issues. I don't care if he never works again. I don't care if the press vilifies him or me or her. I just don't care about any of it.

I sigh heavily, letting as much frustration out as I can in that moment. "You want to blame me and…I can't for the life of me understand where I hold the fault in your decisions, but there's not a chance in hell that I'm coming back to California because of this."

"I won't sign the papers."

"Then don't. I'll wait the six months and get my contested divorce. I'm sure Whitney will love that. She really handled our vacation well, didn't she?"

Whitney is who leaked the photos of them. She didn't like seeing the very staged photos of Dylan and me on vacation. Apparently she was texting him nonstop while we were away, and when she didn't get what she wanted, she made the divorce happen the best way she could.

Whitney sounds like a real peach.

"Okay, fine, then I'll sign the papers this week, but you should want to salvage this too."

He really is delusional. "Sign the papers and I'll consider it," I lie.

Then I hang up, again taken aback by the absolute selfishness of the man I once loved.

I can do this.
I'm fine.
This isn't a date. It's dinner with a neighbor.

I look down at my jeans, tank, and long cardigan and nod. It's casual. Totally casual.

Then why do I feel like my heart might beat right out of my chest?

I hear a car door close, take a few deep breaths, and smile as I walk to the front door, opening it before he can knock.

"Hey," Everett says with a grin.

"Hey."

"The benefits of living in a small town, you always hear when a car arrives."

I smile and nod. "Very true."

He hands me a bottle of wine. "Thank you for having me."

I take it, grateful for something to hold on to. "I think you're the one being thanked, so thanking me kind of negates the first part."

He chuckles. "My bad."

"You're forgiven."

Everett follows me in and lets out a small laugh. "This place is exactly like I remember."

I smile. "Some of my favorite times were in this house. When Granny died, I knew I didn't want to change anything. It's the best decision I made to keep it frozen the way I remembered. Well, other than the lumpy seat cushions and the really uncomfortable bed. Otherwise, I love it all."

When I think back on my life, this is where I was always happy.

Sure, it was a vacation of sorts, but there was more than that. It was a place where I could just be who I was. Granny never tried to mold me into what my parents wanted or force me to be something I wasn't. She was happy for me to wade through life, figuring out which way the waves were going to take me.

"Maybe upgrading the heating wouldn't have been a bad choice."

I laugh. "No, I'm already in the process of doing some small things, like the stove is ancient, and I'm not sure it's actually close to the temperature it says it is."

That was my lesson from yesterday. I am a nervous baker. When my life feels out of control, I can always rely on the chemistry and the oven to provide a consistent outcome. I put the batter in, take the baked goods out, and it's edible.

I went grocery shopping after the heat was on, grabbed my supplies, and then had to run out to get a thermometer and realized the oven is about eighteen degrees off. As shitty as my day of experimenting was, I'm grateful I figured it out before I tried to make us dinner.

Lasagna wouldn't exactly be one of those dishes I could just finish on the stove.

"I'm sure at your house in California you had top-of-the-line appliances."

While I don't think he means it with any form of judgment, I feel the condemnation in my chest.

The people of Ember Falls aren't like the celebrities and wealthy people I spent time around. They don't care about designer labels or what kind of car you drive. They care about people and helping your neighbor, not one-upping them.

"We did, but I don't miss that."

Everett leans against the counter. "You don't?"

"I mean, I miss some stuff. Having a working oven was a plus."

He laughs. "I'd imagine so. What else? There has to be some good stuff there."

There was, for sure. I try to think of the one thing I miss the most since coming here. I miss Ana and Eleanor, but...oh, I know. "I really loved this bakery that was down the street. It had the best pastries, and I swear they imported dough or water to make it taste so good. I used to go every day and the owners were so nice. They'd constantly add new things to the menu so I wouldn't get bored of it. It was the best part of my day."

"I can't compete with that, but we do have cows."

I snort a laugh. "That is something."

Ember Falls also has him.

No, no, no, we are not going there. Uh-uh. Nope. This is dinner to thank him for literally saving me from the cold.

"Are you okay?" Everett asks.

I push out a deep breath and smile. "Of course. Are you hungry?"

"Famished."

Everett helps me carry the bowls out to the dining room. I take the seat across from him, and we pass the plates back and forth, adding different food items on it. We laugh and catch up on small things, like how Hazel decided to open the store and how Miles ended up becoming the principal. For some reason, everything feels easy.

Maybe it's the food. Maybe it's the glass of wine, but the awkwardness is easing somewhat.

Everything is very surface level, and it's been nice to just catch up.

Everett leans back, his arm resting on the chair next to him. "Can I ask some personal questions now?"

And my previous thought about how nice this was just went for a nosedive.

As much as I'd like to have avoided this, it really can't go on forever. "If you must."

"I can keep reading the tabloids if you'd rather."

I groan and take a sip of wine. "No. Ask away, but for every question you ask, I get one back."

"Fair enough. You met your husband in college?"

This is at least an easy one.

"I did. We met my senior year of college."

"I see."

God, maybe it wasn't so easy. We had plans for when I was going to college, and I abandoned them and Everett. He deserves to know what happened and how I feel about it.

As much as tonight was a way to thank him for helping me with the fact that I didn't have heat, it was also a way to open up the lines of communication and hopefully get some of this behind us.

Everett was an amazing guy, and I've always hated myself for what I did to him.

I lean forward, resting my hand on his. "I need to say this to you, and I want you to know that I'm sorry, Everett. I mean that. I was young and stupid and unable to communicate. I didn't know how to tell you that I was terrified that I would follow you and then you'd get your shot at the major leagues, leaving me behind. So I just didn't say anything at all. I thought about reaching out a bunch of times, but then I was afraid I wouldn't say the right things, or that you didn't even want to hear from me."

He rests his other hand on mine. "You were seventeen, Vi. I was asking you to follow me to college, and it wasn't fair."

"That doesn't excuse how I handled it."

"Or the way I did."

That rocks me back. I stare at him, waiting, but he doesn't say anything. "How did you handle it poorly?"

He scoffs. "Well, you told me that you didn't want to go to Florida a few times. Then you finally said that you'd go, but you really wanted to go to school elsewhere, and I didn't care."

No, he didn't.

I remember when we'd talk and I would beg him to consider another option that had the school I wanted. He'd shut me down, saying this was his best chance for the major leagues.

"Again, we were young. So young, Everett. We didn't know anything, and we were so stupid to think it would just magically work out because we loved each other. Still, I should've talked to you. I wanted to, but I was scared. Then there was the fact that my parents kept saying you were going to be some big star and I was going to lose who I was. I was stupid. I was also one hundred percent sure if I did tell you, and I explained what I wanted and why I wanted to go to California instead, you'd convince me to go to Florida. You could convince me to do just about anything."

Everett smiles. "I don't know about *anything*."

I laugh. "Well, I seem to remember a few things we did that I recall required a lot of coaxing from you."

"If we're talking about our first time, I'd like to have the record show that you were the one who told me you were ready and wanted it to be me," Everett says with one brow raised.

That is true. "I meant when you had me skinny-dip in the falls."

"Oh, yeah, that was all me."

I grin. "Okay, you had your question that led to a rather long road. Here's mine. Did you ever get married or were engaged? Are you with someone now?"

That probably should've been my first question, but Hazel had alluded to the idea that he wasn't dating anyone.

Everett drains his wine and places the glass down. "Nope. I honestly just haven't thought about it. When things with us ended, I wasn't in a good place to date. I won't lie, I had no shortage of women interested and I didn't say no often. I was angry and stupid, but no dating, really. Walking away from baseball sort of made me a little bit more of a dickhead, and Hazel acted as a cockblock—to help the women around me. Then I got my head out of my ass and focused on school, which brought me back home and to being a veterinarian."

"I love that you're all still friends and she helped you."

"Me too." He refills his glass and tops mine. "Okay, my question… has your husband suffered a head injury?"

I put the glass down after starting to take a drink, as I'm extremely confused. "A head injury?"

I've heard a lot of things through the tabloids, but that's a new one.

"Or maybe he's suffering from a medical condition they haven't fully come to understand yet?"

I must be in the middle of a really weird and detailed dream, because nothing he's saying makes any sense. "How many glasses of wine have you had?"

He chuckles. "Just one. I have a point."

"I can't wait to hear it."

"If that man doesn't have something wrong with him, there is no logical reason why any man on earth would let you go."

"Well, there clearly is."

He shakes his head. "No. Don't argue. You're beautiful, smart, resourceful, and I lost you fifteen years ago and I'm still not able to date anyone else. So, I don't buy it or at least he'll regret it."

I sit back in my seat, ducking my head as my cheeks warm. "Everett…"

"All I'm saying is that I don't get it. It's been a long time, and there's a lot I don't know about you, but I know you're not a girl that someone could just walk away from."

Oh, how I wish that was true.

I lift my eyes to meet his. "Apparently I am."

Everett shakes his head. "I don't think so."

"Like you said, you don't know me anymore."

"Then tell me why he'd walk away."

What do I even say? I'm not really sure why he left. I'm not sure what was so terrible about me that he felt the need to step out and fuck his coworker. None of it has made sense and, really, I don't know that I care. He did what he did and clearly has no remorse. And he's an idiot for wanting me to go back to California to help him put out the fire he started.

Still, there's clearly something that's wrong with me or at least undesirable.

"You want me to tell you my faults?" I ask.

"Lay 'em all out."

If this isn't the most awkward dinner I've ever had, then I don't know what is. "Well, I snore, according to him. I have ambition, and I wasn't content to just stay home and do whatever he wanted. I wasn't teaching, but I was doing some tutoring online under my maiden name, and he hated that. I hated having *staff*. I can't walk in heels, no matter how many stylists have tried to get me in them for the red carpet. I hated his agent, and while his publicist was nice and all, she was obviously on his side, regardless of how it hurt me. Although he fired her, so maybe she wasn't on his side."

"So far I'm hearing a lot of nothing. I want *faults*."

I cross my arms over my chest and sit back. "They are faults."

"They sure as hell aren't valid reasons a man cheats on his hot wife."

I grin. "You think I'm hot?"

"Absolutely."

I swear I might cry. How absolutely stupid will I look when I break down in tears? Here I am, though, getting misty-eyed. "You mean that?"

"Tell me you really don't know that you're still stunning."

"I don't know that I've ever been called *stunning*," I admit.

Everett stares at me. "You...you what?"

This was part of why I wanted to leave Dylan years ago. "I always felt small when I was with him. It was Dylan's life, his career, his wants and needs, and I just existed."

He wasn't mean or degrading, he just didn't care.

"Please tell me you're joking. You are not small. Jesus, he's more of an asshole than I thought before."

I shrug. "I honestly can't remember the last time anyone other than my best friend told me I was pretty or complimented me."

Everett sits up and clears his throat. "Violet, hear me when I say this, you are absolutely breathtaking. You were the day I saw you when you were fourteen and you still are today. Your husband is a fucking moron for not spending every waking moment telling you how goddamn lucky he was to be with you. He should've counted every star in the sky and thanked each one for having the chance to hold you, love you, touch you. And I can say with all the confidence that he will never forgive himself for letting you go. Never."

It has to be the wine talking. I have to remind myself of that.

He doesn't know the me of today, regardless of what I tell him.

"I appreciate you saying it, truly, but whether Dylan thought I was beautiful or a horse's ass, it doesn't matter. He cheated and I got to learn about it with millions of other people."

Everett leans forward. "I can't imagine that was easy."

I snort. "Yeah, it was definitely not. I thought it was a lie. You live in this sort of alternate reality in Hollywood. Everything is sensationalized and twisted into these clickable moments. Like, if they can get the right hook, then you're locked in. It doesn't matter if any of it's true. It just matters that people will stop and read it or watch it. I'm aware of that fact, so when it started to break, I thought, *Here we go again*. When I kept seeing the photos and finally believed it was true"—I laugh once—"I realized that my life was about to be completely changed."

"So you came here?"

I nod. "I went and stayed with my best friend, Analeigh, for a few days. But I couldn't do that forever, and I couldn't be in LA. I was…drowning in the photos and the news reports. I told her I had to leave and Ember Falls was the first place I wanted to be. I came, I saw a job opening at Ember Falls High School, and it happened quickly. I filed for divorce when I went back to pack the rest of my stuff, and I've been here since."

It was the only place I could run to. Here I'm not Dylan Leone's soon-to-be ex-wife who was cheated on.

I'm Violet, or I'm Ms. Stewart at school. Even though half the kids know exactly who I am.

"I knew you missed me," Everett says with a grin.

I laugh, so grateful for the break in seriousness. "Yes, you were the number-one reason. I thought, *Let me go back to where the boy I loved was, even though he's probably married by now, and I can torture myself in an entirely new way.*"

"I think it's you who wanted to inflict the torture. My ass is falling asleep in this hard chair. How about we go in the living room?"

I let out a quick laugh. My grandmother's furniture is sturdy, but not the most comfortable. When I got here, the cushions on the chairs had to make their way to the trash. Regardless of the woman who came to clean once a month, they were not worth keeping.

"Okay. Let's go."

I grab the wine bottle, and we head into the living room. Everett stokes the fire, adding another log, and we curl up on opposite ends of the love seat, both turned into each other a little and our knees just barely touching.

"Okay, my next question," Everett says, refilling his glass. "How did you meet him?"

"Do you really want to talk about Dylan?"

"Not really, but I've been curious."

I sigh, staring at the flames. "We had a class together. I spent the first three years trying to wrap my mind around how I could be so stupid as to walk away from you. I loved you, Everett. I loved you to the depths of my soul, please know that." His Adam's apple bobs and then he nods, so I continue. "I didn't date or sleep around. I just sort of spent three years trying to be invisible. I met him at a party that my roommate dragged me to, and I can't explain it, because looking back, I was just desperate to not be alone anymore. I was so sad and angry at myself. Here was this guy who was charismatic and had this plan for a life I dreamed of."

"Dreamed of how?" he asks with a tightness in his voice.

Laying all of this out is so difficult, but at least, once we talk about it, maybe the slate can be clean and he can see that it was never about him. It was me. "I spent my entire life moving around from one archaeological site to another. I didn't have any security, and here you were, this incredible athlete who was going to take the world by storm. I was so proud of you, but it terrified me. That we would never have any stability."

He laughs once. "So you married an actor?"

"He graduated with an accounting degree. Dylan never had aspirations for anything more than making a great living and providing a stable home. I thought that's what we were going to have. A marriage, two kids, a dog, and a white picket fence. Then, about two years into our marriage, he just quit his job because he was going to be an actor. It...well, it was not what I thought, but we were married and I wanted to support him."

Everett leans forward, his hand moving to my knee. "I'm sorry. I didn't know that baseball was causing you fear. I wish you'd have talked to me."

"I wish I had too. Not because of the current state of my life, but because I loved you, and I can't help but laugh, because I ended up leaving you to get exactly what I was afraid of, only with a person who sold me lies."

His brown eyes shine with a hint of sadness. "I appreciate you saying all of this. I always wondered what I did wrong."

"It was never you," I reassure him. Everett's hand stays on my leg as our eyes are locked. Immediately, I go back in time to when we sat just like this as kids, and he leaned in to kiss me for the first time.

I glance over at him, seeing that boy again, as he stares back.

"What are you thinking right now?" Everett's deep voice crackles like the fire.

"Is that your question?"

"Yes."

"I'm remembering something that happened on this couch."

His arm drapes across the back. "What do you remember?"

"You kissed me."

"I did."

The rasp in his voice causes my stomach to clench. "It was my first kiss."

"It was mine too."

We were young and naive, but he made me feel so special. "I know, we were all teeth and tongues." I laugh, looking down and shaking my head.

He doesn't say anything for a few minutes, and I slowly bring my eyes back to his. Everett's gaze is serious, and the heat in the room goes up twenty degrees, but it's not from the fire. The desire to kiss him is so great I can barely think straight.

I lean forward, as though we're two magnets and the force is too great to resist. His hand moves to my arm, and my heart is racing.

I need this.

I want him.

I don't care if it's wrong or stupid, it just feels so right.

I shift and move in more. Our lips are so close, and then his hand moves up to cup my cheek. He cradles my face tenderly, and then the other hand comes up, holding me in place. Our gazes are locked, and I wonder whether he can read my thoughts.

I'm scared.

I don't know if we should.

I don't know if I care.

Kiss me. Please. Show me that someone in this world wants me and I'm worthy.

Everett brushes his thumb against my cheek. "I want to kiss you more than you can even know, but the last thing I want to do is mess with your head. You have to make the final move, Violet."

My hand rests on his chest, and I can feel the pounding of his heart. I can't do this. I can't give my shattered heart to this man who is so wonderful. My life is falling apart at the seams and there is not enough thread to hold it together.

He brings his forehead to rest on mine and I inhale his scent, letting it fill me as I try to grapple with my racing mind.

Before I can say anything, his phone rings. "Shit," he grumbles and leans back, breaking this moment.

Thank God. I…wasn't ready or maybe I was, but I'm too afraid to let myself hope.

Everett clears his throat. "I have to take this."

He's on his feet, walking toward the kitchen. "I see. Yes. I'll be right there," he says and then walks to me. "I have to go."

I nod. "Is everything okay?"

"It's fine…I just have to deal with something."

The way he says it causes my heart to race. "Of course. I'm sorry."

He grabs his jacket, pulling it on. "I'm sorry too. We'll talk soon."

And then he's gone, and I'm left feeling like the closing of the door means so much more.

CHAPTER 6
EVERETT

"Dr. Finnegan, you don't understand. Karen complains all the time. And I mean all the time. She's never happy. She hates everything and everyone."

"Yes, but you said she's not complaining," I say slowly, looking down at the docile cat.

"That's my point. She's sick."

Some days I really question my life choices. This is one of those. "Mrs. Pavlov, I understand that you're concerned about Karen."

"Yes, I am. She's not being a Karen."

"But that doesn't mean she's sick."

Mrs. Pavlov strokes the cat's back. "She's letting me touch her. Do you see this? She's possessed, or maybe she was switched with a replica."

I clear my throat. "Okay, so I want to be sure I understand. Karen, the cat, isn't acting like a Karen who is a drama queen? You're worried this means something is wrong."

She nods. "Yes, exactly. You have to fix her. Find out why she's suddenly letting. Me. Touch. Her."

"All right, let's take a look."

I complete an exam with Karen not hissing at me once—not a normal occurrence—but I don't find anything out of the ordinary. Everything looks normal, and there's nothing that I could even try to blame it on.

"Karen looks great, Mrs. P. I think that we can just keep an eye on it, see if over the next week or so she returns to her typical self, and if not, maybe be happy that she's being nice."

That's really all I got.

She picks up Karen and puts her back in the carrier. "I would've sworn we'd find something."

"Cats are cats, you know? Maybe she had a change of heart and just decided being a Karen wasn't for her anymore."

I wish more people would follow that lead.

"I hope so."

"Call the office if you notice any changes. We'll take another look if we need to."

Thankfully, that was my last client of the day, and now I can head to do something fun that keeps my mind from constantly drifting to that damn almost kiss and then the fact that I was once again reminded why I like the routine of my life.

My mother was falling apart and I wasn't there.

She was alone, scared, and couldn't remember where I went because I thought I could change things up and go have dinner with a friend. I should've secured someone to be there, but I figured it was short, and she'd been doing better.

Once again, thank you universe for showing me my ass.

"Dr. Finnegan?" calls Darlene, my tech.

"Yes?"

"There was a request to go to Mr. Thorn's ranch. The trainer called and asked if you could go look at one of the horses before you come into the office."

"Not a problem. I'll let Killian know at practice tonight that I can go by there."

"Great. Have a good night."

"You too."

Once I'm finished with some notes I needed to do, I change and then head to Prose & Perk before the field.

All day I was slammed and couldn't get my normal lunchtime brew. The door dings as I enter, and Penelope and Hazel come out from behind the counter.

"Hello, gorgeous girls," I say with my most charming smile.

Hazel rolls her eyes. "Hello, freeloader."

"Do you treat all your customers this way, or am I just the lucky one?"

"Just you," Hazel says with a shrug.

"I'm so blessed."

"You're something."

She puts a coffee on the counter, and I reach in my pocket and put a twenty down. "Here, this should cover me for today and tomorrow."

Hazel laughs. "That's not even one day's worth of your coffee consumption. It's six dollars a latte, and you have about seven a day."

"Six dollars?" I ask incredulously. "What the hell is in this coffee? Gold?"

"Liquid gold, depending on who you ask," Penny says as she leans against the counter.

"I can't even argue, because I would agree."

"Don't you have practice in two minutes?" she asks.

I'm already going to be late, so I'm not worried about another five minutes. "I'm heading there next. I just missed you both."

Hazel narrows her eyes. "Why don't I believe you?"

"Why else would I come here?"

"Maybe you were hoping to run into someone…"

Hazel and I have been best friends since we were five. She pushed me off the seesaw at recess, I threw dirt at her, and that was the beginning of a lifelong friendship. There is probably no one in this world who knows me better.

This time she's wrong.

If anything, I'm hoping to avoid that someone.

"Not even close," I tell her.

"She was here about fifteen minutes ago," Penelope offers up.

I glare at Hazel. "You told her?"

Hazel laughs. "You think I had to? Who is she living with?" Miles. Bastard is going to pay for this during practice, that's for damn sure. "Besides, what is there to tell?"

I walked right into that one.

"Nothing."

"Really?" she challenges. "I heard that you guys had dinner last night."

"You heard that from where?"

Nothing in this town can ever be kept as a secret. I swear, people talk more than anywhere else.

She shrugs. "Around."

"As much as I'd love to stay here and continue this conversation, I have a practice to get to."

They both wave, and I return the gesture with a lift of my cup and get in the car. On my way, I call Justine, checking on my mom and how her day went. Thankfully, it's one of her better days. She had no real issues and Donna Anderson, Miles's grandmother, is on her way over to relieve Justine for the day.

Donna and my mother are still very close. She comes by on the nights I have practice. They usually watch a movie, knit, or work on whatever craft she brings, and it's always those days that my mother is happiest, which alleviates the guilt I had about playing Frisbee to begin with.

It was even Donna who insisted I join a team. After the accident, I wasn't in a good place. Losing my father was hard, but watching my mother struggle ate me alive. I just wanted to fix it, to get her some semblance of life, but nothing I did helped. It wasn't until I joined the Disc Jocks that I found a part of myself returning.

Thankfully the park is empty, except for us, and I get a spot close to the field. The three guys are already out there, tossing the disc back and forth in a triangle.

"Oh, look who showed up," Lachlan says first.

Of course it's Lachlan who has something to say. Not that if the roles were reversed I wouldn't be the one to give him shit, but he's the second-most jaded out of this quad.

I open my arms wide as I keep walking. "I'm sorry you were so bereft without me. I'm here, princess. I'll make it all better now."

Miles chuckles. "I didn't miss you."

"I'm still not sure I'm talking to you."

Killian snorts. "Lovers' quarrel?"

"Something like that," Miles replies. "He's mad because I forgot to tell him that his ex-girlfriend from fifteen years ago was back in town."

"You forgot?" I say with disbelief.

"Yes, I was kind of dealing with a lot," he tries to defend.

Lachlan walks over, placing his hand on Miles's shoulder. "I've got your back, buddy. For all the shit Everett has given us over the years, he deserves a little discomfort. I heard you guys had dinner last night."

What the fuck? "How the hell did you hear that?"

Bunch of gossiping assholes they are.

"I went to check on Violet's house since I knew it was closed up for a while. I wanted to be sure her fire alarms worked and the chimneys weren't a fire hazard."

"Well, aren't you just the nicest fire chief to ever live," I toss back.

I should've done that. I make a mental note to make a list of things she might need to do and people to contact if something goes wrong.

Lachlan continues as though I didn't even speak. "While I was there, she was cooking and said she was having dinner with her neighbor to thank him. She went on and on about how nice the people are in Ember Falls and what a difference it is. Since you're her closest neighbor, it didn't take much to figure out the rest."

"Did she say anything else?" I ask.

What is wrong with me?

Why the hell did I just ask that?

I wonder what the chances are that they pretend I never said anything.

Lachlan and Miles share a grin.

The chances are a big fat zero.

"She mentioned something today at work," Miles informs me.

Don't ask. Don't ask. Do not ask him or you'll regret it.

"She did?"

I'm a fucking idiot.

"No, she didn't say shit!" He bursts out laughing, and the other two follow. Miles sobers the fastest. "I'm sorry, that was mean. I couldn't help myself. Anyway, I didn't see her today. I had three students who thought it would be funny to paint a mural of a penis in the bathroom. I was tied up with that, so I didn't see Violet."

Killian shakes his head. "Are we going to practice today or what? I have to head back to Boston tomorrow."

"Fine, let's play."

After two hours of running up and down the field, I swear my legs are going to break in half. We have an indoor tournament coming up, since we were able to find a winter league, much to Ainsley's and Penelope's dismay. They both hoped they'd get their significant others back at the end of the last tournament.

I'm sitting on the bench, working to catch my breath while Lachlan is laid out like a star on the ground. Miles is on the bench beside me, panting. It's only Killian, who is the oldest out of us, who looks like he could go for another hour.

How is that even possible?

"Dude, are you on some kind of performance-enhancing drugs?" Miles asks him, clearly thinking the same as me.

Killian chuckles. "No, it's called exercise other than just at practice."

Lachlan lifts his head. "I'm in the gym every day. Everything hurts right now, and I want to die."

"Do it quietly," I toss back.

He gives me the finger. "Sit and spin, fucker."

"Only if you promise to be gentle."

We all chuckle.

Miles pushes up off the bench. "All right, I need to get home. Don't forget the high school football team's home game Friday. Brutus's presence is required."

"Yeah, yeah, we'll be there with bells on."

It's the only time Brutus actually likes me. Anytime I say football, he'll perk up, walk to the door, and allow me the privilege of his company. Otherwise, he just glares at me in the way only he can.

Lachlan and Miles head out while Killian and I change out of our cleats.

"Do you want to grab a drink?" he asks.

"Tonight?"

"Yeah, if you don't have plans."

I shake my head. "Nope, no plans. Donna is with Mom for at least another two hours."

"Perfect. I'll meet you at the bar."

This day is ending up exactly like I needed—Violet-free.

CHAPTER 7
VIOLET

I'M SITTING ON MY LUMPY BED, STARING AROUND THE ROOM, trying to decide which paint swatch I like better.

I'm debating between a cooler blue or a creamy beige with warmer undertones.

My grandmother had a very deep love for yellow, and while I understand it's supposed to be a happy color, it just makes the house feel dirty.

It's time for a refresh.

I purse my lips, tilting my head, and squint.

I think beige is the better choice. The wood accents in the house are warm, and I worry the blue will be too stark.

Yes, beige it is. Thankfully I bought a can of each, so I'll use the blue in the bathroom and it won't go to waste.

I hear Everett's voice outside: "Brutus! Get back here, you dumdum!"

It's been a week since our dinner and the "almost kiss." I haven't been able to stop thinking about it and wondering what it would've felt like.

Would it be like coming home?
Would it feel awkward?
Would the feelings I thought I'd buried rise again?

I know that last one is true, because they already have.

I push the curtain back and see him walking toward the house. Without hesitating another second, I rush down the stairs, taking them two at a time, not wanting to waste the opportunity to see him.

I push out the back door, and a huge bulldog is sitting on my step. Since I'm rushing, I don't have enough time to stop, so to avoid kicking him, I try to jump, but I misjudge and I'm going to hit the ground face-first.

Instead of slamming into the concrete, I hit a hard male chest, sending us both flying.

"Shit!" I say, and he makes an oof noise. "Are you okay? Oh my God, did you hit your head?" I ask quickly. His arms are around me, holding me to his solid chest and protecting me from the fall. I touch his face, checking for any signs of injury. "Anything hurt?"

"Just my pride," he says, his voice strained.

I smile, staring down into his warm brown eyes. Everett looks like he hasn't slept, there are dark circles under his eyes, and the scruff on his cheek looks maybe a day or two older than I've seen him wear it.

He rests his head on the ground, groaning slightly. "What hurts?" I ask again, and he tightens his arms around me just a little more. I inhale his deep woodsy scent, and it smells as though he's been outside working, chopping wood by the campfire.

It's incredibly sexy.

Everett sighs. "I'm fine. That damn dog is trying to kill me. Are you okay?"

"You broke my fall."

He grunts, shifting his body, and I realize that I'm still lying on top of him as he's on the cold, damp concrete. I quickly scramble to get off him and help him sit up. "I wasn't sure I was going to get to you in time. Thanks for that, Brutus," he says to the dog, who looks completely unaffected by the commotion he caused.

"Wait, is that Brutus like the Ember Falls mascot?" I ask as it dawns on me.

"That's him."

I push up and walk over, sitting on the step, and pet him. "Hey, Brutus, you're a very sweet boy, aren't you?"

"No, he's not sweet. He's a turd. I need to bring him to the office today for his shots, and he took off. Of course I didn't have my shoes on, so I had to get those, which is how he got over here so fast."

I smile. "You wanted to hide from the mean vet, huh?"

Everett huffs. "Yeah, the mean vet who pays for his treats, food, and takes him to the f-o-o-t-b-a-l-l game," he says, spelling it out.

"Well, Brutus knew where to hide out. You can come here anytime you want. As a bulldog myself, we have to stick together," I tell the dog, who then flops to his side, offering me his belly to scratch.

"Great, another woman he's got wrapped around his rolls."

I laugh and shake my head. "Here, hand me the leash."

Everett gives it over, and I snap it onto his collar and hand the loop to Everett. He tugs on the leash. "Come on, Brutus. We need to go."

Brutus does not move. In fact, he becomes even more deadweight than before.

"Aren't you supposed to be good with animals?" I tease, trying to contain my laughter.

"All but this one. Come on, boy. Want a treat?"

The dog lets out a snort and I giggle. Everett huffs. "I give up."

Seems Brutus has no intention of moving either. "If his shots aren't urgent, he can hang out here. I'm just painting."

"Painting?"

"Yeah, the house needs a fresh coat of paint. You know, out with the old and all that."

"The inside or outside?" Everett asks.

"Inside first. I don't think I'm adventurous enough to tackle painting the outside of a house yet."

He grins. "I don't suggest it. I tried once and had to call a professional to come fix my mess."

"I'm only doing things I feel like I can manage. Painting seems like a good place to start."

Everett eyes me warily. "Have you ever painted before?"

"No, but it's paint and a wall. Put it up and then it dries."

I spent two hours in the hardware store getting all the information the two old men were willing to disperse. A lot of it contradicted the other, but the basics were there. I need to tape the ceiling, put cloths down, cover everything, then roll.

"I mean, sure, that's the goal, but you have to make sure you tape off everything, trim, and use the right roller."

"Oh, I'm not using rollers. The guys at the store said they leave streaks."

His eyes widen. "Please tell me you didn't go to Sanders."

"That's the only store around here that had paint," I say, feeling a little worried.

I asked Miles where to go before I left work yesterday, and he recommended there. He did say something about asking for help, and that I should ignore it or maybe not ignore it. I wasn't paying close attention as I was writing down the name and how to get there.

He chuckles. "Let me guess, you met Ray and Lou?"

"Yes, they were really sweet."

"Oh, they're sweet and love to give out shitty advice so you have to return twenty times."

My jaw drops. "What? Those cute little old guys?"

Everett sighs and sits beside me, which causes Brutus to make a huffing noise and roll slightly away from him. "Man's best friend my ass."

I fight back a laugh and fail. "Okay, so back to the paint. I *should* use a roller?"

"Help me get Brutus back home, since he's now sworn his allegiance to you, and I'll bring some supplies to help."

"You don't have to do that," I say quickly.

"I know, but I worry what might happen if I don't supervise this experiment."

I roll my eyes, but honestly I could use the help. Plus, maybe Everett and I can talk again, and I can put this attraction to him to rest.

Or find the courage to kiss him, which would be a terrible idea—so we will not be doing that.

Nope.

This will be easy, and I'll get through it without any hiccups.

What a lie that was.

We're four hours into this painting experiment, and I want to slap myself for agreeing to it. Not only has it been one mishap after another, but I'm realizing that the feelings I thought were gone are still very much there.

"Oh no!" I say, looking at my ponytail, which now has streaks of beige in it.

"You painted yourself?"

"Apparently." I sigh, waiting for the biting remark about how stupid I am and that this is why we hire people.

Everett chuckles and grabs the paintbrush, slapping it on his chest. "There, now we both have paint on us."

I rest my hand on my throat, so confused by his reaction. He didn't berate me, which is exactly what Dylan would have done. I wait a little longer, preparing myself for what is sure to come, but he doesn't.

"Oh my God! You got paint all over you!"

"So did you."

I laugh once. "By accident."

"Really? I thought you said you wanted streaks in your hair. Oh, well. Although we should probably not waste any more since I don't have much left in my tray, and the paint can is empty."

This man is the complete opposite of what my ex is.

I forced myself to forget just how great Everett is. I convinced myself that we were just kids, and I had created this fictitious version of who he was.

But he's always been this way. Silly, quick to joke, always willing to do something to help a friend or someone he loves.

Even with the mess that this entire project has been, he's never put me down.

First, I got the wrong kind of paint. I asked for a flat paint, but Ray said I absolutely didn't want a flat paint, that I needed something with a little shine so it didn't look like chalk, to which Lou agreed and said everyone with flat paint regrets it.

I had to go back to the store while Everett stayed at the house, taping everything except the ceiling. He was confused when he saw me start there. I explained about the advice, and he quickly stopped me.

"Wait, we're out?" I ask. They were absolutely certain I would only need one can to do the bedroom.

"Well, three walls are better than none," Everett says as he crosses his arms over his chest.

"Four walls would be preferable."

He chuckles. "I told you, they just want you to go back another time. It's their MO."

I huff. "I don't even have a choice. This is my only place to sleep. I figured since I was at the store at nine this morning, I'd be done before bed."

Everett shakes his head. "How about we take a break, go grab some lunch, and we'll head to Sanders, where I will put my foot in their ass?"

The offer is tempting, but I don't want to hold him up all day.

"What about Brutus?" I ask as he lies on the floor by the empty paint can. We tried to get him to go back to Everett's, but he wasn't having it. Instead, when I went to open my back door to show Everett the paint, he ran in and made himself comfortable.

"Brutus will be fine. He likes you better anyway."

"That is true. Still, don't you have plans or something to do?"

"Helping you is always more important," he says with a smile. "Besides, you owe me another dinner or lunch or something."

I laugh. "So feeding you is the payment for help?"

"Hey, you started it."

"Fine, we'll plan another dinner."

He grins. "Perfect, let's go get you more paint and put the room back together."

Maybe they'll have something at the store to deal with crushes too.

CHAPTER 8
VIOLET

"Violet Stewart, is that you?"

I place the box of cereal back on the shelf and turn. I smile, instantly recognizing the woman before me. "Mrs. Anderson."

"Hello, dear, it is you. Miles said you were back in town, but I hadn't run into you."

"I'm sorry, it's been a hectic few weeks."

She steps closer, shaking her head. "Don't you apologize. How are you settling in?"

"Good, it's been a…culture shock," I say with a laugh.

I've absolutely loved being back in town. My students, the other teachers, my friends, and everyone have been wonderful, but I forgot just how different it is being in the mountains.

In Ember Falls there are limited food and entertainment options. The closest movie theater is thirty minutes away. We don't have a major grocery store, and while the corner mart does have some stuff, it doesn't have my favorite things.

Besides, when I get home from work, I typically crash. I'm so damn tired after being on my feet and dealing with teenagers.

"I'm absolutely sure of that," Mrs. Anderson agrees on a laugh. "You were in California, where I'm sure everything was at your fingertips."

"Yes, that part was nice. I would absolutely love to find a makeup store close."

Her shoulders shake with her giggle. "I'm afraid that's impossible, but you can at least get most things delivered."

"I used to get four-hour delivery online. Now it's four days. I'm learning to plan a little further ahead."

She nods. "That is definitely helpful. So, tell me, how are your parents?"

I haven't really spoken to them since my life went to shit. I did get an email from my mother asking if the news article her friend sent her was true, so I guess that's something.

"They're good. They're on an expedition in South America." At least the last I heard. In her email she didn't say anything other than they were hoping to have a call with me soon.

Her knowing eyes narrow just slightly. "They didn't come home when they heard about your…situation?"

I shake my head. "You know they don't do that. It's fine, though."

It's really not. It's just never going to change. My parents aren't bad. They just don't know how to put people before their work. I've learned how to deal with it my entire life and expect nothing from anyone.

That was the mistake I made with Dylan. I trusted him, believed that he would put me—us—first.

There was only one person who truly did that, and I threw him away.

"Well, I would love it if you wanted to come visit. Do you still bake?"

"I do." I smile, remembering that Donna and my grandmother always liked to bake. Donna had a bakery for a while when I was a kid.

"I miss your grandmother. She was my baking buddy."

"I miss her too."

"I won't keep you," Mrs. Anderson says with a hint of sadness. "I need to get home before Eloise brings the kids over."

Eloise is Miles's twin sister, and we never really hung out. She had her own friends, who were the cool kids, and they didn't like us. Eloise was never mean to any of us—she just didn't want to spend time with us.

"Eloise has kids?" I ask, surprised. She never seemed as though she liked kids—or people.

Donna smiles. "She does. She has a six-year-old boy and just gave birth to a little girl. She actually married one of Miles's best friends from the military."

"Wow."

"Isn't it funny how life doesn't ever go the way we think? However, I think that things work out exactly how they're supposed to. Don't you agree?" she asks with a warm smile.

I would love to argue that my life is absolutely not working out the way it was supposed to. Having your marriage end on television isn't really part of the plan. Still, she appears to believe in that, so I just force myself to nod.

She pats my arm. "It was great to see you. Don't be a stranger."

"Great seeing you too."

I finish my shopping and start my drive home. My phone rings and I see it's my lawyer. I hope she's calling to give me the good news that Dylan signed the paperwork. It's been three and a half weeks since I left, and I was hoping for an expedient divorce.

I should've known that Dylan would never do anything to make my life easier.

"Hi, Gail," I say as I answer her call.

"Hey, Violet, I just wanted to let you know that all of the paperwork is finalized. It just needs to go before the judge," my lawyer explains.

"He signed it?"

"He did. It was delivered back to me this morning."

Maybe some things are working out the way they were supposed to. At least I can put this behind me.

"I really wish you would've pushed for more financial compensation."

She and everyone else.

"I just wanted it to be over. I don't care about the money."

Dylan agreed to my terms that I would get half of whatever assets we have, which is what the judge would've awarded anyway, and I waived spousal support. I really don't want anything from him except to be out of my damn life.

"I'll let you know when it's finalized, but for all intents and purposes, you're divorced."

"How long does it usually take to be official?" I ask.

"At least thirty days. They allow time for either party to make changes and renegotiate. If you do decide you want to amend anything, you can, but it would just delay things."

"There won't be any changes. Thanks for all your help."

"You're welcome. I've requested the settlement be paid at the time of finalization," she says before hanging up.

It'll be nice when I get some money so I can buy some things for the house. Three days ago, a new stove, refrigerator, and dishwasher were delivered. I couldn't handle the nonfunctioning appliances.

I spent last week painting the rest of the bedrooms and bathrooms, on my own I might add. Which I am pretty damn proud of. I didn't even need to make six runs to the store either.

I have a few other small upgrades I'd like to make, but my lawyer advised me not to use any of our joint accounts, as it could be seen in a poor light, so I used part of my inheritance. Although I really don't like touching it, since there's not much to it, and I'd like to have an emergency fund.

I pull down my driveway and my jaw drops.

What the hell?

There's a sealed mattress leaning against my door. I open my car door, thoroughly confused. I didn't order one.

At least I don't remember doing it.

Maybe I did in the middle of the night…

No, I wouldn't because I didn't want to spend the money on

one right now. That was one of the things I planned to purchase once I get money from Dylan, because sleeping on that mattress is absolutely going to be the death of me. The springs and lumps are terrible.

I climb the steps, incredibly confused, and there's a piece of paper taped to it.

Vi,

Two things, first, here is a list of people you need to keep in case of any further housing mishaps, which seems to be your thing.
- *Electrician: James Constantino 1–888-ELE-TRIC (don't ask, just go with it)*
- *Tree removal: Justin, he's a bit of an idiot, but the nicest guy. Tell him you know me. 1-888-555-TREE (look, the town people like to be obvious)*
- *Snow: Call me. I have a plow and I'm not afraid to use it.*

The second thing is:

No one should sleep on an uncomfortable bed. Call me when you're home and I'll move it in for you and no, this is not on my list of things I do, just for you.

E

What? Why?

He bought me a bed? I didn't even complain about it, did I?

I think I passively mentioned that the bed was uncomfortable when he helped me paint, but that was it. I grab my phone and dial his number.

"Hey, are you home?"

I blink, still trying to get my thoughts right. "I am, but what? You bought me a mattress?"

"I had an extra one in the upstairs room. I planned to make it into a guest room, but I ended up turning it into a movie room. A bed didn't make much sense."

None of this makes sense. "Everett, I can't accept this…"

"What? You need a new mattress. You said yours was uncomfortable. I'll be there in three minutes and I'll bring it in for you."

He hangs up and I just keep looking at the mattress.

He did this for me?

I'm so unaccustomed to anyone just doing something like this that I can't even process it. I can feel the moisture welling behind my eyes. This is so sweet.

So unexpected.

He continues to surprise me at every turn. Helping me with painting, the dinner, the almost kiss, and now this…

Everett walks up the steps with a smile. "Hey."

My heart is pounding as I look at him. "I don't know what to say," I confess.

"How about, *Let me get the door?*"

I laugh and shake my head. "That's one option, but you didn't need to do this."

"Is the mattress you're sleeping on comfortable?"

"No, but…"

"But what? You need a new bed, I have a mattress, I want to give you this. Think of it as a housewarming gift."

I force myself to take a deep breath. "And it's incredibly sweet. I really appreciate it. I just feel like it's too much."

He shrugs and walks forward. "It's not."

But it is. "I get paid this week, if you let me know how much it is."

"I didn't bring it over here to sell it to you." Everett looks slightly offended.

"I know that, but…"

I don't know how to accept this. I know how much a mattress costs. It's why I've held off a little bit, because the other things in the house were more pressing. You would think that considering who I'm married to that money wouldn't be an issue, but when you haven't worked in four years, it changes your personal financial situation.

However, I'll pull more from my inheritance to cover this.

Everett huffs a laugh. "No, I don't want your money. Now can you get the door for me? Let's get the old mattress out first."

"Everett..."

"Violet, please get the door."

Right.

I open the door, and we head up to the newly painted bedroom. Everett takes a second, looking around the space. "This color is great in here."

"Thanks to you."

"I think the only thing I can take credit for is that you're still not painting it by hand with a brush."

I sigh. I grab all the pillows, blankets, and sheets off the bed, tossing them in the corner. "I'll never live that down, will I?"

"Probably not. Grab that side." He points to the top of the mattress.

I get ahold of it, and when Everett goes to grab his side, one of the coils nearly pops out. "Jesus, you slept on this?"

"The bed in my old room had a weird smell, so I figured this was a better risk."

He shakes his head and mutters something under his breath, but I don't catch what he said.

We get the old mattress out and the new one in without any issues.

Everett stands against the doorjamb as I finish adding back the pillows.

"You know you only have one head, right?" he asks as I arrange the lumbar one.

"Yes, I am aware of that."

"Okay, so why the thirty-two pillows?"

I roll my eyes. "I have six."

"Okay, same point applies."

"It makes the bed look pretty."

He grins. "I see."

Men never understand these things. There is something about getting in a made bed that looks inviting and comfortable. Also, I needed the pillows to help with the errant springs, but I guess that won't be a problem now.

I sit on the bed and smile. "Thank you for this."

He steps into the room a little more. "Is it comfortable?"

"I hope so," I say, not having a clue whether it is, but no matter what, it's better than what I had.

"Test it."

I pull my lower lip between my teeth and then flop back. Oh, it's heavenly. The bed has no lumps or sharp metal pieces jutting out. There is a plush pillow top attached to it, and it seems to just cocoon me perfectly. I roll back and forth and sigh.

Everett chuckles, much closer now, and I lift my head to see him standing by the bed.

"This is a really good mattress."

"I'll take your word for it," he says.

I reach out, grab his wrists, and pull him down next to me. "See, great bed."

"Very comfortable, lacking any protruding springs."

"And you really won't take anything for it?" I ask, rolling to my side.

"It's a gift, Violet. You don't pay for gifts. Haven't you ever had someone just do something nice for you and not expect anything in return?"

"Yes, but it's just uncomfortable in a way for me."

"You owe me nothing," he says firmly. "This is what you do for people you care about."

I care about you, too, I want to say but keep the words to myself.

His eyes find mine, and the way they brighten causes an electric shock to run through me. Everett and I are lying in bed, and suddenly I see a very different picture. One where his body is over mine, his lips…his touch.

The air suddenly feels harder to get into my lungs, and he seems to be struggling with the same thing. I want to kiss him. Badly. I know I just need to say the words, but I let the desire shine through my eyes instead.

I lean closer, not by a lot, just slightly testing myself, but then he abruptly pushes up, getting to his feet. "I should go. Enjoy the bed," he says hurriedly before walking out.

Leaving me alone on my new mattress and my head an absolute mess.

CHAPTER 9
VIOLET

"All right, everyone, please take your seats," I say, calling the class to order.

A few students look away, but they at least do as I ask.

I pull up the topic of today's lesson on the smart board and hear a collective groan. For the first two weeks of school, I took it easy on them—not anymore. It's September and we are ready to get down to business.

I fight back a smile. "Do we not like Shakespeare?"

One of the boys groans. "No."

"Why do you dislike him, Bryan?"

"Because he's boring as f—" I raise a brow and he stops there.

"Boring or not, he's one of the best storytellers who has ever lived," I say, loving this topic, and *Romeo and Juliet* is my absolute favorite to discuss.

"Thank God he's dead," Bryan says, and the class joins in laughing. He then turns and claps his best friend Mike's hand.

"Ahh, but his words live on," I say and click the button to slide to the text portion showing the balcony scene. "This scene is one of the most iconic, but it's not my favorite."

"It's not?" Jessie, my quiet and top student in the class, asks. "It's so romantic, though, Romeo speaking to her, professing his love. It's so beautiful."

I nod. "It is, but while they're declaring their love at this moment, I don't think it's actually the most romantic or poignant."

Jessie shakes her head. "The wedding?"

"That's one, but I actually think the most profoundly beautiful scene is when she awakes to find Romeo beside her, dead."

There are varying degrees of surprise on the kids' faces. "You think them both dying is beautiful?" Bryan questions. "Nice."

I laugh because boys are all the same, no matter the age. "Imagine, right now, you have someone you love. You're in high school even though Romeo and Juliet were around fourteen and seventeen years old. Now, back then, they'd be living in a time when you'd be thinking about marriage and courting, so let's age them up to what you are now. Bryan, do you have a girlfriend?" I know he does, as he's sitting next to her.

His eyes move to Samantha and he smiles. "I do."

"Okay, Samantha, can you imagine awakening from faking your own death to be with Bryan, your one true love, the man you would defy your family, society, hell, the world to have, only to see him lying beside you, having killed himself because the sheer idea of a world without you was too much for him to bear?"

Samantha stares at Bryan. "Would you do that for me?"

His eyes widen. "Umm..."

I take pity on them and step in. "Imagine, Samantha, because, trust me, you wouldn't want him to do that."

Her eyes go back to me. "Right."

Okay, maybe she would. "My point is, Juliet, being young with an entire life before her, would rather follow him to heaven or hell than be walking on earth without Romeo. It's beautiful and tragic and incredibly sad, but the depths of their love is what leaves generations reading, watching, and discussing this story."

Lord knows I've dreamed of it myself. I idolized their love, the sheer strength of it. How two people were willing to give up everything they knew and their families just to have each other.

Even though they ended in tragedy, they loved in a way that was so deep.

"Okay, but the dude offed himself for a girl," Bryan cuts in.

Jessie talks. "He loved her."

"I love a lot of things. That doesn't mean I would die for them. Sorry, babe," Bryan says to Samantha.

She shrugs. "It's fine. I wouldn't for you either."

This is going to take a bad turn, and I regret calling them out. "The point is, it still can elicit such deep and strong feelings as we talk about it. It's why love stories are still written. Why we hope for a love that would make someone give up all they have for another."

I turn to start writing on the smart board, and when I turn back around, half the class is on their phones.

"Guys, do I need to bring out the phone basket?" I ask.

A few students, at least, look chagrined, but the others are staring at me with a mix of horror and...pity.

My stomach drops, and I can only imagine what the hell they're staring at. "What is it?"

Samantha shakes her head. "Nothing, it's stupid."

I doubt that very much. I glance around the class. "Clearly it's something if you're all looking at me."

Jessie gets out of her seat and hands me her phone.

When I see the headline, it feels as though I've been punched through the chest.

Sitting on her screen is the headline: "Dylan Leone and America's Sweetheart Are ENGAGED!"

"Hit me, Max," I say to the bartender as I sit at the corner of the bar. Max is my new best friend. I came in about an hour ago, and since it was literally just me and him, we spent that time chatting a little.

It's been a day.

A really horrible day.

It didn't start that way, but it sure as hell is ending that way. I still haven't said any of it aloud, because I still can't believe it.

He's engaged before the ink is even dry.

Max places a vodka and diet soda down in front of me and leans against the counter. "All right, Violet. Let's hear it."

I look into his warm green eyes. "Hear what?"

"What's got you sitting alone drinking?"

I sigh and pull my phone out, showing him the wonderful gossip rag's story. While I wish this was a lie, the big honking diamond ring on Whitney's hand doesn't exactly allow it.

Max huffs a laugh. "Let me guess. You're devastated because you're in love with him?"

"I was," I answer and then take a sip.

He shakes his head. "The guy isn't all that great. I heard he cheated on his wife to be with that girl."

My lips turn up into a sarcastic smile. "Yeah, he did. He's also pretty shitty in bed, but you know, no one wants to believe a heart-throb has a small dick."

I bet I could make some money off that story.

His brows lift and he laughs. "You know this personally?"

I close out the social media post and pull up my wedding picture, then show him the phone. "I do." I laugh. "No pun intended."

"Wait, you were married to him? You're the ex-wife?"

"Well, current wife, actually. We're not divorced yet. I just need another three weeks before that is done."

Max leans back. "I'm sorry…"

"Don't be, it's why I'm in Ember Falls. I filed for divorce and came here to put my life back together, but…that was the happy news I learned today with my entire class." I take another sip. "You know, I'm starting to think that's the way he communicates. That's also how I found out that he and little miss America's Slutheart were banging during our marriage. Why not learn about their upcoming nuptials the same way?" I lift my glass in a mock cheers. "Here's to the happy couple."

"Who are we toasting?" a deep voice asks from beside me, and I gasp.

When I turn to look, it's Everett, a strange look in his eyes.

Immediately warmth rushes to my cheeks, and I can't even blame the alcohol, since I've only had two sips. My stomach has been upset since I arrived, and when I took the first sip, I almost puked. "Everett."

"We're toasting to me? Well, that's something since I don't think I did anything worthy of it, but I'll go with it."

I clear my throat, dropping my glass to the bar. The last thing I want to do is show him what a loser I am.

I came here hoping I could avoid seeing him. In fact, I was hoping I'd never see him again, because then I don't have to think about the horrific way he walked out of my room after I almost kissed him—again.

Although the almost kiss at the dinner was worse. Maybe.

Yeah, they're both bad in their own way.

That magical moment in time when I could've had a romantic and beautiful kiss with a man I once loved and who loved me after he called me beautiful, stunning, breathtaking, and I—froze.

Like a loser.

The second one wasn't as charged, but still bad. I was so grateful that he thought of me, wanted to make me happy, but then he pulled away.

Max speaks first. "Do you know Violet?"

"I sure do. We go back a long time."

"Really?" Max asks.

Everett rests one arm on the bar. "Her grandma was Doreen Stewart."

"No way!"

I nod. "Did you know her?"

"Know her? Doreen was everyone's favorite person here. She used to bring brownies to the school once a week for anyone the teachers thought deserved one. It was…my favorite thing."

I smile, remembering baking with her as a child. She knew every recipe by heart and would just go in the kitchen and whip something up, as though it was no big deal. The best part was trying to stump her and naming some weird dessert, but somehow Granny just knew, and she'd make it.

God, I miss her so much.

I smile at Max. "I'm glad you were one who got them then. I loved everything she baked."

Everett clears his throat. "Are you here because the heat went out again?"

"Nope."

"Electrical this time?"

I shake my head.

"Tried to paint another room?"

I snort. "Nope, none of those. It actually isn't any housing catastrophe this time."

There's not a chance I'm admitting the real reason. I don't need to look any more ridiculous than I already do.

"Okay, I'll bite. Why are you at the bar?"

"Why are you?" I deflect.

He points over at a table to the right. "That's one of my teammates, Killian. We came to grab a drink after practice so he can pay me back for waking up at the ass crack of dawn tomorrow to check on his horse."

"You're going to see a horse tomorrow? And help it?"

That's so sweet.

He chuckles. "Well, yes, I am a vet."

"I know, but I figured you just dealt with a lot of dogs and cats."

Everett's smile widens. "I do that too. Do you have a thing against them?"

"Of course not!" I say quickly. "You know that since your dog and I are very close."

He laughs. "Brutus is easily won over. If I told you I also saved a cat today, would you get all excited?"

"Yes. Duh."

He chuckles. "All right, now that I told you why I'm here, I'd like to know what has you here."

Of course he does. "Can't a girl just walk to the local bar for a drink?"

"She can. Is that what you're doing?"

I could lie. It would honestly be the easiest thing, but I hate liars.

"I'm drowning my sorrows," I admit.

"And what sorrows might those be?"

I should've kissed you. I dream every night about kissing you while I lie on my new mattress that you gave me.

My husband is engaged—to his mistress.

Take your pick.

I sigh and open up my phone to show him the article. "Here."

He reads it and huffs. "Well, that would do it."

"It sure does."

"All right, well, your day sucks, but you're not sitting here drinking alone. Come on." Everett grabs my drink and starts to walk away.

"Hey!" I call after him but get off the barstool, chasing my drink.

When we get to the table, his friend stands, like a gentleman. "Killian, this is Violet. She and I have been friends forever. She's going to join us if that's cool?"

Killian smiles warmly. "Of course, welcome."

"Thank you. I didn't plan to be around anyone, so I'm sorry if I'm in a mood. This asshole stole my drink and forced me to interrupt."

"You're not interrupting at all. I'm glad to have someone other than Everett to hang out with, and he totally is a prick. You stole her drink?"

"I did. She would've fought me about sitting with us, so this was easier."

"I swear, you're on a roll lately with your friends."

I grin. "Seems you annoy everyone lately. Hazel said you drive her nuts, and Miles says the same."

"I'm an equal opportunity ballbuster," Everett admits.

I turn to Killian. "So you're a member of his sports team? Do you play baseball too?"

Killian shakes his head. "No, we don't…umm…play baseball."

"Oh? Football?"

"Nope, not football either."

Okay, why is he being so weird? "What do you guys play?" I ask.

"Ultimate Frisbee," Everett answers as he leans back in his seat.

I didn't know that was even a thing. "And what exactly is Ultimate Frisbee?"

Killian jumps in. "It's like football, with a disc. Think of it as a merging of those sports."

"I see."

"It's a lot of fun. Hazel is riveted by the games. She comes to a lot of them," Everett informs me.

"You have groupies?" I ask.

"Of course. I'm kind of a big deal in the Frisbee world."

Killian chokes on his drink. "You are?"

Everett gives him a look. "Aren't I?"

"I'm sure, in some obscure section of the Ultimate Frisbee world—yes."

I laugh softly and try to cover it with a cough. However, Everett sees through it and just smiles at me. "I'm sorry, I'm just really shocked. You went from being really good in baseball to this. It's just a little jarring, that's all."

"I'm good at a lot of things," Everett says, his voice low.

Killian drains his drink and then places the bottle down. "I just remembered that I have a meeting tomorrow morning, and I need to run some reports. Will you guys be okay if I dip out now?"

Everett looks over, disbelief on his face. "You have a meeting?"

"Yes."

"That you *forgot* about?"

"Yup," Killian says with a grin and turns to me. "It was wonderful meeting you, Violet. I'm sure I'll see you around, and hopefully you'll come to one of our tournaments so you can really see Everett in all his Frisbee glory."

Everett glares at him and I fight back a laugh. "Thank you. It was nice to meet you."

Killian nods and then leaves me alone with Everett. That whole plan I had about avoiding him is clearly not going to happen now.

"Did that feel weird to you?" I ask.

"Yes, subtlety is clearly not Killian's strong suit. Honestly, I'd be surprised if anyone in this town could even spell it."

I grin. "At least you know they're always coming at it from a place of kindness. Unlike where I lived, where it was all about schemes and malice."

"I couldn't do it," he admits. "As much as Ember Falls has a lot of problems or things that make life difficult, we mean what we say and we do what we promise. I never understood it until…a few years ago. How lucky I was. How much a community matters more than money or what you have. It's more about who you are."

The idea of that causes me to smile. "It's why I wanted to come here. I can remember Granny talking about how lucky she was. She would tell me about having a family here, even though not a single person shared her blood."

"You're a part of that too, Violet."

My chest grows tighter as I let those words walk over me. How beautiful of a thought that is. "I don't know about that."

"I do."

"How so?"

Everett reaches his hand out to rest over mine. "I get to decide who is a part of it. I'm one of the head decision-makers of all town matters, didn't you know?"

"I didn't. You're so important."

"That I am."

I laugh and then sigh heavily. "I don't know why I'm even upset about it—the engagement. They deserve each other, and I don't even want him. Not once have I missed him or thought, *Wouldn't it be great to talk to him?* Our marriage ended years ago, but we were just unwilling to do anything."

"Because no matter what, you were married to him."

I shrug. "I guess maybe it's more that this is how I found out. It's only been a little over a month, and already he's engaged? We aren't even officially divorced! How does anyone think this is so okay? I don't know, I mean, whatever."

Everett drains his beer and then sits, watching me. "Come on."

I blink in confusion. "Where?"

"Take my hand. Trust me."

Trust. What a funny word. Five letters and yet it means so much. To give trust to another that they won't hurt you is a difficult thing.

But this is Everett.

He's never hurt me. Not once.

It was me who hurt him.

I place my hand in his and he pulls me up, leading me to a space in the middle of the bar. "What are you doing?" I whisper.

"What does it look like?"

I'm not sure, that's why I asked. "Everett."

He grins and pulls me to his chest, his hand on my back. "Dance with me."

Dear God. "This is not a dance floor."

"It's a floor and we're dancing on it. That's pretty much the definition."

Out of mortification, I bury my face in his chest and let him sway me to the sounds of the bar. There are people talking, glasses clinking, and then, suddenly, music playing.

I look up and his eyes meet mine. "See, now we even have music."

I laugh softly and shake my head. "You're a mess."

"That's true, but I'm a cute one."

"Says you."

"Says everyone," Everett corrects.

I don't argue. Instead, I lay my head on his shoulder and dance with him. The song ends, but he doesn't let me go. Another two couples end up joining us, which makes this all slightly less uncomfortable.

The music shifts to something more lively and I step back, but he grips my hand tighter. "Where do you think you're going?"

My eyes widen as I stare at him. "Umm…"

"We're not done." Everett grips my other hand and starts to move like an octopus. His arms move up and down as he waves his lower body.

Truly, it's not dancing. It's more of a flailing, but I can't stop laughing.

We laugh and move, not caring about anyone else in the bar. It's just us, and all my worries melt away as Everett spins me around.

CHAPTER 10
EVERETT

Violet rests her head to the side, staring out the window. "Thanks for driving me home," she says absently.

"Of course."

She walked all the way into town, fueled by rage. There wasn't a chance in hell she was walking down these streets at night, even if she had only one drink.

She glances over. "I had fun."

"I did too."

I can't remember the last time I had so much fun. I'm not a dancer—at all—but when she started to smile and forget her piece-of-shit husband, I didn't care. I just wanted her to be happy, to let go, to remember the girl she once was who lived without fear.

I saw *her*, even if it was just for a sliver of time, so she's still in there.

"I made a cake today," Violet says distractedly.

"Cake is always a good idea."

"And brownies and cupcakes and lemon bars and cookies."

"Okay, that might be a bit excessive," I say with a laugh.

She shrugs. "I was going to make a pie, too, but I was out of sugar and I wasn't going to show up at your house again."

It's probably a good thing, because then I'd have to explain about my mother. While I don't hide her condition, it's not something I talk about freely. There's always a big explanation, and then pity, and honestly, I'm not ready to talk about it with Violet.

"I don't think I have any in the house," I confess.

We turn down her driveway, and she sighs heavily. "It's for the best."

Only it isn't like she thinks it is. She sounds sad, and I fucking hate that she's sad.

I pull up behind her car, putting my truck in park. "Are you going to be okay?"

She nods. "I think so."

That doesn't put me completely at ease, but it's better than the girl I found at the end of the bar.

She looked heartbroken.

Right now, Violet just looks resigned.

"Do you need me to sing for you?" I joke. Lord knows I'm terrible, but I'm going for anything to make her smile again.

She laughs. "No, I'm good."

I smile. "Good, I really fucking suck at it, but I'd try."

"You know you really are a great guy."

Only I'm not, just for her. I want to be a great guy, because I have always loved her.

"Tell Hazel that. Maybe she'll go back to giving me free coffee," I say with a grin, needing some levity so I don't think about how much I still love Violet.

"I'd be happy to put in a good word. However, I make no promises. Hazel is a tough cookie."

I reach my hand out, gently brushing her cheek with my thumb. "So are you, Vi."

Her eyes glimmer in the moonlight, and there's a vulnerability that makes my chest ache. It's as though she doesn't believe anything good about her.

Violet turns her head to look out the window. Her voice is quiet as she breaks the silence. "Why?"

"Why what?"

"Why didn't I see this all coming? Why did I put blinders on?"

"Only you can answer that."

She turns back to me. "I should've left years ago."

"Why didn't you?"

Violet twists her fingers as she sighs heavily. "It doesn't matter, I stayed. I guess I deserve this in some ways for being so stupid. You must think this is karma at its finest."

I jerk my head back. "I don't think you deserve this."

Her eyes move back to me, and there's so much regret in them it makes my heart ache. "But I do. I hurt you, and I didn't give you the courtesy of a conversation, and now look at me."

"Violet, we talked about this. We were kids, and I don't hate you or think this is some penance you owe. Fucking hell, I'd kill him if he were here, but I don't have to do that, karma will. He's going to wake up one day and know you moved on, that's his fucking karma. Trust me, I know how it feels to wake up one day and know you let the woman you love go. I've lived it and he will regret it, just like I did."

Making this woman feel small and insignificant pisses me off beyond words.

He's a coward, and I would do anything to show her what a real man would do for her.

A real man would risk his heart, his soul, his very breath to just be with her.

I would know.

I'm that man.

"Thank you for saying that."

"I mean it," I tell her, hoping she believes it.

She sighs and looks at the door. "I should go inside."

I wish she'd stay.

"Yes," I say, knowing she shouldn't. I want her too much and she's too vulnerable.

She doesn't move. "It's getting late."

The air is thick, and each breath is a little harder than the last. If she doesn't go now, I'm not sure I'll be able to stop myself from kissing her.

I use the last threads of decency I have, keeping my voice steady amid the chaos of my mind. "It is. I have to be up early."

Although I doubt I'm going to sleep. No, I'm going to remember her lying on that bed, smiling and looking at me like all she wanted in the world was for me to kiss her.

I wanted it more than I've wanted anything else, but not like that. Not when she already felt indebted to me.

"Do you want to come in? I have baked goods. Lots of them."

I learned my lesson the last time I came over here, thinking things could be different, but I'll go inside.

Because it's her.

Because I've never been able to say no to her and even if all I get is now, I'll take it.

"Do you want that?"

She looks to her door and back to me. "Yes."

This is one of those times that will define a lot of things in my life. I can either let her walk out, go into that house alone, and have a chance of my heart remaining intact, or I can decide to go in, no matter the consequences.

Although it's not really a choice.

It's Violet, and there is nothing I won't do to make her happy. She's always been the girl that I'd split myself apart for.

Then her voice is small as she looks up at me. "I don't want to be alone."

Well, fuck me. No way I'm saying no now.

I open the car door and come around, meeting her at the front.

We walk inside, and she stops at the kitchen. "I'll bring a plate into the living room."

"Okay."

I head in there, sitting on the couch and regretting all my life choices, and then my phone pings.

> **Lachlan:** I just got an interesting text that I wanted to share with you guys.
> **Miles:** Oh?
> **Killian:** Anyone else have a feeling interesting is going to end up being a euphemism?
> **Me:** Look at you and your big words.
> **Killian:** Bite me.
> **Miles:** Shut up, you two, I want to see what interesting text Lachlan got.
> **Lachlan:** It seems our lover boy was dancing at the bar and left with a very pretty woman.

I should've known.

> **Miles:** Killian finally met a girl? Who knew.
> **Lachlan:** Other loser of the group.
> **Miles:** Everett? He just texted us... I can't imagine he's with a girl and doing that.
> **Killian:** I can vouch that he was with Violet when I left.
> **Miles:** Now that is interesting.
> **Me:** Seriously, this is what you find interesting?
> **Lachlan:** Is it true?
> **Me:** I'm not even dignifying that with an answer.
> **Miles:** Well, that means he's still with her, but it's probably not going well if he's texting. Did you get shot down?

I roll my eyes and put the phone away as Violet walks back in with a plate that's heaping with all kinds of desserts.

"You weren't kidding, were you?" I ask as she places it on the coffee table.

"I can't even imagine what it would've been if I didn't run out of supplies."

I grin. "If you hadn't, then you'd never have gone to the bar."

"And that would've been a shame to miss your dancing." She sits beside me.

"It would've."

Violet pulls her lower lip between her teeth and then stares down at her clasped hands. "Everett?"

"Yes?"

She lifts her gaze to meet mine. "You said all I had to do was say the word."

I swallow and nod. "Yes."

All she has to do is ask me, and I'll give her anything she wants.

"Kiss me."

I want to, more than I want air, but I don't want her to regret it. "Are you sure?"

"I was sure the other night. I was sure the day in my room. I've never been more sure that I want something than I do right now."

That's all I needed to hear. I lean forward, taking her face between my hands, holding her so that her gaze has nowhere else to land other than on me. Violet's cognac eyes turn heated, and I move in infinitesimal amounts, allowing her a chance to back out at any point. Her lids slowly lower, and there's a breath between us.

I can hear her struggling to keep her breathing even, and I linger, drawing out the anticipation.

If I only ever get this one more time, I'm going to make it count. I'm going to pour everything I have into this kiss and make it one she'll never forget.

"Violet," I say her name softly. "Breathe or you might miss the whole thing."

She inhales and then closes the gap, kissing me.

It's like fire and ice. The warmth of her lips is thawing the parts of me that have been frozen, and the other parts of me that have been burning feel as though I'm numb from the cold.

Everything inside me is at war.

I slant her head to the right, and she opens up for me. My tongue slides into her mouth, tasting her again for the first time in years. She's the same and yet different. She tastes like a sun shower that is both humid and prickles the skin.

"Everett." She sighs my name as her hands tangle in my hair, holding me to her.

I kiss her again, moving together in a dance not unlike the one we had at the bar. Violet scoots forward, pressing her chest to mine, and I'm on fire for her.

I pull her closer, forcing her to wrap her legs around my middle. God, I can feel the heat of her against my cock.

I'm like a virgin all over again with Violet in my arms as we're on her couch. I groan and kiss down her neck.

"Yes," she says quietly. She drops her head back, giving me access to kiss her wherever I please.

"Tell me what you want, Violet."

"We shouldn't," she says, but at the same time she kisses me again.

"Then you have to tell me to stop," I tell her.

I will kiss her, touch her, taste her, and fuck her if she lets me. Since the second she walked back into my life, she's *been* all I want.

She hesitates as I kiss her neck, and I realize what a fucking prick I am right now. I want her, but not like this.

Not when she had a day like this.

Not when I can see the way this story ends and I'll be the villain.

I pull back and she rests her forehead on mine. "I want you," she says.

"You have no idea how much I want this, but…" I have to work extremely hard to say the next words. "Not tonight. Not like this."

She leans back. "I don't want to stop."

"Trust me, I don't either." My cock is rock hard, and the heat of her against me is too fucking much. "But tomorrow, I'm not sure you won't regret it."

"I won't."

"I can't believe I'm saying this, but I think you will. I won't be another guy who doesn't think about you. Who takes what he wants and doesn't care about the aftermath."

Violet lets out a half laugh and half sigh and climbs off me. "I can't even do this right."

"Violet, it's not that. Did you hear what I said?"

"Yes, you worry about my feelings, but I want this, Everett. I want you. I want..."

If anyone ever heard the fact that I'm turning away a woman who is literally asking for me to fuck her, they'd have me committed.

I take her hand, pulling it over my aching cock. "Do you feel that? Do you feel how much I want you? I'm torturing myself right now because I can't be something you'll regret in the morning. You tell me tomorrow that you want this, and I promise, I'll spend however much time it takes to erase every memory you have of any other man. I'll make sure that the only thing you remember is how good I made you feel. You won't be able to walk when I'm done with you. So I'm going to go home, and you're going to go to bed—without me, and knowing I'm hating every word I'm saying now. Then I'll try to fall asleep not remembering the way you moaned when you kissed me. And if, tomorrow, you tell me that you still want this, then buckle up, sweetheart, because I won't have the strength to walk away." I stand before I lose the nerve.

Her amber eyes look up. "I never should've let you go."

I grin. "If you hadn't, I wouldn't be the man standing here today."

If we hadn't lost each other when we did, she might not have come back to Ember Falls, and I wouldn't be who I am. All of this is a chain of events, and she'll never know how grateful I am that it's me in front of her.

Violet stands, her hand pressing against my face. "I'll see you tomorrow."

"I really fucking hope so."

CHAPTER 11
VIOLET

"Please tell me you're going to call him tomorrow. If you don't, I might find a way to clone your number and do it myself."

I laugh, lying on my bed, unable to think of anything else except that kiss. "My head is a mess."

Analeigh laughs. "Then let's unfuck it."

I roll my eyes, glad she can't see my face because we're not on video. "I'm not even sure I can."

"It's worth a try."

I lean back against the headboard and sigh. "Give it your best shot."

"Okay, when you were straddling him, was he hard?"

"Analeigh!"

"What?"

He was. So hard. So big. So much more than I remember, but I won't tell her that.

"I'm not talking about that, and it's not why he stopped it."

"I'm sure he didn't want to be the guy you fucked while you thought about your husband, who is newly engaged to the woman he was banging during your marriage."

I huff. "I'm sure too."

"Well, were you?"

"No! I didn't even think about Dylan. All I've thought about since being here is Everett."

Honestly, I hadn't thought about Dylan since the moment I saw Everett. I was too busy laughing, smiling, dancing, kissing...oh, the kissing...

"Did you tell him that?"

"No."

"Okay, so maybe your head isn't a mess as much as you just really suck at communicating," Ana says with a note of judgment. "You have to tell guys. They're really not all that smart when it comes to reading a woman's mind. They are far too literal."

"Nick seems to have no issues understanding what you want," I toss back.

She bursts out laughing. "Nick? Are you kidding me? I literally text him what I want, and then it shows up. We don't expect the other to read our minds, and we talk about everything. Yes, he *tries* so hard to be romantic and surprise me, which is cute, but when it's the big things, I tell him exactly what I want."

That was never the case for me. I've always been...embarrassed about what I want. My parents didn't care or ask me for my opinion when it came to things that mattered, so I learned to not have one.

Granny was the only one who would ask and push me to state my desires.

As a kid, whenever Hazel, Miles, Everett, and I would play or make plans, I never was the one who made the suggestion.

I just went with the pack.

"I'm not sure I can do that."

"Why not?"

I really hate that she pushes me to feel vulnerable. She knows why, but I guess I have to spell it out.

"What if he doesn't want to? What if he rejects me? He walked out that day in my bedroom."

Analeigh chuckles. "I'm going to say there's a fat chance of him rejecting you this time. Didn't he say something about buckling up?"

"Yes, but it's awkward."

"Okay, I think you need to practice," she says as though this is the best idea she's ever come up with.

I groan because there's no way this isn't going to end up without me hating my life. "Ana, I don't think..."

"That's right, don't think. Just do what I say. I want you to open up your text messages and write to me, pretending I'm Everett."

Yeah, that's not going to happen. "No."

"Violet, you need to learn to ask for what you want. You're sending it to me. You know there's nothing you're going to say that will shock me. So take a deep breath, open the text, and tell me what you want."

I open the text because I know this will never ever end, and Ana will just keep pushing.

Me: I want you to stop pushing me.
Ana: I bet you do, but that's a big fat no.

I sigh. "You're annoying, you know that?"

"You called me because you wanted my advice," Ana says with her stern tone laced in each word. "I know that you're afraid and that telling people what you want or need is foreign to you, and I love you, so know that when I say this, but it's why you're in this position. You would never tell Dylan how you felt. You let him decide your life. The last real decision you made on your own was the college you went to, and even that, you just ran from the confrontation of your feelings. I get it, Vi. I really do. You're so easygoing and don't ever push back, but you have to fight for yourself now."

I stay silent as my throat grows tight. Tears build behind my eyes, and I want so badly to shove them back, but instead I let them fall. "I don't know how."

"Oh, my sweet friend, you are right now. You're in Ember Falls, you filed for divorce, you didn't let Dylan convince you to let him make you out to be the villain or whatever bullshit his PR team would've pushed for. You got a job thousands of miles away. You did that. Look at how you handled today. You're fighting, but now you have to push against the instinct to protect yourself and take what you want."

An unease sits in my chest, making it hard to breathe just thinking about it. Every instinct in me says to just slink away and be the good girl who is quiet and accommodating.

But that girl was broken.

That girl was used, and it wasn't good. It was horrible.

It led me here, and I don't want to be her anymore.

It won't be easy, that's for damn sure. I'm not even sure I can do it, but Ana's right. I did all those things, and I didn't ask a single person for permission.

I did it for me.

I glance at the clock on my bedside table and smile when I notice it's officially tomorrow.

"Okay, here's what I would say to him."

I pull up my text message and tell Ana exactly what I would say to Everett.

Me: It's tomorrow, and I want you. Come to my bed and let me show you what I regret.

I hit send.

"Too stupid?" I ask her.

"What?"

"The text!"

Ana clears her throat. "You didn't send me a text."

My eyes go wide and I pull my phone down. "Oh God," I breathe.

"No! You didn't!" Ana says with a laugh. "You sent it to him?"

"I did. Oh, God."

I'm going to have to move. Sell my grandmother's house and be homeless. No way in hell can I face this man ever again.

"What did it say?" she screeches.
I read it back to her and she is silent.
"Ana? What do I do now?"
"I think you better go unlock your front door…"

CHAPTER 12
EVERETT

I'm a goddamn idiot.

I walked out of that house and the second I breathed the cold night air, I wanted to slap myself.

Also, I think I deserve a medal.

That was a Herculean effort to say any of that and then actually leave her when she looked all mussed and beautiful.

However, what I said was the truth. I will want her any day, and being with her when she's hurting from something that douchebag did isn't exactly what I want our first time in years to be built around. So I came back to my house, cursing everyone and everything.

I roll to my side, punching the pillow in hopes I can get comfortable now that it's after midnight and I have to be up in four hours.

Great.

I am trying to close my eyes when my phone pings, and I sit up quickly. It could be the alarm company informing me my mother opened the doors again.

It is not that, though.

No, it's much more…surprising.

Violet: It's tomorrow, and I want you. Come to my bed and let me show you what I regret.

I stare at the text, and then I'm throwing the covers off and getting to my feet before I can even think about it.

Well, there goes all the restraint I thought I had.

I'm out the door before I can even get my sweatshirt on over my head. This time, it doesn't take me ten minutes.

No, I'm through the brush that separates our houses in less than one and across her lawn in another.

Two fucking minutes and if I had been on the first floor, I would've been here in one.

I'm not sure if I should knock since she told me to come to her bed, but I do, and the door opens within a second.

We stand here, staring at each other, and I clear my throat.

"Are you sure?" Giving her one last out.

Her chest rises and falls as I watch a million emotions dance in her eyes. Finally she speaks. "Yes. I want you to kiss me, because with you, I feel alive."

I don't know whether I'm dreaming or what, but I hope I never wake up so that this is not just a fantasy. I take a step forward and she does at the same time, wrapping her arms around my neck, and then our lips come together.

And it feels like home, despite the years between us.

I kick the door shut and then spin her so she's pressed against it, kissing her like a starved man, which I am. I slide my knee between her legs, holding her up just a little.

My hands move from her hips to cup her breasts. She gasps as I squeeze them gently. "I remember the first time I saw you shirtless," I say, as my thumb moves across where her nipple would be. "I remember thinking there was nothing in the world as beautiful as you."

"You made me feel good."

She stares at me, her gaze molten. "Do you want me to make you feel good now, Violet?" I ask again, giving her another out.

"Yes," she replies without any hesitation.

Thank God.

Without wasting another second, I lift her shirt up and toss it to the floor. She arches her back, rubbing my hard cock. If I thought I was hard before, I'm granite now.

I move my hands to her back and undo the hook of her bra in seconds, pulling the straps down, and while I may still remember her all those years ago, it's nothing compared to the woman in front of me now.

She's so fucking gorgeous.

"You are perfect," I say with a knot in my throat. "*So* perfect. Tonight is for you, Violet. Whatever you want, let me be the man to give it to you."

Violet shakes her head, but I don't let her say anything. I lean down, my mouth watering as I swirl my tongue around her nipple before sucking it in my mouth. Then I start to flick it and alternate between the two movements, listening to the sounds she makes.

"Everett," she moans.

When she says my name, I feel it everywhere.

I move to the other side, giving it the same attention. After a few seconds, she moves her hands to my face, pulling it back.

Her chest is heaving and she kisses me again. I groan as we devour each other. I rub my cock against her front, and she hitches her thigh around my hip. I do it again, and she gasps against my mouth.

I stare down at her, cheeks flushed and eyes swimming with desire. "More?"

"This…I don't…I don't want to use you. I don't want to hurt you."

She has no idea that I've only ever been hers. She can't use me or hurt me. She's just putting a piece of me back together.

"Fucking use me, Violet."

"It's you I want," she says. "But this is all I can give you for now. I'm not ready for more."

Jesus, could this be any more perfect? No strings, no promises, no demands, just fucking pleasure with the woman I've dreamed of for years. With my life as up in the air as it is with my mother, my job, and everything else I take care of, I've never had the ability to give more to a woman.

"I don't need more. I can't give you a future, Violet. I can't make you any promises other than the sex will be good."

"Then make me feel good."

And that's all I needed to hear.

CHAPTER 13
VIOLET

I push at Everett's chest before he kisses me again, and confusion spreads across his face.

I'm not pushing him away, though.

All I want is him, and tonight, for once in my life, I'll be doing something for me.

I'm going to have him.

I've thought of nothing else but being with him. How he makes me smile. How I'm not the worthless woman I've felt for years. With him, all of that disappears.

With him, I'm just Violet.

"Let's go upstairs," I say with a soft smile. "I did promise my bed."

He grins. "Thank God. The things I plan to do to you will be much better in a bed."

I lead him up the stairs, and with each one I take, my heart races faster. I can't believe I'm going to do this. I know being with Everett isn't wrong. My marriage is over—it has been for a long time—and I deserve to be touched by someone who sees me as more than a burden.

When we get into my bedroom, he turns me to face him, and his mouth is instantly on mine again. We kiss, and the notes of his beer from earlier and his familiar peppermint taste sweep against my tongue. He walks me backward as I cling to him, my bare chest against his.

Everett's hands move to my pajama shorts, and he slides them slowly down my legs, leaving me in nothing but a pair of black panties. He's on his knees before me, and I shiver when he kisses my leg.

He stares up at me, his eyes filled with lust. "God, you're beautiful," he whispers, his voice thick, and he kisses up my body.

When he's standing, I hook my fingers in the waistband of his sweats and push them down. "Just tonight," I say again.

"Or anytime you want," he says with a cocky smile.

I have a feeling if this is half as good as I think it will be, I'm going to be begging for more.

The backs of my legs hit the mattress. "Lie down, Violet."

I do as he asks and wait for him to climb up to me, but he doesn't. He stands there, staring down at me, the heat in his eyes felt all through my body.

"If I might only have tonight, then I'm going to make the most of it." Those words send a shiver down my spine, and I don't think I've ever heard anything hotter. He pulls my panties down, leaving me completely bare to him. "*Fuck.* Yeah, I'm going to have you every way I can."

"Everett." I sigh his name.

"Do you know what I regretted the most after I lost you?"

I shake my head.

"That I never had a chance to know what your cunt tasted like on my tongue. I'm going to rectify that mistake tonight. I'm going to make you come that way and then on my cock and maybe my fingers."

I feel like I unleashed a beast I didn't know before. "Three times?"

He chuckles. "We'll see if I can beat that before the sun comes up."

If he only knew I've never had multiples. In fact, I haven't been able to orgasm without help in a long time, which was something that always pissed my husband off.

"You should know something," I say carefully.

"What?"

This is so embarrassing, but if I don't say it, I know I'll regret it. "I don't...come...easily. I struggle and I... it's not going to be you. It's me."

He laughs once. "Are you saying that you don't think I can do it?"

"No, that's not it."

"If you're saying it might take all night, then we're wasting time. Open your legs for me."

"But..."

"Open your legs, Violet. I have nothing but time, and I promise, it's not a hardship to have to spend hours between your thighs if that's what it takes."

My heart is racing, but I do as he says, spreading myself to his gaze. His head lowers, and he kisses the inside of my knee. "What time is it?"

What the hell does he care about the time for? "Does it matter?"

"Look at the clock," he commands.

I turn my head. "It's twelve-oh-seven."

"Got it."

"Got what?"

Everett doesn't respond though. Instead his mouth is doing other things like kissing his way down my thigh, and then I feel his tongue swipe against my clit. My eyes close at the sensation. Everett's hands move to my knees, pushing them down against the bed, and he literally eats me out. His tongue makes circle after circle, and then pushes inside, all while he holds me immobile. I try to move my hips, but I'm completely trapped by his weight.

I can feel my limbs trembling as my orgasm races.

No way.

I can't.

It never happens like this.

But here I am, thrashing my head back and forth as the pleasure builds faster than expected.

He moans, and I feel his teeth taking my clit and gently biting. "Oh, God. Oh my God!" I pant over and over, my fingers sliding in his thick hair.

Everett releases one leg, and I feel his finger enter me. He slides in and out of my cunt as his tongue continues to make circles and patterns.

I can no longer think.

My brain is completely disconnected from my body. All I feel is pleasure. All I know is this rising tide that's threatening to take me under.

I scream out his name when it crests, taking me under, but at the same time giving me life.

I feel him kissing up my stomach and the valley between my breasts, all while he continues to finger me. I whimper as I work to bring my breathing back to normal. When I finally open my eyes, he's leaning over me with a shit-eating grin on his face.

My back bows as his thumb rubs my clit. It's too much. "I can't…"

"You can," he counters. "Feel how wet you are. It's dripping down your leg. You want more, baby. You want to come again. I can feel your cunt pulsing, begging for my cock to grip onto it." His dirty mouth is new, and I'm not complaining at all. "And that was just the first one." He pulls his finger almost all the way out before pushing back in. "I think maybe I'll make you come like this now."

I shake my head, unable to even entertain that it's possible, but then, oh God, he curls his finger and keeps going.

"Everett," I pant. "Please."

He just keeps going, his thumb now hitting my clit when he pulls back. It's too much.

I'm unable to stop it. I can't even think because another orgasm hits me so hard that I can't breathe. My body writhes and shudders as it tears through me. All the while he keeps going, not giving me any reprieve.

It's a mix of pleasure and pain, each warring with each other. I want to laugh and cry and everything in between, but all I can do is fall slightly limp and struggle for breath.

"What time is it?" he asks again.

Somehow I manage to open my eyes to look at him, wondering what the hell he cares about the time for, and since he could very easily look at it since it's in his view, but I turn my head.

"Twelve fifteen," I say, still panting.

"Two orgasms in eight minutes, now I bet we can get another one before half past."

Oh my God. That's never happened before. I continue to stare at it, thinking maybe it froze, but then it moves to twelve sixteen.

Wow.

I stare into his eyes, pushing the dark-brown hair off his face and grin because now it's my turn. "Only if I get to ride your cock."

"Your wish is my command." He pulls his fingers out and then slowly licks each one, his eyes staying on me the entire time, and I think I might come just from watching him. "Mmm, delicious."

I need him inside me right now. "Please tell me you brought a condom," I say, praying he did because I don't have any and I have to have him.

He chuckles and rises, moving to his sweats, pulling a condom out of the pocket. "It was the first thing I grabbed. Hell, I even left my phone." At least one of us is prepared. He stands in front of me and I rise onto my knees, my hand resting on his hard stomach. "I want you to put it on me."

I move my hands down, pulling his boxers off and staring at him in all his glory. His thick, hard cock stands at attention, and my mouth waters.

Yeah, he may have thought I was perfect, but he is a goddamn Adonis.

I bite my lip and take the condom from him, but I want something else first. "You had regrets about us when we were younger," I remind him. "I did too. You were the first in so many things, but I never was brave enough to do one thing."

I keep hearing Ana in my head telling me to ask for what I want.

"What is that, baby?"

I look up at him with a seductive smile. "I want to suck your cock."

He climbs on the bed and lies beside me with his hands behind his head. "By all means, I wouldn't want to deprive you."

I lean down, kissing him, and feel his hard chest before wrapping my hand around his dick, stroking him slowly. He moves one hand to the back of my head, keeping me right against his mouth before I break away.

My kisses move down his neck to his chest, and then I keep going lower. When I reach his cock, I kiss along the shaft and then lick the crown, tasting his precum.

"Violet," he groans, and then I take him deep.

I hollow my cheeks, bobbing up and down, using my tongue on the underside. My hand pumping in time with my mouth.

Each gasp, each moan, every sound he releases drives me to make this the best thing he's ever experienced. I want Everett to never forget tonight.

His fingers lace in my hair again, and he pushes me a little deeper, but not enough that I choke. I do my best to relax the muscles in my throat so I can go even further.

"That's it, baby," he murmurs. "You're taking me so well."

The next time down I'm able to swallow deeper, but not much. I keep going, sucking, licking, and when I moan, his groan is so deep I feel it in every part of me.

"Violet, baby, you have to stop. I want to be inside of you."

I pull my mouth away and straddle him, but he immediately flips me on my back and grabs for the condom.

"You're going to come again, and I'm going to watch every second of it when I take you."

"Everett," I say softly as his words send a tingle across my heated skin, and I watch him wrap the condom over his length.

"Look at me, Violet." I meet his gaze. "Watch your pussy wrap around my cock."

He adjusts his cock and I feel the tip enter. "Oh God."

"Do you know how long I've wanted this? Do you even have a clue how long I've dreamed of being with you again?"

My chin trembles as I fight back tears. I want to confess that I've always thought of him, that a piece of my heart has always been his, but I can't.

"You have me now," I say, rubbing his cheek with my thumb.

"Do you want more, baby?"

I nod. Yes, I want this so much.

I want him—all of him.

Everett Finnegan stole my heart when I was fourteen. He was my first kiss, the first boy to touch me and claim me as his. And when I close my eyes, I'm that girl again.

The one who dreamed of a lifetime of this. A world where Everett was always mine.

I never thought I'd feel this again.

"Open your eyes for me, Violet. Look at how good we fit."

He pushes deeper, my body accepting him, and I glance down where we're joined, feeling so many emotions it's hard to control them.

My eyes move back to Everett as he moves his hips, driving into me in slow, controlled thrusts.

Our eyes stay locked as he moves, the feeling of him inside me is too much. The building starts again, between the emotions and the intense friction, driving me back toward an orgasm.

My fingers dig into his back and then score down his sides. He groans, moving his hand between us, rubbing my clit as he keeps pumping his hips.

"Oh, oh, it's coming again."

"That's it, Vi, feel it. Feel me fucking you, me touching you. You're so fucking beautiful. Grip my cock and let me feel you come for me, baby."

It keeps building, climbing, and Everett doesn't relent. He grips my hips, adjusting the angle, and then I fall apart.

I cry out, my head thrashing side to side as my orgasm takes over.

Everett follows right after, collapsing on top of me, and there's not a chance in hell that's going to be the only time we do this.

CHAPTER 14
EVERETT

I stare out the window, watching the sky at the earliest parts of the morning, where night and day are at war and the dark blues are starting to lighten. I maybe slept an hour, but it'll be worth every minute of exhaustion I feel.

I pull Violet closer before I kiss the top of her head. To have her again was everything and more.

Her arm is draped across my chest while the heat of her breath dances across my skin. Her scent, vanilla and cinnamon, fills me, warming me from the inside out.

In my thoughts, I had this belief that if we did this, I'd somehow have exorcised her from my head. That was a lie.

If anything, I just want her more now.

She stirs and then looks up at me. Her warm eyes widen, and then she blushes. "Good morning."

I smile. "Good morning."

"What time is it?" she asks.

"Just about five thirty."

She lifts up onto her elbow. "Shit, didn't you have to go to Killian's farm?"

I pull her back down. "I'll be fine. I'd rather stay like this a little longer."

She nestles back in, her hand resting over my heart. "Okay."

We lie like this, and I do my best not to think about how I'm going to spend the next year around her and not have her this way.

"You were right," I tell her.

"I was?"

"This bed really is comfortable."

She grins. "It's all the pillows."

I laugh once. "Yes, that has to be it."

What Violet doesn't know is that I didn't have this mattress lying around. I ordered it the day we painted her room after I remembered her saying she couldn't sleep well on her old one. When I sat on the edge, it sagged more than I've ever seen a mattress sag before.

I just wanted to make her smile and not have to worry about one more thing.

Violet's alarm starts to beep, and she rolls away before sitting up. "We should get moving."

Yeah, we should. "I need to get home anyway," I say reluctantly. I really have to get my mother set up, but I'd much rather stay here with her lying next to me.

She gets up, pulling the sheet with her, and just watches me as I pull on my pants. "Everett?"

"Yeah?"

"Are we okay?"

I laugh once. "That's supposed to be my line, Twinkle."

For a second my heart stops. That came out way too easy. That nickname hasn't been said in fifteen years, but she's not just some girl I picked up in a bar. There's a lot of history, and while that's probably why we fell into each other's arms so easily, it's complicated as fuck.

Violet watches me, swallowing once before smiling. "Well, that makes me feel better."

If there's anyone in this situation who is going to end up hurt, it's me.

As I lay awake, I kept thinking what a fucking idiot I was.

She's…I don't know, vulnerable? Her entire world has come down around her, and here I am, walking right into it.

Yes, we said no promises and all that, but come on. There's always going to be feelings between people who loved each other once. Plus, she'll leave, go find whatever peace she is looking for, and I'll be here. I can't leave Ember Falls and we both know it. Even knowing this, I won't resist her. I've wanted her for too long and one taste of her will never be enough.

"Come here, Vi." I watch her walk around the bed before she's in front of me, and she tilts her head back to meet my gaze. "Are you okay?"

Her lashes flutter, and she bobs her head slightly. "I am."

"Truly?" I hook my finger under her chin, not allowing her to look away.

"I've never done this. I've never slept with someone I wasn't in a relationship with, but at the same time, you're different. You know? We were in love. I've kissed you before. I've been with you before. It's not casual, but at the same time, it…is?"

"I get what you mean. If you were just some girl, I would've bounced before the sun came up, but I didn't want that."

She laughs and then turns her head. "We're a pair, aren't we?"

"We sure are."

Her eyes move back to mine. "I don't know how to…like I don't want to say thank you, because it wasn't like a service, you know?"

"No, it wasn't. It was something much more than that."

"But at the same time…it's not like we can say I'll see you tonight or make plans, because we said no strings."

I pull her close, my arms wrapping around her, wanting it to happen again, but I won't push. "Shut up and kiss me goodbye."

Her hands move up to my face, and our lips meet. It's a soft, gentle kiss, not nearly like the lust-filled and frantic ones we shared all night.

I pull back and then lean in again to give her a peck. "I'll see you later, okay?"

"Okay."

I wink. "Okay."

I grab my shirt, throwing it on, then my sweatpants and shoes. I turn back, and Violet is still standing there, the sun now poking out more, and I know I'll never forget how she looks right now.

She's so beautiful with her brown hair falling around her face, framing her sleepy eyes and slightly swollen lips.

Her delicate hand lifts in a wave and I do the same, then turn before I tackle her back on the bed and we both miss work.

"So, how did last night go?" Killian asks as we're walking out to the barn.

"It was fine. How is the horse?"

He laughs. "Deflecting much?"

As if I would give them any ammunition to use against me? Absolutely not. I'll lie before I tell them a damn thing.

"Here, I brought you coffee. Hazel insisted." I hand him the cup.

"Thanks, but it's half gone."

"Oops."

Killian snorts. "Anyway, the horse is better. He was moving around a little earlier."

"That's good. Does the trainer know how he could've injured it?"

"He wasn't overly forthcoming—you know how Travis is. He knows everything, and he only produces winners."

Killian owns part of this horse farm with his friend who breeds and boards racehorses. It's an amazing facility, and the care his horses receive is top-notch, but his head trainer is an egotistical asshole. If I can avoid dealing with him, it's for the best.

"He's something, all right," I say as we enter the stall.

The horse shifts back and forth as we approach. "Hey there,

buddy." I lift my hands as I open the door. "I'm not going to hurt you, I just want to see what that mean trainer did to your leg."

He snorts and lifts his head a few times before stepping back. I've looked at him a few times over the years, and he's always been a little skittish. I can only imagine, now that he's in pain, that I'll have to work a little harder.

Killian steps over to the side a little out of view, and the horse settles slightly. "You're putting weight on that leg, so that's a good thing," I say in my most soothing voice. "I'd like to take a look. Will you let me closer?"

I lift my hand and brush his neck, continuing to let him know I'm not such a bad guy. After another minute of that, he moves his head to bump my shoulder, and I see we're going to be friends.

The exam doesn't last long, since it's pretty clear, based on the swelling, it's a joint issue. I exit the stall and Killian comes around. "He needs stall rest and no training or races for a while. I'd like to do an injection to help with the healing, but I'm serious that Travis needs to give him a break."

"I'll take care of it," Killian promises. "He's still young, and I think Travis sees something in him and is just pushing him a little harder than he needs to."

"He is. Tell him to relax or you're going to have more issues than just this."

"Thanks, Ev."

"Of course."

We start to walk back, and Killian just can't help himself, apparently. "So you were childhood sweethearts with Violet?"

"Yes."

Maybe if I keep to one-word answers he'll give up.

"How is being around her now?"

It's conflicting and terrifying because I could see myself easily falling back in love with her.

"It's fine."

Okay, that was two words.

"Sure it is."

"We're just friends. There's nothing there." That's the biggest lie I've said. There's definitely something there.

"It didn't look like that last night. You looked like you were ready to lasso the moon for her."

"You need glasses, old man. I don't have the time or the energy to put into any relationship. Between work, my mother, Frisbee, and sleep, there's not a chance in hell I can dedicate more of myself. Not to mention, Violet and I have already failed once, and she's leaving in a year, and then she'll probably move back to California."

Which is what she's alluded to and I have to remember if I feel myself slipping.

"Did she say that?" Killian asks. "Hazel was talking about her staying around longer."

No, no, no. I can do a year. I can't do forever with her here.

I'll fucking lose my mind.

"That's news to me."

Killian clasps me on the shoulder. "It's a good thing, then, that you guys are just friends."

Yeah…just friends.

CHAPTER 15
VIOLET

I MADE IT THROUGH THE DAY WITHOUT ANY MAJOR CATASTROphes, which is a win in my book. The kids behaved, we made it through more of *Romeo and Juliet*, and tonight I don't have to cook.

When I stopped in Prose & Perk for some required caffeine, Hazel invited me for a girls' night where I can get to know Penelope and Ainsley better. I'm really excited because I miss Ana and that close friendship with other women.

I drop my bag and head upstairs, flopping on the bed.

The bed.

This bed.

The bed he gave me and where last night there was very little sleeping. I roll over, burying my head in the pillow, and catch the remnants of all things Emmett. Fresh air, woodsy, and a little bit of farm, but when you bundle it together, it's just him.

I flop back over, refusing to be a pillow sniffer, and grab my phone as it rings. Well, this should be eventful.

"Hi, Mom," I say in a sweet, singsong voice.

Whenever I talk to her, this is how I sound. My mother doesn't like unpleasant people, so I've spent my entire life being—happy.

"Hello, Violet. How are you?"

"I'm good. You?"

"Wonderful. Your father is off on a hike today while I stayed back at the village."

"And you're in Peru?"

"Yes, it's wonderful here. Very hot, but we've made some interesting findings that could lead to a real discovery."

I love my mother, but this is the script she follows all the time. Not that she hasn't already done some incredible work, but she's had a lot more misses than wins.

"I'm sure that no matter what, the work you're doing is meaningful."

"Yes, dear, that's why I continue to do this. How is teaching? Have you spoken to Dylan?"

"Teaching is great, I love my students. I haven't spoken to Dylan in a while other than when he called me asking for me to get him out of the PR nightmare he was in, but he fixed it."

By getting engaged.

Mom huffs. "Did he?"

"Yes, and I have nothing more to say to him."

"That's your decision."

One she doesn't agree with. Although that's nothing new. Mom is my biggest critic. "It is and I'm content with it."

"Good, then. And Ember Falls? Have you seen any of your old friends or Gran's old neighbors?"

I smile at that, because yes, I have seen Gran's neighbor. "A lot of the people we knew here are still in the town. Hazel is doing great, Miles is the principal, which I told you, and I saw Everett as well."

"I hope you stop by to see their families, and when you do, be sure to send them our love."

"I will, Mom. I know Dad will want me to do that as well."

My father grew up in Ember Falls, but he never felt like he belonged here. He was into digging holes and finding buried treasure. He would tell me about how the other boys wanted to ride bikes and play sports, but he'd rather dissect something.

However, this place was his home.

"Yes, he would. Now, I'm curious, did you file for divorce, or are you and Dylan going to find a way to work through your issues?"

My head drops and the exhaustion overwhelms me. Not just because I'm running on only a few hours of sleep, but because talking to her always drains me.

There are expectations I can never meet. I don't do things well enough. I don't work hard enough. I don't put the effort in required to be a success. *"It takes a lot of work to be at the top, Violet. You can't worry about boys and makeup, you need to focus on what matters."* I heard it over and over or I got: *"Marriage isn't for quitters. You have to give more of yourself than you take."*

I gave all and was left with nothing.

"Mom, there is no marriage to save. He cheated on me, and he's now engaged to another woman," I say, using the firmest voice I can manage with her.

She's silent for a moment. "That's that then."

"Yes, that's that."

It should've ended years ago, but when I went to my parents to talk about how I was feeling, they nearly blew a gasket about walking away from a marriage. It's unforgivable for them.

"I'd love to stay and chat, darling, but I need to meet your father and get things organized for the dig. We're finding that doing it a little later is proving to be better."

As if I knew what that meant. "I'm glad you're finding success."

"Take care of yourself, okay?"

"I will, Mom. Give Dad a kiss for me and tell him I love him."

"I will. Bye."

"Bye."

I hang up. "I love you too, Mom," I say quietly.

After I take a twenty-minute power nap, I hop in the shower and get ready to head to Hazel's. Once I'm in my jeans and USC hoodie, I make the fifteen-minute drive. Hazel moved out of her family's home and into her own that's closer to the center of town. It's small, but super cute.

"You made it!" Hazel says as she sees me climbing the stairs. She and the girls are out on the porch, which has an adorable swing and two chairs.

"Oh wow! Your porch is to die for."

She smiles as she closes the distance between us. "It's why I bought this place. I loved the porch and figured I could fix whatever I hated inside. Luckily, I love the inside just as much."

"I love it."

Hazel takes my hand in hers, leading me up the stairs. "Ainsley, Penny, you guys have all met Violet."

They both come over and give me hugs. "It's great to see you outside of the coffee shop," Penny says.

"I know we've met a few times, but it'll be so nice to get to know you for real." Ainsley's warmth is laced in each word.

"Thank you for letting me crash your girls' night."

Ainsley scoffs and waves her hand. "You're not crashing! You're a welcomed member to our little squad."

"Well, I'm grateful to be welcomed into the fold then." I've been in Ember Falls for a little over a month, and this place has started to feel more like home.

"You may have regrets about that," Penny says with a grin. "These two are relentless, and while both are amazing, you'll find it hard to say no to them."

"I'm a delight," Ainsley says while batting her lashes.

I laugh, instantly loving her. She reminds me of Analeigh. "You sound like my best friend. I swear that's her catchphrase."

"It's a good one."

"It is and also completely untrue about her," I tell Ainsley.

She grins, wrapping her arm around my shoulder. "My fiancé would agree that it also does not apply to me, but…I don't give a shit."

"Neither would Analeigh."

"Then when she comes to visit, you have to bring her."

The idea of Analeigh in Ember Falls is almost funnier than anything. She would absolutely lose her mind here. "If that ever happens, I definitely will."

Hazel's eyes narrow slightly as though she's figured something out. "Analeigh? Like as in Analeigh Walsh?"

I nod. "That's the same one, only now she's married."

"Oh my God! I loved her dad!"

I laugh because everyone does. Her dad was a famous boy band member whom my grandmother loved before he became an actor. There are generations of women who adore Eli Walsh. "He's really a sweet guy."

"That makes me so happy to hear," Hazel says with a dreamy sigh. "So many times you find out a person you idolize is a dick, and that ruins the fantasy."

"Don't I know it." I married one.

"Yes, well, don't worry. We all hate Dylan now," Ainsley says.

I love that they have my back without even knowing me. Besides Analeigh, I never really had someone watch out for me like that. "I appreciate the solidarity."

We spend the next hour laughing and talking about life and some fun gossip about Ember Falls. I laugh way too hard when Ainsley talks about the fire at the cabin she was staying in when she first got here.

"That cabin should've been condemned when I used to visit," I say between giggles.

"The listing online didn't mention any of the issues it had," Ainsley says with a sigh.

"And then it caught fire?"

"Well, it caught smoke. It didn't get to a fire, but without that event, I wouldn't have been forced to stay with Lachlan."

Aww, that's sweet. "When is the wedding?" I ask.

"If you ask Lachlan, he'd say tomorrow, but we really don't have a plan. I'd like to have a small wedding, on the beach, with just our families there. However, his daughter, Rose, wants a huge wedding where she can be the flower girl who wears a tiara. She also demands I have a very big dress."

"That is something to consider," Penny says. "I mean, she's a princess."

Ainsley turns to me. "She really is. She's so adorable and I love her so much. Most likely, we'll find a compromise." Then she looks at Penny. "And what about you guys?"

"Oh, we'll have a bigger wedding. According to Miles, I've spent way too many years hiding away, and I'm going to have a day where I'm the center of attention. Even though we all know I'm not all that excited about it."

Hazel sighs dramatically. "Oh, the horrors you both face."

"I had a big wedding and an even bigger marriage implosion," I say absently.

My wedding was truly one for the books. My parents, being as conventional as they were, had a lot of things they felt were necessary for their only—virginal—daughter. Yeah, that conversation was hilarious to sit and listen to, since I stopped being a virgin when I was sixteen.

I really didn't care about any of the things they asked for, but my mom suddenly was the mother I always wanted. She was so much fun during the planning. I think it was a lot like an expedition for her, so I let her have control and enjoyed our time together.

Hazel reaches over, taking my hand. "It brought you back to Ember Falls, and I know that there are several people truly happy about that."

I think about last night and the way he touched me, kissed me, how he made me scream his name and how I could feel my body temperature rise.

I do my best to hide my thoughts, but Hazel is close and she studies me. "I wonder if you're happy about someone too?"

"Oh, Everett and you were a thing as kids, right?" Ainsley asks.

Hazel shifts. "They were so gross. Seriously, Miles and I would have to go in other rooms because they were horny teenagers."

"Hazel!" I protest. "It was not like that."

"Ha! You were always making out, and after you and he finally"—she makes a very clear sexual innuendo with her hands—"it was even worse. Then you guys would actually ask us to go away."

I hide my face in shame. "Oh my God."

The girls laugh and Hazel nudges me. "Don't be embarrassed, Vi, you guys were actually super cute."

I peek through my fingers. "Cute? You just said we were gross."

"Okay, maybe *gross* isn't the right word. However, let's not get away from my original point. Are you happy to be back because of someone else?"

"Am I happy to see Everett? Of course. I loved him with my whole heart, and I've always had regrets around how that all ended. I'm really glad we've been able to talk and work it out, find a new... friendship. He was a huge concern when I decided to come back here. I wasn't sure if he was married or had kids, so I was really uncomfortable."

Ainsley smiles. "I get that. I knew Lachlan since I was a kid. He and my brother are best friends, and I remember wanting to puke thinking I'd have to come here and find him with someone and pretend I didn't care. Not that I would've been upset if he was happy, but facing it is super hard when you loved them."

I'm glad someone understands. "Exactly. I want him to be happy, and it seems like his life is pretty great here. It's going to make it easier when I have to leave."

"Why do you have to leave?" Penny asks.

"My contract here is just one school year."

Penelope pulls her legs up, wrapping her arms around them. "Talk to Miles before you decide anything. The worst he can say is no."

I nod even though I know that won't happen. Besides my contract being valid for only one year, I can't stay because there's no way I'll be able to resist wanting something more with Everett, and he's made it clear he doesn't want that.

Just like I have.

"I don't know that I can hide away here forever."

"Is it hiding?" Penelope asks. "I know all about hiding, but it seems like I found myself here more than anything. Maybe the same can be for you."

"I hope I find myself, but on the heels of this ordeal with my ex, I don't know that love will be what I find," I confess.

Not that a part of me won't always love Everett, because there will always be a part of my heart that's been reserved for him.

You can't love someone that much and not be forever altered by it.

"He's always missed you, Vi," Hazel says cautiously. "Please just be careful, because the two of you could very easily fall back together, and when you leave, I don't want to pick him back up again."

Yeah, I need to be careful for myself too.

I'm blaring my favorite song, singing as loud as I can as I drive back home. The sun has set, the stars are shining, and I'm still singing my silly heart out when I put the car in park. You don't just shut the car off in the middle of a ballad.

The song finishes and I've grabbed my purse to exit the car when I see a shadow of someone moving on my porch.

My heart starts to race, and all the blood drains from my face.

Oh, God. I'm going to die.

I try to remember what to do from those self-defense classes.

However, my brain seems to have gone blank. I should do something. I should…run or use my car. That's what I should do.

I start my car back up and then the shadow is at my window, the hood is pushed back, and I realize it's not a serial killer or someone who wanted to abduct me. It's Everett.

I let out a very heavy breath and pry my fingers from the death grip I have on the steering wheel.

I manage to get out of the car on shaky legs. "Everett, you scared the crap out of me."

"I was sitting right there. You probably didn't notice me as it was all coming back to you, huh?"

Great. He heard me singing. Fabulous.

"After a good girls' night out, you should always end it with a song."

He chuckles. "I'll take your word for it."

My heart is finally beating at a normal pace. I lean against my car door, wondering why he's here and also hoping it's for the same reason I thought about turning down his driveway when I was coming home.

I lift my gaze, our eyes meeting, and it feels as though we're both saying a million things.

Do you want me still?

Did we make a mistake?

Should we make another one?

Neither of us speak, and then I feel the brush of his knuckles against my face. My eyes close as I lean into the touch. So soft. So gentle. So perfect.

"Everett, why are you here?" I ask, barely a whisper.

He holds my face in his hands, tilting it up until I'm looking into his gorgeous brown eyes. "It's still tomorrow."

CHAPTER 16
EVERETT

Call me stupid.

Call me whatever you want, but I sat on her porch step for an hour talking myself in and out of being there.

I even left once, but then found myself right back there.

All day I convinced myself that coming here, seeing her, would be a mistake.

But I don't fucking care.

I'll deal with the consequences later. Tonight, I want every second I can have of her. If this story ends in tragedy, then by God, I'm going to enjoy myself before that hits.

Violet doesn't say anything. She lifts up on her toes, her lips brushing mine. "What if we just say one more time?"

I lean down, cupping her thighs and hoisting her up. She giggles and wraps her arms around my neck as I carry her up the stairs. "How about we say one more night. I plan to fuck you several times tonight."

"Promises, promises," Violet says before she crushes her lips to mine, kissing me deeper with each passing second.

I bump into the couch and decide that'll work. I turn, sitting, all while her tongue continues to rub mine. She's straddling me, her long brown hair creating a curtain around us, like there's no one else in the world—and right now, there's not.

My worries.

My business.

My mother.

My life all disappears, and all that exists is Violet.

Her hands are in my hair, and my hands are on her ass, pulling her tighter against my erection.

She starts to rub back and forth, and I help set the pace.

It's like we're fifteen again, dry humping on her grandmother's couch.

So much has changed, and yet it's the same in many ways. She's a siren, an Achilles' heel, a woman who has the potential to leave me in ruins.

But I'm not stopping. We know the rules.

This will be the last time.

I move my hand between us, undoing her button, then her zipper. "Are you wet for me?" I ask, my hand reaching toward her underwear.

"Yes," she moans and rocks harder. "Touch me."

I slip my finger down, and a low rumble comes from my chest when I rub against her cunt. "So wet, so fucking hot."

"For you."

"Yes, baby, just for me." I push my finger in, feeling the way she grips me.

Unfortunately for me, in order to remove her pants, I have to stop. I quickly remove her jeans and underwear, and once they're gone, I pull her back to being on top, sliding back inside her warmth.

My thumb rubs her clit and her head falls back, the long waves brushing my leg. I lift my hand, placing it against her long, exposed neck. "Is this okay?" I ask softly when she flinches.

She nods.

I keep a light pressure, and watching her riding my hand is so hot. "You're so beautiful. I love being inside of you, watching you as I pleasure you. Do you wish it was my cock?"

"Yes."

"Yeah, Violet, I know that's what you want." I push another finger in and she gasps. "I want to feel you around me so badly."

She looks down at me. "Please."

I release her and move my hand to slide my pants down. I grab the condom in the pocket but Violet stops me before I put it on.

"Let me. I didn't get to earlier."

I grin and hand it to her. Her delicate hand wraps around my cock as she pulls it between us. She tears the packet, and then my head drops to the back of the couch when she strokes me softly.

"I think you want me too."

"So much."

"How much?" she asks.

I lift my head and give her the truth. "I waited on your porch for an hour."

That seems to make her happy, as there's a smile on her lips. "I debated turning down your driveway when I was on my way home," she confesses.

I brush my thumb against her lower lip. "Why?"

"Because…the same reason you're here now."

She slips the condom on and then rolls it down.

I lean forward so my lips are right against her ear. "Fuck me, Violet."

I hold my cock, lining it up, feeling the scorching heat of her before she sinks down.

We both let out a long moan as her tight cunt grips me. After a moment, she starts to rock and it feels so goddamn good. I can't think straight with the pleasure of her on top of me.

My hand goes to her shirt, and I rip it off. After removing her bra, I cup her breasts and bring my mouth to them where I suck and lick, while she rocks against me.

"Everett!" she yells, her fingers gripping my hair, holding me against her.

I keep going, doing my best to hold back because I'm so fucking turned on. She feels incredible, and I don't want this to end.

I want more of this—of her.

But it's like a train that can't be stopped. "Are you close?" I ask against her skin.

"So close."

I clench my jaw and think of anything I can to avoid release too soon. "I'm close, baby," I warn. "Fuck me harder."

I put my finger on her clit and rub fast. She's panting, her moves becoming more frantic as she chases her release.

Her muscles clench around my cock and I groan, my other hand digging into her ass. "Yes, fuck me. Yes. Harder. So fucking good." My words slip out, and then I feel her grip me tighter before she screams out, her hand falling to my shoulder.

I jerk my hips up a few seconds later, no longer able to hold back.

Fuck my life, I'm never going to get enough of this girl.

We're sitting on the floor, the fire going, eating some of the desserts still left over. "I brought some to school for the teachers, and Miles took some for Kai, Penelope's son. I even brought some tonight to Hazel's, and there's still so much left."

"How did the girl party go?" I ask.

"It was great. They're all sweet."

I chuckle at that. "They're all diabolical. Ask the men they're with."

Violet tucks her leg up, wrapping one arm around it. "I'm going to assume your friends are the victims in this?"

"Absolutely not. They deserve every minute of torment they endure and then some."

She shakes her head and pops part of a brownie in her mouth, making the sexiest moan ever. "I swear, chocolate can solve any problem."

I clear my throat and try not to picture that sound as something else in her mouth. "If only that was true." I would use it daily if I believed it could do anything to help the people in my life.

"I mean, I guess it can't solve them, but it does make it better." Violet leans her head on the couch cushion. "I ate a lot of chocolate...like, a lot in the days after Dylan's affair broke. Ana actually was worried at one point."

Talking about her ex-to-be husband after fucking her brains out isn't exactly high on my list of things to do, but I'm not sure where or what this thing is going to be, so I might as well say it now.

"Is there any chance of you going back to him?" I do my best to sound like the answer really doesn't matter, which it shouldn't. She's not mine anymore. She hasn't been for a long time.

Violet's eyes lock onto mine, and the steel in her voice is impressive. "Not ever."

"Because he cheated?"

She shakes her head. "No. Because I don't want to be with him. Yes, the affair was the catalyst, but there was so much wrong in our marriage that I was just pretending wasn't there. He's selfish, beyond measure. He even called to ask me to come back to LA because *we* have a PR problem. Apparently the stories aren't painting him in the best light."

What the fuck? "He asked you to come help?"

"Yup."

"I'm hoping you said no."

Violet smiles. "I said unequivocally no." She takes another bite and then continues: "Then the idiot got engaged. Not sure how that is supposed to help him, but it's not my issue. Being back there is too much for me. I don't fit in there. You can't even begin to imagine the things people say about me. Things that are cruel and horrific."

"About you?"

What the hell can anyone say bad about her? She's beautiful, smart, kind, and has a heart of gold.

Her sigh causes my chest to ache. "Anytime they posted a picture of us on the red carpet or at a premiere, the comments on those photos would make me sob for hours. I did my best not to look, I really did, but there were times I couldn't avoid it. People who don't know me just...ripping me apart. When the affair broke, I wouldn't even open my phone unless it was a text message, but one of my college friends sent me a screenshot, and I literally was sick."

I lean forward, my hand resting against the side of her neck. "Those people are fucking idiots."

"Maybe, but the comment was so gross, so unkind. I didn't deserve him cheating because I'm a fat bitch. I didn't ask for it. I didn't do anything to him. No one deserves this kind of humiliation. If he was unhappy, he could've just said the word and ended it. I would've been sad, sure, but not mortified at the same time."

"Violet, it's his embarrassment."

She snorts. "Apparently it's mine. I'm the villain in this story. I didn't satisfy him. I was too controlling. I was too plain. I was too ugly. I didn't give him what he needed, and of course he should've gone elsewhere. Do you have your phone?" she asks.

"It's over there."

She reaches around me, grabbing it. "Here, open a social media site."

"I don't..."

"It's fine. I have chocolate." Her voice is soft and encouraging.

Still, it feels like a trap. You know, when your mother would tell you to go ahead, do what you wanted, but you knew that if you did what you wanted, you'd be in trouble. Women are always good at those.

I give her a side-eye and decide not to open the phone. "I don't need to see what they say about you, I know the truth. I've also learned that people who don't have any influence in your life don't matter. People can say what they want, because at the end of the day, we all just do the best we can. I make mistakes, you make mistakes, but isn't that the point of life?"

Her gaze softens. "Maybe I don't need chocolate. I just need to record that and play it back."

"If you tell anyone I said that, I'll deny it. I have an image to uphold."

"Oh? What's that?"

"The evasive bachelor who is sarcastic and nothing bothers him."

Violet snorts a laugh. "And how is that working for you?"

"So far, it's been great."

Only the people in my life who actually know the real me are aware that none of it is true.

She smiles and takes my hand. "Thank you. It's been a very strange twenty-four hours."

"How so? You've had amazing sex, girl time, and more amazing sex." I remind her of that second part again because it deserves another mention.

"That is all true. I've also dissected more of *Romeo and Juliet* with a bunch of teenagers who are intent on making points that aren't at all relevant, and I talked to my mother."

I really hope Violet's relationship with her parents has gotten better. When we were young, she was always so sad when it came time to go back with them. She loved her parents, but they worked all the time and she was alone so much.

"Are you guys closer now?"

She shakes her head. "No, it's just the way we'll always be. They don't understand me, and I'm always disappointing them." She shrugs. "It is what it is. What about your parents? I'm so sorry I didn't even ask about them."

I rub the top of her hand with my thumb. I don't talk about this with anyone. I haven't really had to, to be honest. The entire town was there, doing what they could to help me and Mom. They made meals, cleaned the house, and when I realized she wasn't going to get better and she and I both needed to have a little separation, they were at my property every single day, helping to build the barn for her.

Some people will ask, but most know that there's no change, and it usually sets me off to have to keep saying it.

While I'm not angry all the time about it, I also don't go out of my way to discuss it. To tell Violet will be one of the first times in years that I'll have to go into the entire story.

"Everett?" Her soft voice breaks the silence. "What's wrong?"

"Six years ago, my father died."

She instantly shifts up onto her knees. "Oh my God. I didn't know. I'm so…I feel like…God, I should've known. How?"

Her eyes are filled with unshed tears and I pull her to me, wrapping my arm around her. There's no way I'll get through this if she starts crying. Her tears will break me. "My parents were in a car accident. It was bad. The car flipped, and Mom can only remember certain parts of it. She remembers him swerving to avoid something, I'm guessing a deer, and then the flashes of light and the sounds. She talked about the sounds a lot. At some point, she lost consciousness, and when she woke up, the car was upside down." Violet tries to sit up, but I hold her there. "Please, I won't be able to get through this if I have to see you sad."

"Okay," she breathes, staying against my chest.

I steel myself to get into the rest. "My mother said he was breathing when she woke. That he told her it was okay." My heart is pounding, and the pain of that night comes back so intense, it aches. "That he loved her. He loved me…" I have to stop and choke back the emotions. Violet wraps her arm around my middle, holding me more than I'm holding her. "He died at some point, and Mom screamed for so long she couldn't speak when they found her."

Violet moves, no longer against my chest, but now back to straddling me. She keeps her gaze away from mine and buries her head in my neck. I can feel the moisture against my skin, but her arms are like a vise around me, as if she can hold me together with her small body.

I'm quiet, letting her hold me as I tighten my arms around her.

This is why I loved her so fucking much.

She just knew what to do.

She could make any situation better just by being near me. If I was angry, she made me laugh. There weren't dark skies when Violet was with me.

Even now, as I'm recounting one of the worst nights in my life, she's giving me something I didn't even know I needed.

After a few minutes, she pulls back, and saltwater tracks run down her cheeks in rivulets. I wipe them. "Why are you crying?" I ask, a faint smile forming on my lips.

"Because you loved your dad so much. He was your best friend."

Yes, he was. My father loved me more than anyone in the world. There wasn't a problem he couldn't fix. Except death.

"He still is," I admit. "I miss him."

She cups my face. "I'm sorry I wasn't here. I'm sorry I didn't know. It sounds so stupid to say this aloud, but if I did know, I would've come back."

I lean forward and kiss the tip of her nose. "No you wouldn't, but I appreciate you saying it."

Violet was married, living her new life, and while I love the sentiment that she'd have been here for me, we both know that's not true.

"Maybe I wouldn't because I'm stupid, but my heart would've been. I'm even more sorry I didn't think to ask about them. We kind of skated around parent talk. How is your mom now?"

"The accident was bad, and Mom isn't the same," I start. "She suffered a very serious head injury. She was out of it for days, and we weren't sure how severe the damage would be long term. It was impossible in the beginning for the neurologists to even make a determination. Each day something changed, but her traumatic brain injury has left her with a lot of short-term memory issues. She knows who we are, that Dad died, the accident, but she can't remember where she put her shoes or if she made tea and left the kettle burning."

"Where is she now?"

"She lives with me, I built her an apartment in a barn. It's actually nicer than my house, and I offered for her to stay in the main house, but she said she couldn't, she couldn't find Dad."

Violet's frame falls a little. "Oh, Everett."

I smile a little, because she looks so damn cute. "It's okay. She has good and bad days, but we have a plan in place."

"You are such a good man to take care of her like that," Violet says before she leans in and kisses me. "She's so lucky to have you as her son."

Violet is one of the only people in the world who knows the truth. She was visiting her grandmother the day I found out that I wasn't really their child, not blood related, at least.

I was broken beyond belief and I ran out of the house, needing to be alone, but when I walked down to the back of the property, Violet was there, and I lost it.

She listened, hugged me, and then told me that she would give anything to have parents who loved her the way mine loved me. That love doesn't come from blood—it's from the soul—and I was lucky to have two parents who were so willing to give me theirs.

"I wish I could give her more. I wish I could go back and tell my dad how much he meant to me."

"He knew, Ev."

"I know he did, but...I could really use some advice at times. I wish I could tell him all the things I didn't get a chance to."

Violet shifts off my lap, curling up into my side. We both stare at the fire, the crackling sound filling the space. I pull the blanket off the couch and wrap it around us.

She tilts her head up, her amber eyes even warmer thanks to the glow of the fire. "I think when we love someone so much, they're always with us, even when they're gone."

Yeah, I think she's right, because no matter how far Violet went, she has always been in my heart.

"And sometimes they come back."

She grins. "Sometimes tomorrow comes again…"

"Tomorrow."

"Tomorrow."

CHAPTER 17
VIOLET

"You're pregnant," the doctor says as she sits in the chair across from me.

I blink, my mind completely blank for half a second before it catches up. "What?" The word escapes out like a breath. "No."

I can't have a baby.

This must be some kind of horrible joke. Or they made an error.

"I'm guessing this is unexpected?"

She can say that again. "Are you sure this isn't a mistake? I just had sex like six days ago. Isn't it too soon?"

"When was the last time you had your period?"

My head shakes back and forth as I do the math. Oh, God, I haven't had a period since I got home from my trip.

It's been almost two months.

"This can't be happening," I say frantically. I'm not in any freaking place in my life for a child. "Can you run another test? Maybe there's another reason I'm feeling this shitty. The flu or maybe something else?"

That's the reason I'm here. I kept getting sick. I vomit, feel nauseated all day, and yesterday was the worst. I couldn't keep anything down, so I came here, hoping for some answers or ideas.

The doctor puts the file on her lap and her hands on top of it. "I'm afraid the test will show the same thing. I can tell this is upsetting."

I laugh once. "I'm pregnant with my husband's baby who's now engaged to the girl he cheated on me with, and I'm sleeping with my ex while waiting for my divorce to go through. Yeah, upsetting is a good word."

Instead of censure or judgment, the doctor looks sympathetic. "Do you have a support system in place? Family or friends who are around?"

"No, I'm...I mean, I have a few friends in Ember Falls, but... God, I'm going to have to tell him."

And I don't even know which him I mean. I have no idea how Dylan will react, but I can only imagine Everett will be absolutely done with me.

She reaches out, resting her hand on mine. "Take a few days, Violet. I recommend that you talk to your friends, and you have options. Just know that, okay?"

I nod. Because what else is there to say?

Although, for me, it doesn't feel like options. In theory, I wanted a baby. I thought about a family and that was my plan. My choice is to raise this baby or give him or her up for adoption, and I don't want to do that either.

So, really, it's option one.

"Good, you'll want to follow up with an ob-gyn soon."

"Right. Okay." My chin trembles, but I hold back. I don't want to cry. I don't want to feel anything.

"Okay. I'll have the nurse bring in a list of doctors in the area," the general practitioner says softly and then rises, leaving the room.

The nurse returns with the list, and I somehow manage to walk out the door and make it to my car.

As I sit in the seat, the tears I was able to hold back in the office begin to stream down my face. I move my hand to my stomach, resting over the child that's growing inside.

I'm pregnant. I'm going to be a single mom.

And I have no idea what our future looks like.

I don't even know if I will be a good mom, but I'll try. Then there's the money, where we'll live.

God, then I have to consider whether Dylan will want to be a part of this. Will he even care? Not to mention that this baby will create an entire media circus, and once again I'm going to be thrown back to the wolves.

Despite all the uncertainty, I'm firm in the fact that I want this child. I may not know any of the answers, but I know that I will do whatever I have to. I don't know that I'll ever have another chance to be a mother, and, regardless, this child will be loved.

"I'll protect you," I promise. "I'll figure it out and we'll be okay."

Before driving home, I glance down at my phone, where there are two text messages.

Ana: How did the appointment go?
Everett: Are you feeling better? Did you go to the doctor to see what's upsetting your stomach?

My stomach roils, feeling the mix of pregnancy and sorrow. All my life had to fall apart at one time? I couldn't have it spaced out a little more? Or maybe not at all?

You know, that would've been great.

I was finally starting to feel more like myself. Everett and I were having fun, and there wasn't anything I had to worry about other than just the next time we'd be together.

I wish I could undo every decision I made. I should've stayed in California, not come back and seen him. Sure, it would've been awful, my life would still be in this mess, but at least I wouldn't have another layer to take care of. I wouldn't know what it feels like to be absolutely adored, worshipped, and cared for.

Now I need to give that up and get my shit together.

Not that I have a clue what that looks like, because it all feels so uncertain.

I take a deep breath. *One thing at a time, Violet.*

I text Analeigh first, letting her know I'm going home to rest and I'll talk to her later.

My best friend is amazing and I love her, but right now I can't handle her reaction. She was good dealing with the cheating because she could be a maniac, but this…no, I need sane and rational.

Then I reply to the reason I've started to smile again.

Me: I'm okay. Do you think we could have dinner or I can just come over later?
Everett: Sure, I have practice with the boys so do you want to come around eight? I know that's a late dinner.

I'd like to put this off for as long as I possibly can, but I want Everett to know, and I unfortunately need to tell Dylan. God knows that's going to go over like a lead balloon.

I stare at my phone, my nausea not because of the newfound pregnancy this time. It's all nerves from having to talk to Dylan.

My lawyer suggested that we pause the divorce finalization. She was almost giddy at the idea that we could finally get some real compensation. She also thinks paternity needs to be established, so she suggested maybe even holding the divorce off for a year and keeping the information from Dylan.

I can't do that. I wasn't with anyone else until a few days ago. I don't need to wait to be sure.

Not only that, but that's what his mother did. Dylan didn't meet his father until he was eight, because she was angry at him. In the end it hurt him, and his father had to battle to get visitation. So when we'd talk about our fictional children, their names, who they might look like, he would always talk about how he wanted to be there through it all.

How he wouldn't be like his father.

Gail reiterated that talking through the lawyers would be better, but I can't. I may hate him in so many ways, but I can't rob him of this, and he deserves to know the truth.

Before, when I thought about telling him we were going to have a baby, I had plans to wrap up a onesie and that we'd be so happy.

Everything was a dream.

This is a nightmare.

I'm going to bring a child into this world in the middle of a divorce because their father is a cheating asshole who is now engaged to his mistress.

Great.

But no matter how I feel about this situation, it's the reality I'm choosing, and I need to face it.

I exhale deeply and press the number on my phone to call him.

It rings, and rings, each one causing my anxiety to spike higher and higher. Finally, right when I'm about to hang up, he answers.

"Violet."

"Hi, Dylan."

"What do you want?"

He isn't making this easy with his attitude. "Believe me, I wish this was a phone call I wasn't making, and it's actually against the expressed wishes of my lawyer, but I thought you deserved the right to know."

He's quiet for a few seconds and then clears his throat. "Know what?" he asks with what almost sounds like concern.

"I'm pregnant."

This time the silence is much longer, and I actually pull my phone down to look at it. Maybe I lost service.

Nope, the clock is still moving, so I continue to tell him what I do know. "I was feeling shitty the last few days, nothing out of the ordinary, and then I got sick at work, thought maybe I was coming down with something, so I went to the doctor today. Turns out I'm not sick. I'm probably about two months or so pregnant."

"I have to ask…"

"Don't ask, Dylan. Don't ask if the baby is yours. Do not do that to me. I didn't cheat on you." Regardless of the legal status of our marriage, we are not married. We are not a couple. We are no longer anything but strangers who legally are tangled. So whatever has happened in the last few days does not hold any bearing on this.

"Okay, so what do you want from me?" he asks, almost detached, and I blink.

"What?"

"What do you want? Money? Is this a way to get more out of the divorce? The very generous settlement I offered isn't enough? Now you have to have a baby to ruin the life I'm building?"

There is so much to unpack there, and I take a few seconds to try to make any of the things he said make sense. First of all, the settlement was an absolute joke. He offered me $200,000 for our $7 million home and to pay off my student loans. Not that I want to take an unfair amount of money, but there's no way I was going to take that when I also contributed to building our life.

I paid for things when he was out of work. I took care of us, and now that I know there's a baby I have to think about, there's no way I'd accept that. We finally agreed to split the sale of the house in half, or he can buy me out.

What I'm more focused on is the part about me ruining his life. I'll start there.

"I shouldn't be surprised by anything you say at this point, but here I am, once again just completely baffled. I didn't think this was going to go over with you being overjoyed, but I didn't think you were going to accuse me of trying to ruin your life considering not once did I ask for a damn thing. I'm letting *you* know that *you're* going to be a father because I know what that meant for you. As for the money, I don't even know what to say to that. Do you not want to help your baby?"

"If it's even really happening and this isn't just some ploy to ruin my new life."

I laugh out a huff. "Do you really think I'd make up a baby to what? Win you back? I don't want you back. If you think for one second that I'm happy about this, you're even more of a narcissist than I ever believed. The baby is real. It's yours."

He lets out a long sigh. "I can't have a baby now."

"And you think this timing is great for me?"

"I'm happy, Violet. I found someone who sees me and loves me. She's not trying to change me and turn me back into the weak man who was struggling. She loves my fame and revels in it."

I roll my eyes. "I don't give a flying fuck that you're happy. I've been perfectly happy here as well."

Seriously, the last couple of months of my life have been amazing. I have friends, freedom, Everett…

"I'm going to have to talk to Whitney. We're building a life, and I don't think she wants a kid right now."

I struggle to breathe. Who the hell is this man? "You're going to have to talk to Whitney?" I ask, praying I didn't hear him correctly. "And ask her what? You're going to have a child, Dylan. This baby isn't contingent on your fucking mistress. Do you get that? I'm going to have a baby in about six or seven months and…you're going to ask for permission?"

"No, Violet, I'm going to ask my fiancée if she wants to be around this or if we keep this quiet. I need to talk to my team. Don't tell anyone until I have an idea of how to handle it. I don't need the press getting wind of it and tearing me down more."

I drop my head, my heart going with it. I didn't expect him to be happy. I just didn't think he'd be this much of a piece of shit. "So you're worried that the baby will ruin your image?"

"Of course I am. I don't need this right now. I'm doing my best to fix what you refused to help with, and this will just make it worse. And you plan to keep the baby?"

"Yes," I say through gritted teeth.

"Right. Are you doing this to punish me? You can't want this baby. We're in the middle of a divorce, and we aren't exactly on the best of terms."

It's always about him.

I really don't know how to reconcile my feelings. They're all over the place as I go from anger to utter despair.

"I'm aware of the current state of our life, but that doesn't change anything. You do whatever you need to do with your team, but regardless, I want this kept out of the press. This baby isn't going to be used for your benefit, and I swear to God, Dylan, if you do anything to leak this, I will go on my own press tour and expose anything I can. If you don't want to be a part of this baby's life, that's perfectly fine. I'm not asking you for a thing, not money, not co-parenting. I just didn't want to be like your mother and keep this from you. You do whatever you need to, and I'll do the same for me and the baby."

Then I hang up and curl into a ball and sob.

CHAPTER 18
VIOLET

I wrap my sweater around me tighter as I walk across the field to the tree line separating my house and Everett's.

After crying for about twenty minutes, I picked myself up and said *enough*. If I'm going to do this on my own, then I need to plan and think about my steps and choices. It felt good to start to have a plan. While my world may be spinning in the wrong direction, I have to be able to adjust, and making lists gives me a place to start.

The first thing I did was call the ob-gyn, and I was absolutely horrified that they didn't want to see me for another three to four weeks.

What in the fresh hell is that?

I'm pregnant and they don't want me to come in right away? I was floored, but they didn't seem concerned at all.

Now I have three weeks to wonder and worry. I also put worrying about the baby on the list.

The next thing I wrote of importance was to tell Everett it's over. That my situation has changed, and I can no longer keep having these "tomorrow" days. Tomorrow is gone. It's now yesterday. The future is going to be a minefield, and I can't bring another person any further in than I already have.

I did allow the tears to fall as I wrote out that one. I know it's the logical decision, but it doesn't make it any easier.

I then have to tell my parents and friends and come up with how I'm going to raise this child on my own.

Somehow.

I get to the front door and knock, but he doesn't answer.

Oh good, I get to prolong this stress.

Then I hear a very familiar voice. "Hello?"

I turn, coming face-to-face with Mrs. Finnegan. Her soft blue eyes are the same, only they look a little tired. Her hair is almost fully gray now, with slight hints of brown still sprinkled in. She steps forward.

"Hello, Mrs. Finnegan," I say, my heart aching a little, not sure whether I should say anything to her. "Is Everett here?"

"Yes, he's…" She looks back toward the house. "He's here."

"Okay. I can wait out here."

"Mom!" I hear him yell from inside. "Mom! Where are you?"

"I'm at the door," she says. "You have a friend here. She's very pretty."

He pulls the door back and sees me. "Hey."

"Hi."

"Everett, don't be rude. Introduce me to your friend, and you're letting all the heat out."

His smile is soft. "Of course. Mom, you've actually met Violet. You haven't seen her in a long time, though."

Mrs. Finnegan's eyes go wide. "Violet Stewart? Is that you?"

"It is."

"Oh!" She ushers me inside and then pulls me into a hug, holding me to her chest, and those stupid tears that I've been really good at keeping at bay for the last three hours come rushing forward. I wrap my arms around her, feeling like a little girl all over again. She rubs my back. "Don't cry, dear."

"I'm sorry." I hiccup. "I'm just…I've missed you and Ember Falls. It's just…"

She pulls back. "Well, we missed you too. I'm sorry about your grandmother. I loved her very much."

"I know, she loved you too." My grandmother felt that she won the lottery with neighbors. The Finnegans always came to check on her, making sure she was never without.

"Well, we know that she absolutely thought you hung the moon." Her hand rests on my cheek.

"I should've come to see her…" I choke on the words, the guilt hitting me so hard.

I went to college and never saw her again. She didn't travel well, so my parents always came to her, and I was too stupid and selfish to return, not wanting to risk seeing Everett.

I've never forgiven myself for it.

She deserved better from me.

"Oh, sweetheart, she didn't need to see you to know you loved her very much. She would come talk to me and tell me just how great you were doing."

"She did?"

Mrs. Finnegan nods. "She came for tea every Sunday morning, and we would talk about you and your schooling. I swear, that woman could go on for hours about the things you were going to do in life. Her love crossed any number of miles and didn't require anything from you."

Everett smiles from behind his mother. "I can also attest to that."

She turns. "Oh, Everett, I didn't know you were behind me. Did you know that Violet is here?"

His eyes meet mine for a heartbeat, and then he turns to his mother. "I did. She's staying next door."

"Doreen would've loved that. She missed you very much," she tells me. "She would come on Sundays for tea and talk about you nonstop."

Everett clears his throat. "Mom, it's getting late. Do you want to go watch your nighttime shows?"

She glances at the clock behind her. "It's almost time for my favorite game shows. Do you know where Brutus is?"

Everett glances over at the couch. "He's over there, waiting for you and glowering at me."

Mrs. Finnegan walks over, petting the big bulldog. "There you are, sweet boy." He lifts his head, allowing her to pet him. "Let's leave Everett with his friend."

"I'll come over before you go to sleep, I promise."

She pats his chest. "Don't you bother. I'll be fine."

He laughs softly. "It's not for your benefit. It's for mine."

"Oh, then, you can come by or bring me back now and say good night."

Everett turns to me with a smile. "I'll be right back. Are you okay to stay here?"

"Of course."

I watch him walk away with his mother and Brutus, and I take this time to compose myself. Jesus, I literally just wept in his mother's arms. I need to get it together or I'm never going to get through any of this.

The list, remember the list. I have reasons besides the pregnancy, and those are what I'm going to have to cling to.

I can do this.

I have to do this.

Everett comes back in, walking to me immediately. "Are you okay?"

I brush off my mini-breakdown with a laugh. "Of course. I didn't expect to see your mom, and I was surprised. I didn't know what to say, and when she hugged me, I just felt so emotional."

"She loves you very much."

"I love her too."

He reaches for me, but I step back a little, my hand going to my stomach. "I'm still not feeling great," I explain.

"What did the doctor say?"

That I'm going to have a baby.

"The nausea will probably go away soon." That is not a lie. She did say that.

"Good, did you want something to drink before we talk?" His voice is hesitant, and I can already sense that he knows this visit isn't going to end with us tangled in his sheets.

I shake my head. Delaying this is only going to be harder for us both. "No, thank you. Look, I wanted to talk because I just think we need to be smarter than this. We have this…shared history, and we say *no strings*, but I don't know if that's really possible, do you?"

"Okay," he says slowly. "I'm not really sure where this is coming from?"

"I've just been thinking, and it feels like it will be so easy for us. We loved each other once. I'm not sure I won't fall in love with you again."

He smiles. "I'm not sure you won't either. I'm a catch."

"Everett, I'm being serious."

"So am I."

I huff and start to pace. This is not going to plan. I go back to the list. "There are other reasons. For one, I'm not in a place to start anything."

"I didn't ask you to. If you remember, I told you I couldn't offer you anything more either."

Yes, okay, he did. "Then there's the fact that if this were to get serious, I'm probably going back to California."

He takes a step toward me. "But we already said we weren't going to get serious. Hence the no strings."

Why is he ruining this with his logic?

"I just can't."

His eyes narrow slightly, watching my reactions. "Then we don't."

Okay. We don't.

He agreed.

All is well…not well…not well at all.

I don't want this to end. I don't want any of this.

God, I feel so broken and scared right now.

I want my granny. I want someone to hold me and tell me it's going to be okay, but I'm alone.

I'm here in front of a man who has made me feel more alive and stronger than anyone ever has, and I have to let him go.

Great, now the tears are coming again.

Everett moves in front of me, stopping my pacing. "You're crying?"

"No. I'm not. These aren't tears. They're just leaking eyes. There's a lot of dust in the room, or maybe it was the pollen when I walked through the field."

"Violet...why don't we stop with the bullshit and you just tell me what the hell is going on? I'm not trying to push you to keep sleeping with me, but I just want to know the truth."

The truth.

God, the truth is so sad. The truth is tearing me apart.

I shake my head. "All I do is cry. All I do is...feel so damn much, and now I know why. I mean, I get it. It all makes sense. I'm not sad, I'm pregnant. I'm fucking pregnant and, God, how am I going to do this?"

There. I told him the truth.

"Well, shit, that was fast."

"Fast?"

He shrugs. "I mean, I didn't know I could get you pregnant in two days. I'm pretty amazing. I bet we'll end up in some kind of book."

Oh my God. He thinks it's his? "Everett, it's not ours."

"I know, Violet," he says with a soft chuckle. "I was just trying to get you to relax for a second. I may not be a human doctor, but animals usually need a bit before they can be confirmed pregnant too."

I let out a heavy breath and look up at the ceiling. "I keep waiting for this nightmare to end."

"Did you tell...him?"

I stare at him in shock. "You really want to talk about this?" I ask.

Everett lifts a shoulder. "Do you have someone else you can talk to right now?"

"No."

He's honestly the only person I needed, and all I thought was I should push him away to avoid ever hurting him again.

"Come here," he says with his arms open.

I want to fight the pull, but right now I really just want to be held.

Taking the two steps to him is the easiest thing I've done all day. Everett's arms wrap around me and I breathe in his scent, letting it relax me. I don't cry—for what feels like the first time. I just let his strength and warmth engulf me.

"Have you told anyone?" he asks.

I nod against his chest. "I told him."

"And?"

I pull back, swiping at my stupid tears, and push the air out of my lungs. "He was exactly like you'd think. Selfish, angry, worried about his precious new relationship and how Whitney will feel about this. He even said he needs to talk to his team first." I laugh. "He accused me of doing this to keep him or something. I don't know, at some point I just tried to stop thinking."

"The more you tell me about him, the more I really fucking hate him."

I look up into his eyes. "Me too."

And I left Everett to love Dylan. So stupid. I was such an idiot, and in the end this is probably karma.

"What do you want, Vi?"

"Right now, I don't even know what to think. I went home, cried, and then started to make lists."

He releases me just a little and looks down at me. "Was one of them how to get out of whatever this is between us?"

I nod.

"It didn't work," he says with a wink.

"I'm aware. I can't even break off whatever this is the right way."

"I'm not a man who scares easily."

"I was sure the pregnancy would do the trick, but it seems that didn't even get you to budge."

Everett moves closer, his warm palm against my cheek. "I don't think anything could scare me away from you, Violet. Especially not a baby that's half of you."

My heart, that felt completely shattered, mends a little. "Everett, what am I going to do?"

He pulls me to the couch and then against his chest. "Well, you don't have to know today. For now, you can just feel all the shit I'm assuming you're feeling, and then tomorrow, maybe that's when you make some decisions."

I smile, my hand resting on his chest. He is so sweet, and the fact that he is being supportive has my head finally calming. "So you're saying that you want to debate whatever it is we're doing tomorrow?"

"Not debate, just not make any decisions now. Besides, tomorrow seems to work well for us."

Yeah, I guess it does.

"Tomorrow then."

CHAPTER 19
EVERETT

Violet passed out a few minutes after lying on the couch, and I followed shortly after. Yesterday was a long day in general, but last night really added to it.

First, Mom came to the house after wandering the property, saying she couldn't find Brutus, and then Violet and Mom saw each other.

It went better than I thought, but I try not to bring new people around her without at least giving her some prior warning.

She doesn't like surprises.

Neither do I, but, man, I was hit with quite a few in a row.

However, dealing with Mom was so much easier with Violet. Maybe it's not about my days looking different or worrying about the future, but having someone beside me that matters.

I grab the coffeepot, pouring another cup that tastes like shit compared to Prose & Perk. I think Hazel puts some kind of magic in her beans, because no matter what I try, I can't get it to taste the same.

Violet is still passed out, so I head over to see my mother.

When I get inside, I can feel the energy is off. "Mom?"

"I can't handle it!" she yells, and I hear something fall to the floor.

I walk back to where she is and find her pulling everything out of the chest at the end of her bed. "Mom, what are you doing?"

"Where is it? Did you take it, Everett? Where is your father's jacket? He had it with him. I need it."

"Which jacket?" I ask carefully, although I know what she's referring to.

My mother was adamant that, when we cleaned out the main house, my father's belongings also needed to come with her to the barn. She wanted parts of him to remain with her. We kept a few shirts, pants, and his favorite jacket he wore when working on the farm.

We kept everything in that chest to try to avoid my mother falling apart daily if she saw his things hanging in the closet.

"His jacket. I need it."

I crouch down next to her. "I'll help."

Her eyes find mine and I see the tears welling. "I don't know where it is."

"We'll find it."

She shakes her head. "I...I think...I had it."

"His brown one?" I ask.

"Yes, that one."

"Okay, we'll find it," I assure her again.

Sometimes she likes to go through the chest, and then she forgets what she was doing or why the clothes are out. It's very stressful for her when they aren't returned here. If by any chance one of her friends were here when she last went through them, they may not have known how to put them back.

I haven't checked in for at least a week, which is my fault.

I know better than to not go through the rooms every other day to ensure everything is the same.

As I empty the chest, she sits on the bed, her hands clutched in her lap, and she rocks. This is going to send her spiraling if I can't find it soon.

"Check the dresser!" she says quickly.

I go there first. I check the drawers, but there is only her clothing. "Not here, Mom."

"Oh, Everett, please. I need his things, I can't forget him. Please."

I walk over, resting my hands on her shoulders. "You will never forget him."

"I forget things," she says, and her voice cracks.

"Sometimes you do, but never the important people. Do you always know me?"

She nods. "And do you know your friends and nurses?"

"Yes."

"And when you look at that photo"—I point to the one on her side table, showing the three of us at my last baseball game—"do you know who those people are?"

"Of course," she breathes.

"Okay, then. Don't worry about forgetting Dad. I don't think you ever could."

He lives inside her.

"Everett?" My mother's eyes soften.

"What?"

"I'm sorry."

"For what?"

"For being like this. You should be married and have kids. You shouldn't be living like this. I'm a burden."

I crouch down, taking her hands in mine. "You are never a burden. You took care of me from the day you found me. You and Dad loved me no matter what and worked to always make sure I had whatever I needed. I'm exactly where I need to be, Mom. I love you."

Her lip trembles, and she brushes my hair back like she did when I was a little boy. "I love you with my whole heart."

"Good. Then let's find Dad's jacket, put the room back together, and then we can have breakfast."

I stand and head to her closet. Sure enough, there's a pile on the left of all his clothing. I bring the pile to her, and she sits there and folds his things in neat order, at times brushing the fabric with a smile on her face.

"He loved this shirt."

My heart aches for her and the love they shared. I don't know that there were ever two people who were meant to be together more than them.

I can remember walking in on them kissing in the kitchen, absolutely disgusted, but now I see it so differently.

"I think he loved that you bought it for him."

She chuckles. "That man didn't buy a single thing for himself. If I didn't get him new jeans, he'd wear the torn ones until they'd fall apart. He wanted us to have everything."

Mom extends the shirt to me, and I take it as carefully as she handles it. "He never let me see how hard it was for him."

My baseball aspirations drained them financially. There were games all over the place, travel, new equipment, and leagues that I was adamant I needed to play in. The camp up in New England probably cost half of what they made in a year, but they never said a word. Dad just said he'd make it work.

"Oh, honey, parents don't want their children to know the truth."

"Still, it was hard for you both."

Mom waits for me to look at her again. "Parents do whatever their kids need. It wasn't easy, but you were worth the struggles. To see you smile, to know you had what you needed, that's what a parent does. It's what you'll do someday when you have one. You'll sacrifice for them, no matter what they require. You'll love them and always put their needs and well-being first, even if it means your heartache. Do you think I liked watching you go to camp? No. I hated it, but *you* loved it."

"I think you did a lot more than most would," I tell her, thinking of how they gave up their life to take me in.

"Why?"

"Because you and Dad were resolved to not having kids."

This conversation has gone way deeper than I had planned, but these were things I thought about last night.

She shakes her head. "And? You were my son the moment I held you. The moment I knew you existed."

"I know."

I never felt unloved. I didn't even know I wasn't theirs, to be honest. People would always tell my parents how much I looked like my dad, to which my parents would smile and rub my head, saying they agreed.

When I found out I was adopted, it was so difficult. I felt like I'd been lied to, but at the same time I was so grateful to have known them.

I think I learned a lot about love at that point as well. Because they loved me, I never doubted that.

I think about what all this means now. How I don't know what to feel about Violet having a kid and where I thought my life was going. Can I be in her life? In the baby's life? What would it even look like?

We continue to put the clothes away, both silent as the weight of today's conversation settles around us and also knowing she probably won't remember half of it.

She'll go to watch her show, settle into the routine of today, and forget about the pain of thinking she lost Dad's things. Again, a small blessing from her injury. She doesn't hold on to things for long.

"If you could go back, knowing you'd lose Dad, knowing that nothing would be different, would you still love him?"

Her smile is so honest it causes my chest to ache. "I would love that man if I only ever got one day with him." She walks over to me, placing her hand on my chest. "Just like you would for Violet. Love is a choice, and yet, for others, it's just inevitable. You can be scared of it and run, or you can just feel it and let it take hold. I can promise, if your father walked in this house and all I could ever have was one more day, oh, I would hold on to that day with both hands."

I walk back to the house with more of a fucked-up mind than I had last night after Violet told me she was pregnant.

It was a lot: my mother's breakdown, the talk after, and then watching her go back to the shell of who she was just a few minutes earlier, finally going into the living room and settling into a normal day.

However, for a little while, I had my mom back.

Even if that mother imparted way too much wisdom in a short span. All I can think about is the last thing she said about getting just one more day with my dad.

One more day isn't enough.

That's what I wish I could tell Mom. One more day would only make her wish for one more.

Years ago, when Violet left without a word, I remember yelling about all the things I'd say to her about love and the lies she told.

Then I was just sad, because it felt like I'd lost everything.

When she walked through the door of Prose & Perk a couple of months ago, all of that came back. The emotions, the desire, the love, the anger at how it went, but the biggest part of me felt—hope.

I never stopped loving her.

I sit on my back step, not ready to face her yet.

I don't want one more day. I don't want one more week. I want all the damn days. I want her, this baby, a home, a family, all of it is what I want.

Yes, things are a mess, but what in life worth having isn't a little messy?

One more day will never suffice.

I'm going to be there for her, show her that when you love someone, you fight. She and I can figure this out because I can't survive her leaving me again.

I was a fucking liar to think that we wouldn't have any promises or that I didn't want more.

That's been my downfall with her since we were kids—there is never enough.

My phone rings and it's the emergency vet line.

"Dr. Finnegan," I answer.

"Hello, Doctor F, it's Courtney. I got a call from the Jones farm. They'd like to know if you can come today to check on a few cows?"

I really needed today off to process this and talk to Violet about her plans and make her see that sometimes not having one can lead to more than we dreamed. As much as I want to say no, I won't. I never do. If they're calling the after-hours line, it's something they feel strongly about.

"Is it urgent?"

"Not emergent, but, yes, urgent."

"All right, I'll head there as soon as I can."

Then I need to figure out how to tell Violet that we're going to do this together, because I won't lose her again.

CHAPTER 20
VIOLET

I open my eyes, stretching my arms and glancing around, noticing that I am not in my house.

Shit.

I'm on Everett's couch. I must've passed out last night. I remember us talking, me lying on his chest and feeling so content and… tired.

He held me, letting me have all the emotions I wanted.

I cried, I laughed, I worried, all without needing to explain anything. He just let me feel whatever I felt.

I sit up, causing the blanket to fall to the ground. I rub my eyes and yawn.

"Good morning, sleepyhead," his deep voice says from the entry of the kitchen.

"Hi," I say on a breath. "I'm sorry I fell asleep. I don't even remember when that happened."

He grins. "No worries. I knocked out too, woke up early this morning. You didn't even move. Here." He hands me a cup of coffee.

"Thanks."

"You're welcome."

I take a sip and Everett watches me. "So…"

"So…" he says with a grin.

"So, it's tomorrow." Not that I needed to say that since I'm pretty sure we both know what day it is.

"It is, and do you feel any better after sleeping?" Everett asks as he takes a sip of his coffee.

"Not really, but I can do this, right? I mean, I'm going to be a mom, and that means doing whatever needs to be done, and I'll... do that."

"You really don't have to right now. You have months to figure things out," he says, sitting beside me. "Take that time and figure out things day by day."

I know he's right. I don't have to make all these decisions now. I have time, and besides, I can't make any choices when I don't know what Dylan's role is going to be.

As much as I hate him for all he's done to me, I could never use the baby against him.

If he does want to be around, though, it means I have to move back to California. I could try to stay in Ember Falls, but what does that look like with shared custody? The baby will need to travel across the country to see him? Doing that doesn't make much sense and isn't sustainable long term, but I'm getting ahead of myself. For all I know, he'll do what I expect him to do, which is keep the baby a secret and not have anything to do with it.

His fiancée is never going to want this.

She's all about her social media-worthy lifestyle, and the only baby she'd want around is her own.

At least...I think.

"It's just the unknown is terrifying," I say to him, staring down into my coffee.

"The girl I knew wasn't afraid of anything," Everett reminds me.

"She had no understanding of consequences."

"Nah, she knew, but if it was something important, she'd battle. Find that girl, Vi. She's still inside of you. You just have to bring her out."

I wish it were that simple.

"There are just so many variables to think about, but you're right. I have to battle them all, for me and the baby."

He grins. "There she is. You are stronger than you give yourself credit for."

"And if I'm not? What do I have then, Everett? I'm going to be a single mother regardless. I'm going to be alone through it all. Dylan isn't going to come here, and I'm not going back there right now. Not until the divorce is final and I can have some sort of foundation."

He reaches his hand around me, rubbing my back. "Then take this time to figure out what *you* want."

I wanted whatever this was that we were doing. I wanted to let go of the parts of my past that were hurting me and hold on to the things that brought me joy. Now they're mixing up in all the wrong ways.

"What if I can't have what I want?"

"None of us ever do. I wanted a lot of things that will never be possible. My mother's mind may never heal, and the doctors don't think it ever will. I wanted to move out of Ember Falls, but I will never do that to Mom. She can't move. She can't even get in a car. The doctors come here, and if I have to take her, we have to heavily medicate her, and it takes three of us to handle her."

"She can't go in a car?" I ask.

"She can't handle the idea of a car. It was the most traumatic experience she's ever faced. Bringing her home from the hospital was a nightmare, and she made me promise to never make her do it again."

"I'm so sorry," I say, resting my hand on his.

He laces our fingers together as though it's the most natural thing. "I'm only saying it so you understand—you don't have to get what you want to be happy. Sometimes you find the things you need in the hard times."

Like him again.

If the absolute shit show of my life didn't happen, I wouldn't have come back here. I would've been in California in my big house with my husband who didn't love me. I'd have stayed because it was just easier and there never felt like a way out.

I was trapped, but only because I let myself stay in it.

Until I had no choice.

Then it was my decision to come here. I wanted to find myself again. I wanted to be with Everett. I wanted to be touched, adored, worshipped, and he gave me that.

Without any demands.

Maybe this setback will only bring me something else I never thought to ask for.

"All right, I need to go see a man about a cow." Everett gets to his feet, outstretching his hand to me.

"Is that a euphemism that I just don't know about?"

"No, the farm down the road just got some cows, and I need to run a few tests."

I get up, feeling awful for keeping him. "Oh! I'm sorry. I'm keeping you from work. I'll head home, and again, thank you for last night. You gave me exactly what I needed."

Everett tilts his head. "Come with me."

"What?"

"Come on, you can come to the farm, see the cows, and they have goats. They're cute, even if they're the most absolutely mischievous animals ever."

"Goats?"

He nods. "I swear, they're magicians and can get out of anything they want to. I saw the little fuckers stack on top of each other to hop a fence. I'm not even kidding."

I bite my lower lip, thinking how I have a million other things I need to do, like call my lawyer and best friend, but they'll be there later, and there's a three-hour time difference anyway.

"And you really want to spend the day with an emotional headcase who might puke randomly?"

Everett chuckles. "It's every man's dream."

"Sure it's not."

"Well, I might have to stick my hand inside a cow, so really, I'm just a walking dream come true too."

Oh, that image. "If you don't want me to hurl, I would leave out that part."

"Got it. Are you ready?"

"Now?" I ask in surprise. "No, I need to go home and shower. Do I have time for that?"

"Of course. I'll check on Mom, make sure she's set for the day, and then come pick you up."

"All right, I'll see you soon."

I walk over to kiss his cheek, but as I lift up, he moves his face and our lips touch. His hand moves to my back, holding me against him. After a second, he releases me and grins. "I figured I'd do that before I have to go near the cows and goats."

My stomach flutters, in the good way this time, and I smile broadly. "You really are a walking dream come true. Don't sell yourself short."

I step back, grab my sweater off the back of the couch, and head out the door with a smile on my face.

When I get home, I head upstairs and turn the water on for a quick shower. As I wait for the water to heat up, I stare at myself in the mirror, moving my body right and left, imagining how I'll look when I start to show.

I grab my phone and send off a text to Analeigh, knowing she'll call as soon as she sees it.

Me: SOS 811...or even 911.

We have only ever used up to a 7, so she'll know this means business and I need to talk to her.

Then I hop in the shower and wash away the last twenty-four

hours, ready to see some goats and forget about the circus that is my life.

"Oh my God, I want one!" I say as the baby goat climbs up in my lap. I pet him, giving him kisses. "He's so cute."

Everett laughs once. "Where do you plan to keep him?"

"Umm, in the house, duh. I'm sure he could be potty-trained, couldn't you?" I pick him up, rubbing my nose with his.

I had no idea how therapeutic this would be. The farm is absolutely incredible. The Jones family has pretty much every animal you can imagine. A lot of them are rescues, and the owners are in the process of building an equine therapy program.

Everett was busy with the cow for at least three hours, but I haven't cared in the slightest. I've been in goat heaven.

He squats, rubbing the goat's head. "I promise, you don't want a goat and you definitely don't want one in the house. He absolutely will not be potty-trained. They just poop as they walk, and I don't think you want a newborn baby crawling around shit—literally."

Fine. He's right. I forgot for a second I have to think about those things now. "Yeah, no."

"Maybe you can start small with like a dog."

I sigh dramatically. "It's no animals for me until I figure out my life."

"Good plan. Let's not complicate your situation more. Come on, you need to see the new foal. He's going to be an incredible stud."

I take his hand, and we walk out of the goat pen. "Bye, baby goats! I love you!"

Everett chuckles. "They will undoubtedly try to escape to find you."

"Aww, don't tell me that!"

"You'll be fine, trust me. When you see the foal, you'll forget all about the goats."

I doubt that. I loved those little guys.

"If you say so. Why do you think this baby horse is going to be a good stud?"

"You'll see."

I don't know anything about horses, so I'll just trust him. Everett takes me around the farm, showing me a few different areas that house chickens, ducks, alpacas, and a few peacocks.

As we approach the paddock, the mama horse and her foal come up to the fence, but she angles herself so we can't see the baby. "Hello, Mystic," Everett says, placing his hand on her nose. "How is your baby doing?"

The horse lifts her head and then drops it. "She likes you."

"She does. This little guy was a rough birth, and I had to intervene. I think she knows I was there to save her."

The foal peeks his head around his mother, and I smile. "He's beautiful, from what I can see."

"Can we say hi to him?" Everett asks the horse, and she huffs but shuffles her backside to the left, giving us a view of her baby.

A baby. A little, beautiful baby. One that is close to his mom, knowing she'll protect him, love him, give him all he needs.

I stare at the foal, my heart swelling as I think about how, in months, I'll be the same. I'll hold my child, hoping that I can also provide shelter, love, warmth, and security in a world full of anything but that.

The foal is a true black with just a touch of white on his right leg.

"Wow, his coloring is stunning."

"He's also already bigger than most foals. I think that's why he was such a difficult birth."

I'm hoping I don't endure that.

"How old is he?"

"Four months." He pats Mystic's neck. "Soon they'll wean him and Mystic will get a break, won't you, girl?"

It seems so unbelievable to me that they get separated. "Why do they wean the horses?"

"Well, it's not great for the mother to be the constant food source. We want the foal to learn on their own. It's not so different than humans. They just do it much faster than us."

So it seems Mystic doesn't have it all figured out, either, but she's doing whatever she can for her baby.

I smile. "Can I pet her?"

He smiles and grabs my hand. "Let her sniff your palm and talk to her softly. Let her know your intentions."

"Hi, Mystic, you're beautiful and your baby is too," I tell her. After a few seconds, she touches her nose to my hand.

"She likes you too. Pet the side of her neck."

I do as he says, talking to her and telling her what a good horse she is. After a few minutes, she backs away, raising and lowering her head as though she's waving.

"See you soon," Everett tells her.

We walk back to the barn area, and Everett shows me the cow that was struggling when we got here. She looks much better now, so I guess whatever he did was a good thing.

When we finally get to the car, it's already past lunch. "Do you want anything to eat?" he asks as my stomach rumbles.

"I can eat something when we get back."

"Let me at least buy you lunch after making you spend the day on the farm."

I shake my head. "It's fine. I need to do laundry and get some papers graded."

"Oh, what was the paper on?"

"Romeo and Juliet's decisions that could've changed the outcome."

He laughs and then pulls out onto the main road. "I'm sure they loved that."

"I'd like to think I make it fun."

"I'm sure you do."

I lean against the door, looking over at him. "You know, I never imagined you'd be a veterinarian. I guess I really never saw you as anything other than a baseball player."

"Yeah, I had that one career aspiration, and that was it. But when I was in college, I got a cat."

My voice goes up three octaves. "You got a cat?"

He nods slowly. "Hazel said I needed to learn how to take care of something, because she was tired of always having to take care of me. When I told you I was a fucking mess in college, I'm not even exaggerating. It was my senior year, and I was untouchable in terms of my pitching abilities. I had all these teams coming to watch me, and my scouting reports were impressive."

"And your humility?"

Everett's lips turn up into a cute quirk. "Never that, babe. Never that." He chuckles. "I was so angry. It was wild. I hated baseball by that point and the idea of playing, nursing more injuries. I even had to have another surgery before I could join a farm team. It was...like, for what? For the hope that someday I'd be brought up? To spend years barely scraping by and asking my parents to support me when they were barely making ends meet? Anyway, my cat, Brunhilda, was a nightmare."

If I had water in my mouth, it would've sprayed everywhere when he said the name. "You named your cat Brunhilda?"

He shrugs. "It was that or Hazelette. She refused to allow that."

"Naturally."

"My cat was one that liked to do spiteful shit. I mean, all cats are assholes. They fuck with people and have attitudes like no other animal. Traveling with Brunhilda in a car was a whole other experience. I had no idea about cats when I got her, but I learned fast."

I grin, imagining a twenty-two-year-old college kid with a cat.

Not just any college kid, either, a jock who was probably partying more than he was sober.

"So Brunhilda and you formed a bond, and she is why you went into being a vet?"

"Kind of. She and I had a very contentious relationship until she got sick. I really didn't think I liked her all that much, but when we were faced with something being seriously wrong, I was a mess. The parasite she caught can be very serious and even lead to death. You would've thought I was out of my mind. I drove to three different doctors, and finally the last one spoke to me rationally and gave me clear instructions. I held her, fed her with a syringe, and nursed her back to health. After that, I had this passion to do that for someone else. To save someone's pet or give them hope."

I smile, hearing the devotion in his voice. He truly loves what he does. "That's really sweet, and where is Brunhilda now?"

"She's not good with dogs at all, so when we got Brutus, she went to live with my lead tech, who she loves so much more than me anyway. Erin brings her to the office twice a week so I can see her and be ignored properly."

I can't help the laugh that falls from my lips. I just imagine this beautiful cat walking right past him.

"Do you love it?"

"Being a vet? Yes, every day is truly special. Even the days when I can't give good news or there's nothing I can do to save the animal, I do what I can to make it easier for them and the owner. What about you with teaching?"

I glance up at the blue sky, remembering my own story and how I decided to go into teaching. "My story isn't as cool as yours, but I was studying English literature and thought I would go into publishing, like all young book lovers do, but I took a teaching class and fell in love with it. It gave me the opportunity to combine the two things I love."

"I think your story is cool."

My eyes move to his and I smile. "Most days are a testament to my patience, but then there are days where a student who struggled just gets it or I see them go from hating to read to suddenly wanting to discuss a new story. Those days are really rewarding. I don't want to give it up again, you know? I stopped when Dylan became this superstar actor because it was too hard with the constant media attention. Getting to teach again has been so rewarding."

Everett reaches over and takes my hand in his, squeezing softly. "Why would you have to give it up again?"

I sigh heavily as he turns down my driveway. I'm sad that our day together is almost over. "Because if Dylan wants to be a part of the baby's life, I'll have to move."

"Why?"

"He's the baby's father and will be awarded visitation, I'm sure. I can't stick a newborn on a plane. It's all so complicated, Everett. I can't pretend that this is all going to just work out. It's why days like this and nights like we've had are dangerous for me."

I can see the wheels turning in his mind. "I don't want to be a source of stress for you. Maybe you're right, and we should stop doing whatever we're doing and just keep it to being friends."

With my hand on the door handle, I look into his beautiful brown eyes, so warm, so familiar, so much history there. I force a sad smile and decide to rip the Band-Aid off. It'll be better this way. "It's not what I want, but I think it's for the best."

I hate this so much.

"Okay, then." He sounds...resigned. Like it's the last thing in the world that he wants, but for me, he'll do it because I'm not in the right place for anything more.

I hate that I have to lose him too.

"Everett?" He stays silent and just waits. "Thank you for today and everything. I can't begin to tell you what all of this has meant to me."

"I'd do anything for you, Violet."

Too bad he can't make this all different. That he can't take us back in time where I would never make the mistake of letting him go.

I nod once and close the car door, heading inside.

Those stupid tears start to build until I gasp as I see someone sitting on my couch. "Hi, honey, I'm home."

"Analeigh!"

CHAPTER 21
VIOLET

"Oh my God! You're here!" I scream as I rush toward her.

She pulls me into her arms. "You said it was an 811. What's wrong?"

"You could have just called."

She shakes her head, laughing, and then pulls me down next to her on the couch. "Like I didn't try that first. You weren't answering, and after an hour and about six hundred attempts, I called my pilot and got the jet ready. Within thirty minutes, I was flying here, all the while still fucking calling you."

I look down at my phone. "I don't have any missed calls."

"Well, I can show you my call log. I was worried. I thought maybe you were abducted or being held at knifepoint."

I laugh because that would be the conclusion she jumped to. She seriously lives on true crime podcasts. Ana is one of those friends that no matter what you need, she's going to make it happen, because instead of waiting, like a normal person would, she got on a plane and came here.

"I live in Ember Falls. This place is safe."

"That's what they all say before they end up swimming with the fish," Ana says, tilting her head. "Obviously it's not that, so what's the emergency?"

I still can't believe she's sitting here. I've missed her so much. I didn't even realize how much until I saw her.

However, this is the hard part. Where I have to tell her what I really wish wasn't my new reality.

"I'm pregnant," I blurt out before I back out from telling her.

Her jaw drops. *"No!"*

"Yes, and it's Dylan's."

"No!" Ana says again, her eyes wide. "Shit, I was hoping it was your sexy vet next door. Ugh, Dylan. Okay, well, I'm here and we're going to sort this shit out."

I lean against her, laughing once. "How are you going to do that?"

"I have no idea, but we have to start somewhere," she says, crossing her legs and turning to face me. "Have you told him?"

"I did, and you can just assume how he reacted."

She rolls her eyes and scoffs. "Asshole. I should've run *him* over with my car."

And I don't doubt that she would've done that either. "It wouldn't have changed this, but I appreciate the sentiment."

"I might do it anyway."

I shake my head. She's here and I'm...alone, no thanks to my own decisions, but if there's anyone who can fix this mess of a life, it's Ana. My voice cracks as I plead with my best friend. "Just tell me what to do. Tell me because I clearly shouldn't be involved in any decision-making."

Ana shifts forward, taking my hand. "What do you want?"

I've asked myself the same question, but I just go in circles. I want Everett. I want the baby. I want to stay here, but I'm pretty sure none of that is possible. So I tell her the easiest answer I can. "I don't know."

"Yes, you do," she chides. "You are just afraid of what you want. You always have been. Dylan did a number on you, and so did your parents. Is your life an absolute dumpster fire? Yup, it sure is. In the span of a few months, your marriage ended publicly, your soon-to-be ex-husband is already engaged, you came face-to-face with your first love that you still have unresolved feelings for, slept with said first love, and now you're pregnant with your ex-husband's baby. I mean, girl, you couldn't get any messier than this."

"Thank you for that lovely breakdown of my life."

She smiles. "You're welcome. My point is, before the last surprise, you were happy, weren't you?"

I think about how I've felt since getting back to Ember Falls. How easy it is here. How much fun it is being around people who mean what they say. I've loved being back here, feeling as though life was going to finally get better.

Not only that, there is Everett.

"I was."

"Okay, then why can't you be happy still? You're having a baby that you want, Violet. It's not a death sentence. Many women have kids or divorce and are single moms. Is yours just a little bit more stressful? Yeah, it is, but you are fully capable of handling it."

I know that I can handle it. I don't doubt that I can do it and that I will do it, but there is the worry of who I'm doing it with.

"I'm all alone, Ana. I'm out here, by myself, no family, and I can't put that on Everett. I mean, sure, he's great and he was here for me the last twenty-four hours."

She lifts her hand. "Wait. You told him?"

I sigh. "Yes, I went to try to break off or at least put the brakes on the whole sleeping together."

Analeigh is on her feet a second later. "You didn't tell me it happened again! Please tell me it was good. I really need you to have at least that."

"It was good."

"Really good?" she asks, sitting back down next to me.

She's never going to relent. "It was the best ever."

"Thank God! I thought you were going to be one of those girls who only ever had bad sex and then blamed it on yourself. It is never your fault."

"Good to know," I say with a sigh. "It just can't keep going."

"Why not?"

Has she been listening at all? I mean, it's pretty damn clear why. "Because I'm pregnant!"

Ana rolls her eyes. "So what? Pregnant people have sex. Plus you don't have to worry about getting knocked up again. You can have all the sex you want without the possible repercussions."

I really don't know why I'm friends with her sometimes. "You give terrible advice."

She laughs loudly. "Please! I give amazing advice. You're just way too uptight. Look, I told you how I felt about the neighbor, and now you've had amazing sex. Did he say he wanted to stop banging you?"

"No," I huff. "He didn't."

"Okay, so you told him and he wasn't like, you're a shit show that I don't want tickets to?"

I think back to last night and how that was definitely not what he said. He was sweet, held me all night, and then made sure I had fun today.

"No, he didn't."

"Then I'm going to ask, again, why can't you be with him."

"Because I can't. I can't even think about being with someone. I can't do that to him. I can't ask him to get involved with me. I'm a mess, Analeigh. A fucking. Complete. Mess. A mess of epic proportions. I'm not even divorced yet and…God, I just…I can't."

She moves toward me, pulling me against her. "It's okay, Vi. I know you're a mess, and…" She pauses, sniffing me. "What the hell is that? You smell like a barn."

"I was at the farm all day today. That's probably why I didn't get your calls. Everett took me there after I woke up. He wanted me to see a cow and goats."

Ana looks absolutely horrified by this idea. "This is what you moved here for? Goats?"

"I didn't know there were goats."

"Okay, while you're all *Little House on the Prairie* here, I'm going to back up a second and ask how he was able to convince you to go on this…trip to the farm when you woke up?"

"I slept at his house. I had an epic meltdown after my call with Dylan, went to tell Everett whatever we were doing was done, and then proceeded to cry on his chest until we fell asleep."

Her concern is now replaced by a large smile. "He held you all night?"

Oh boy. She's going to get that hopeless romantic look in her eyes and start her scheming. "Don't get ahead of yourself."

"Don't you see!" she snaps and then grabs my hands. "Vi, you told him your hot mess of a life story and he didn't just toss you out. He must really like you."

"Or he didn't want to be mean to an emotional pregnant girl."

Although, that doesn't explain why he would take care of me all day. Unless he really was worried I was going to snap, which was totally plausible.

Still, it didn't feel like an obligation, and even when I walked away after our talk in the car, it was more that he was doing what he thought I wanted.

Which really was what I wanted, but then not really because I don't want any of this. If I could've had my way, I wouldn't be pregnant with Dylan's child, and I would keep having mind-blowing sex with Everett, get my divorce finalized, and then maybe we could build something special.

"I'm going to let you in on a secret: Men do not take care of emotional pregnant girls if they don't care about them. You guys are like a second-chance love story for the ages. Girl loves boy, leaves him behind in his dusty little town to fall in love with a douchebag Hollywood star who has a small dick. Then you come back, and…poof…love."

"You have been in Hollywood for too long. This is real life, Ana."

She shrugs. "These stories exist for a reason."

"This isn't that story." I won't allow myself the belief that this ends happily, because all too often—it doesn't.

"Fine. Then why are you staying here?"

I blink, unsure of what the hell to say to that. "Where would I go?"

"You'll come live with me and Nick or I'll buy you a house or something."

"Ana, stop. First of all, I have a job here. I promised Miles a year, and I'm going to uphold my obligation until the end of the school year. Also, I don't want to go back to California. I hated it there, and I really don't want to leave this place. I love this house and the town and the people here."

"And your neighbor?"

"It can't happen," I say, needing her to hear me.

"Okay, then. Well, how about you show me all there is in this cute little town so I can at least feel better when I leave."

I reach out, taking her hand in mine. "I can do that."

"Okay, this store is absolutely adorable! We should franchise it and have one just like this in California," Ana says as she's walking around Prose & Perk.

"You really like it?" Hazel asks. She about lost her shit when she saw Analeigh.

"It's amazing, seriously. I love the entire feel of it."

"Thank you."

The way Hazel looks as though she might explode is really cute. I'm such a dork that when I met Ana, I had no idea who she was. I grew up with two parents who probably had no idea who her father's band was, let alone let me listen to it. Although, my Gran did love him, but I didn't get her musical influence until later.

I had classical music or nothing.

I usually chose nothing.

Instead of music, I read.

Everything and anything I could get my hands on. Shakespeare was my absolute favorite or Jane Austen. I read those stories over and over, which may be the reason I'm in the position I'm in.

The two of them talk about the store, Hazel showing Ana different things, including the section that is meant for anyone who needs to be creative.

"Have you thought about selling books here?" Ana asks.

"Not really," Hazel confesses.

"I think you could also be a bookstore, you know, for like your favorite things. Like, maybe it's only books you love."

Hazel purses her lips. "Well, I only read romance."

"Oh! That's even better! You can be a romance-only bookstore. I bet people would love that." Ana looks around and then jumps to another topic. "Anyway, tell me how you and Vi know each other."

I smile at them both. "Hazel and I were really close when we were kids."

Ana's eyes widen. "Really? So you *all* hung out?"

"We did," Hazel replies. "It was mostly Everett, Violet, and I. Sometimes Miles came with us too."

Analeigh brushes her hand against the counter. "Everett? That name sounds familiar. Have I met him?"

I'm going to kill her. She knows damn well who Everett is and that she hasn't met him. I'm hoping to keep it that way.

Her filter broke a long time ago, and there's no way I want anything to spill out that shouldn't be said, which will happen if they meet.

"You haven't," I say, narrowing my eyes at her.

She grins. "Wait, is that your ex-boyfriend? The guy you were in love with before you met Dickless Dylan?"

"Ana..." I say with a clear warning in my voice.

"What? Maybe that's a common name out here. We are in the forest and shit."

Hazel laughs once. "Everett is that same one, and apparently they've been hanging out a lot lately..."

"Have they?"

I huff loudly, but they continue on as though they didn't hear me.

"Yeah, Everett usually tells me everything, but the last few days he's been really cagey about all his answers. I was just here the other day, pouring coffee, and someone came in talking about Everett and some new girl dancing at the bar." Hazel grins after telling her story.

"You don't say? And, tell me, was this friend pretty?" Ana leans her elbows on the counter and rests her head atop her fists.

"I hear she was. It gets even juicier."

Ana smiles and her face brightens. "Do tell."

"When I went over to see Everett the other day, it was really early, before the coffee shop opened. I needed to bring him something, and I saw him coming across the field from his neighbor's house."

Analeigh looks to me, her hand covering her mouth. "No, wow, Violet, that must make you very uncomfortable that he's sleeping with his neighbor."

I roll my eyes. "Shut up."

She laughs. "Well, I can tell you that our friend over here, she decided to stop living in hell and put herself out there. She met some guy, but they knew each other. It's been a whirlwind ever since."

"Betrayed by both of my closest friends," I say, throwing my hands up in the air.

They both laugh, and Ana wraps her arm around my shoulder, pulling me to her. "Oh, don't be so dramatic. I'm just kidding." Ana's phone rings, and she looks down and squeals. "I have to take this." I already know it's Nick. No one else makes her smile like that.

She walks off to the other side of the coffee shop, giggling and chattering. Hazel is wiping down the machinery and then looks at me. "After Everett's parents' accident, he changed a lot. He was dealing with grief and his mother's condition. It was really hard for him."

I nod. "I can't even imagine."

Hazel puts the rag down and sighs. "He always used his sarcasm and humor as a way to deflect, which is just who he is, right? He's stubborn and wonderful and a moron and too smart for his own good, but he's been really lonely. Whenever I've tried to talk to him about dating or anything, he shoots me down, saying he has enough women in his life with his mother and me."

I stay silent for a second. "I'm not trying to..."

I don't know what I want to say. Not trying to hurt him. Not trying to ruin his life. Not trying to be the mess I am. All of those are true. The last thing I want is to cause more stress in Everett's life, although that seems to be exactly what I'm doing.

"You've made him smile again. I know it's only been a couple of months that you've been back, but already I see him starting to perk up or, I don't know, but I'm glad you guys are hopefully finding whatever it is you need. I always thought you guys were meant to be," she says with a smile.

"I don't know about that," I say with a sigh. "I am a bit of a mess right now."

"We all are."

I laugh. "Yeah, but I'm like a colossal-size one. To the point my best friend just flew six hours after I didn't answer a phone call, because she was worried. Ana is extra and does these things anyway, but she had a gut feeling I needed her."

"Are you okay?"

Yesterday I would've said no. I would've cried and felt the intense grief over the course my life has landed on, but right now it doesn't seem so insurmountable. Between Everett and all his encouragement and Ana today, I know that I'll be okay.

It won't be easy, but nothing in life is.

"I am. Just a little overwhelmed, that's all."

Hazel leans forward, her palm flat on the counter. "I may not be Analeigh, but you can always come talk to me. No matter what, okay?"

"Thank you, Hazel."

Ana walks back over with a huge grin. "What did I miss?"

I rest my hand on Hazel's. "Just my friend reminding me that I'm not so alone here."

CHAPTER 22
EVERETT

"Pass me a beer," I say to Lachlan.

He leans into the cooler, grabbing one and tossing it to me as we sit around the fire pit. "You're not in your usual asshole mood."

I'm not in any kind of mood, I'm just whatever.

I don't know exactly how the fuck they want me to be when I finally got everything I wanted and then had it end before it started.

I shrug. "I didn't realize I had to always be on."

He raises his hands. "Easy, killer. I didn't say anything bad. Just that you seem off."

"I am."

There. That's about all the honesty they're getting. I loved a girl, lost her, got her back, only to lose her again because she wants to leave Ember Falls and I can't.

I could never put my mother in a home, and I can't take her out of this place.

So I'm fucking stuck, and that means letting Violet go.

Miles leans forward, resting his elbows on his knees. "Was it a bad day at work?"

I shake my head, not finding myself able to talk to them about this. I can't tell anyone since it's not my news to spread. I just get to suffer in my head. "I'll be fine. I just need to get back in the swing of things."

Lachlan and Miles glance at each other and then back at me before Lachlan speaks. "Dude, you know you don't have to shoulder everything on your own. I know you're not all about sharing, but we're your friends."

"Seriously, how many times have you been there for us?" Miles says, backing him up.

"I share when I can."

Lachlan lifts one brow. "The fuck you do. You never talk about the shit you're dealing with."

"I'm fine. I appreciate the concern. Let's just drink beer and talk about sports."

Lachlan takes a long swig of his beer before going right back into it. "I think it's about Violet," he says to Miles.

I sigh heavily and turn my head.

"Probably, you know he has issues with women," Miles informs him. "I'm not sure if it also includes performance issues."

"I have an issue with you two dickheads," I mutter under my breath.

"Do you remember when Ainsley came to town? He was the one offering all his unsolicited advice," Lachlan jokes.

"I think I gave very solid advice considering you're engaged and living with her…"

Idiot was so sure that it couldn't work and look at them now. Happy and living in domestic bliss. I should get a thank-you card instead of this treatment.

Miles scoffs. "Oh, he had plenty of opinions about Penelope too."

"Again, you're now living together, and I'm sure you're going to be married before we know it. I don't want to hear shit."

"So maybe you're just good at giving the advice and not taking it," Miles counters.

"Maybe I don't need advice from two fools who couldn't get their heads out of their asses."

Although it's not the baby part for me. I mean, sure, it's not ideal and I really didn't plan on becoming a father anytime soon, but I know I could love that child. I watched my parents do it without a thought. I've lived that love, and I could provide that to a baby regardless of whether they were technically mine.

Love is not born from blood, but by a person's willingness to give it freely.

And unlike what I would have initially thought, I want everything with Violet, including this child that is half of her and will be wholly loved.

Right now, she's scared, and I get it. Once again, her life is flipped upside down. She needs time, which is what I'm giving her, but I'm not walking away.

"Come on!" I hear a woman yell in the background, and the three of us turn our heads.

"*Ana!* No!" Violet is trying to be quiet, but I'd know her voice anywhere.

"Oh, please!" the other girl says. "You're no fun!"

Lachlan and Miles both turn their gazes to me, and I shrug. "Violet?" I call out.

"Shit," I hear her say under her breath. "Hey, Ev, umm, I was just outside and... we saw the fire... and my *friend* wanted to come make sure it wasn't a house fire."

The three of us all snort at the same time. "Not a house fire," I say. "Besides, we have the fire chief here, so if it was, we'd be fine."

"Come over and join us!" Miles yells, and I punch him in the arm. "Ouch! Fucker, that hurt."

"It's okay! We don't want to bother you guys," Violet says. "My God, *Ana*, stop."

Instead of stopping, a girl pops her head around the side of the house. "Hey, I'm Ana, a friend of Violet's from California, and we would love to come join you guys."

Lachlan chuckles. "It looks like Violet would rather do anything else."

"Violet would. Hi, Lachlan," she answers and turns to her boss. "Hey, Miles."

"Vi."

She looks to me. "I'm so sorry. Ana is...unrelenting."

I grin. "It's fine, we were just having a few beers and talking about this weekend's tournament."

I'd been doing my best not to think about her, which isn't working out well. I've already debated going to her house sixteen times to convince her that we can work this out. She has no idea how much I care for her, or maybe she does know but doesn't want me to feel that way.

I don't know what the fuck I'm thinking anymore. I go in circles, confusing myself even more.

"Oh? Tournament for what?" Ana asks.

"Ultimate Frisbee," Lachlan says.

Her eyes widen. "What is that?"

"It's a sport," Miles explains. "We play in a league."

"Ohhh," Ana says, nodding. "I see, it's an old-guy thing. Sorry, I didn't know that was big here in Umber Falls."

Violet sighs heavily and looks up at the sky. "Ember Falls, Ana! I swear, I want to hit the reset button on my life."

"Control, alt, delete, babe," Ana replies to her.

"I regret texting you," Violet tells her and then turns to me. "I sent a text to her before we went to the farm that I needed to talk to her, and she couldn't get ahold of me during the day."

"Yeah, the service is terrible at the farm."

It's really annoying for my staff if they ever need to reach me, but they just call their barn line if it's urgent and they know I'm there.

Violet smiles softly. "My very impulsive friend here got on a plane and flew here."

Wow, that's a bit spontaneous and also impressive. I don't know anyone who would just get on a plane and fly across the country because I didn't answer my phone.

Well, maybe Hazel would.

I turn to look at Ana, who just shrugs. "I have a private jet."

"I see." I chuckle. "That makes it convenient."

"Doesn't it? So you're Everett?" Ana asks, walking over and sitting in the open chair beside me. "It's very nice to meet you."

"You as well."

"Anyone else feel like we're missing something?" Lachlan asks not so subtly.

Ana turns to look at him. "Oh, I just really wanted to meet the guy that Violet said was her first love. She had so many good things to say about him, and now I can see why." Her smile is wide as she looks me up and down.

Violet covers her face with her hands and then drops them. "Anything she says, please just forget."

"That's not going to happen," I tell her and then turn to Ana. "So what else did Violet say?"

Ana glances over at Violet and smiles. "Just that you're a good friend to her, and I really appreciate that. Thank you for helping her out."

I nod once. "Of course."

Miles snorts. "Yeah, he's really a very kind soul. I mean, Violet needed her pipes filled, and he was all too willing."

Lachlan chokes on his beer, and Miles pats his back. "Easy there."

"You're a dead man," I warn him. "It was her propane that didn't work, so I was able to turn it on."

Ana grins. "You turned it on, did you?"

I turn to look at Violet, wondering what exactly she told her. She must've mentioned we slept together.

Violet stands opposite of me, her arms crossed, and raises one brow. "She's just as bad as your friends, so don't look to me for help. She has no filter."

Ana stands and claps her hands, holding them in front of her chest. "Anyway, I didn't mean to ruin your bro night. I just wanted to say hello and make sure you weren't in any fire danger, but I see you're all good."

Lachlan speaks before I can. "You guys are sure you don't want to hang out?"

"No, no," Violet chimes in quickly. "Ana leaves tomorrow, and we had plans to spend time together."

Ana rolls her eyes with a sigh. "Please, you want to bake. This is so much more fun. I would really like to know your neighbor, your boss, and the fire chief."

"Analeigh, we have to go."

I grin, debating whether I should push a little and also encourage them to stay, but I can tell Violet is not in the mood.

I refrain from being a ballbuster for probably the first time in my life.

Then Ana sighs again. "Fine, you're no fun."

Violet rolls her eyes. "Bye, guys."

"Bye, Vi. It was nice to meet you, Analeigh," Miles says quickly.

She waves. "Bye, Everett. I'm sure we'll see each other again."

I nod and lift my hand. "Great meeting you, Ana." I catch Violet's eyes. "Bye, Violet."

She waves at me and then grabs Ana's arm, pulling her toward the house. Once the girls are out of sight, I lean back, seeing that my two friends are watching me intently. "What?"

"Just laughing because I think we just met the female version of you."

"So you're saying she's awesome." I grin and take a long pull from my beer.

Miles shakes his head. "I was focusing more on how you were watching Violet."

"I wasn't watching her."

He laughs once. "The hell you weren't. You basically tracked her the entire time."

I thought I held it together pretty well, but apparently not. Did seeing Violet cause my heart to speed up? Yes, but it always does.

She's been the only woman I've ever known to make it feel as though tunnel vision is a real thing. When she smiles because of something I say, it's like I can run through a wall and have the strength of ten men.

It's too bad I can't do anything to make her life better right now. It's out of my hands, and I have to respect what she wants.

Even if it means not getting to be around her.

"Bye, Mom," I say after going through our morning routine. "I'll see you for dinner."

Tomorrow her doctors are coming to the house to do a few routine tests and let me know that there haven't been any changes.

Like always.

I get outside and walk over to Vi's house. I have with me some of the things the Mommy blogs said help with morning sickness.

Inside the bag is ginger candy, ginger tea, ginger ale, some peppermint aroma therapy shit—not sure how that is going to work, but they all swore by it—and salt. Like a shaker. I wrote out some suggestions they had on how to use them because the salt one was a bit of a mystery to me. Apparently, she's supposed to lick her hand, like she's doing a shot, shake the salt on, lick it, and lay there for ten minutes. No clue, but since she's still miserable, I figure it can't hurt to try.

Not wanting to wake her, I put the bag on the porch and start heading back, but when I get halfway down the drive, I hear someone yelling my name.

"Everett!"

I turn and see someone rushing from Violet's porch, but it's not her. It's Analeigh.

I walk toward her, worry filling me. "Is everything okay with Violet?"

The way she's moving has my chest tight with worry. What if there's something wrong and she needs help? I find myself moving a little faster as the fear mounts.

She smiles. "She's fine. I'm getting ready to head back to the airport, and Vi is in the shower, but I wanted to talk to you and saw you leave something on the porch."

I clear my throat and wait for the lecture that is sure to come. The whole *don't hurt my friend or I'll kill you.*

Not that I want to hurt her friend.

Not that I'd ever try to do that.

"Okay," I say, once I've steeled myself.

"Violet...well, you knew her as a kid, and I'm sure you know all about her parents, so I won't bore you with that, but she's got a lot of trust issues, and I'm afraid Dylan hasn't made that any better."

"I'm sure not."

Ana nods. "You can breathe, you know. I'm not going to threaten you. I really just want to thank you."

"Thank me?"

"Yeah, when I got here, I had no idea what mess I was walking into. Violet isn't prone to hysterics, so when she texted me that she needed me, I was terrified about what happened to her. She's my best friend. My upbringing didn't leave me with a lot of people who liked me for me. It was always about my father or what I could get them, but Violet isn't that way. She practically comes unglued when I do things for her." Ana sighs and then looks down. "She's like a sister to me. I love her and would do anything for her. When she told me she was going to move to Ember Falls, I'm not exaggerating when I say I sobbed. My husband had to hold me for hours the night she left, because I was a mess, but then I got here and I found she wasn't falling apart, and I think that's because of you."

I rock back on my heels, not sure what to say, and then step back. "I haven't done anything that a man shouldn't do."

"I know a lot of men, and trust me, they're not doing these things."

"Then they don't deserve a woman like Violet, even if she doesn't feel the same way."

Ana shakes her head. "Violet is afraid to be hurt. She's afraid Dylan is going to force her hand, and right now it's too new to see it doesn't have to be that way. She just needs someone to show her that."

One more day.

That goes through my mind again and again.

I hear my mother saying how she would grab it with two hands.

Violet may leave again. She may walk out of my life, leaving me, but…I will regret not spending every single day I could have with her now.

Analeigh steps closer and gently touches my arm. "I guess what I'm trying to say is that I can leave here and not feel sick to my stomach every day. She has people who care about her. Maybe even love her enough to fight for her."

I nod because I don't trust myself to say anything aloud.

She smiles. "Also, please, do me one favor."

"What's that?"

"Don't let that woman get a goat. Dear God, I had to hear about them all night as she baked enough to fill a store."

I laugh at that. "She really loved that goat."

Ana steps closer and grins. "I think she liked the man who took her more, but what do I know?"

Then she walks away, leaving me wondering how the hell I get my girl back.

CHAPTER 23
VIOLET

This week has been one of those weeks. Where everything sucks, something inevitably breaks—my coffee machine, for example—and you can't find your shoes as you're running out the door.

However, I don't have a first period today, so I'm popping into Prose & Perk. Otherwise, I'm going to be a really terrible teacher.

I pull the door open, both hoping Everett will and won't be here.

I haven't seen him since the night at the fire pit, and each night I lie in bed—the one he gifted me—I think of him.

Of how he looked at me, touched me, made me feel cherished. How we were starting to build something new and amazing, and then I pushed him away.

"Good morning, Vi," Hazel says with a big smile.

"Good morning. Can you save me by giving me a very large coffee, light and sweet?"

"Coming right up." She turns to the machine, hits a bunch of buttons, and talks to me from over her shoulder. "I haven't seen you in a bit. Everything okay?"

Oh, I'm fine, just nursing my broken heart and waiting for my ex to tell me what he wants. All is great.

"Yeah, just working. It's essay week, which means all the students had to write three-page papers on Shakespeare."

She laughs. "I bet they loved that."

"I see the error of my ways now," I say with a sigh.

The kids are great—their papers, not so much. We spent two weeks going over different plays and the facts we know about Shakespeare's life. All they needed to do was show which plays might have been based on real parts of his life and where the similarities were.

I hoped for a little better than this.

"You always loved Shakespeare," Hazel says as she hands me the coffee.

"Yes, she did," a deep, masculine voice that has been haunting me says from behind.

I take a moment, trying to calm my racing heart before turning to see him. "Hi."

Everett smiles. "Hi to you. So you're forcing the students to learn about Shakespeare?"

"Forcing?" I say with a bit of indignance.

"I don't know many teenagers who are all that eager to sit and listen to his inflated stories."

My jaw drops. "Inflated?"

"Are you just picking one word that you want to zero in on?"

I inhale deeply through my nose. "I'll have you know that Shakespeare lives on to this day because his work speaks for itself. Why do you think we still see it performed? Not because they are inflated or we're forcing it, but because the stories are beautiful, tragic, poignant, and make the reader feel something. You suffer along with the characters. You see their flaws and can relate."

He raises one brow. "Relate to what? I've never considered murdering my friends in order to become king."

Hazel snorts. "I'm going to call bullshit. I'm pretty sure you've considered murdering me, or at least Miles, a few times."

"That last one is definitely true, but not because I was greedy or had a wife who had aspirations to climb as well. It's usually just because he's an idiot." He turns back to me. "Don't even get me started on *Hamlet*. That's just a mess that could've been cleared up in the beginning, and I really couldn't handle the tediousness of *Othello*. You know, there's a pattern where he paints men to be idiots."

I tilt my head. "I wonder why that is."

He grins. "I left myself open for that one."

"It was too easy."

Hazel snorts again. "You notice he didn't have a damn thing to say about *Romeo and Juliet*, though."

Everett turns to her, pinning Hazel with a look that indicates he's not interested in this conversation any further. "Coffee, please."

I grin, deciding that I do want to continue. "Yes, I did notice. Why is that?"

"No reason."

Hazel places two cups of coffee down. "It's because he's totally Romeo and can't remotely critique himself."

"Yes, I'm so Romeo," Everett says with an abundance of sarcasm.

"Aren't you?" she counters.

"I can see it," I say, half joking and half wanting to hear what he's going to say.

We used to joke about being Romeo and Juliet, without the death and feuding family part. The way we felt instantly for each other when we were younger. The fact that we had to part, but promised to return, the way a single kiss changed our entire lives, but we promised our story wouldn't end.

"Considering I'm still alive proves I'm not as much of an idiot as him."

"Oh, please," Hazel jumps in. "That's not what made him stupid. That's what made him the hero. He died for her, and I'd bet there's a woman you'd do the same for."

Our eyes meet, and I look away just as quickly. No, that's not...no.

Everett chuckles and then grabs his coffee. "Parting is such sweet sorrow. Until tomorrow." He winks and then heads out the door.

It takes me a second to unscramble my brain and remember I actually have to go to work. I take my card out to pay, and Hazel lifts her hand. "This one's on the house."

"Hazel, I can pay."

"And I can give my friend a cup of coffee. Now, go before you're late."

"Thank you!" I say and then rush out the door.

When I get to my car, I turn the key, but nothing.

"No, no, no! Not today," I yell and try again. Once again, the engine doesn't kick over. I huff, pop the hood, and go to the front as though I have a clue what I'm looking at.

Of course this is my day.

When I step back, Everett is exiting his truck that's parked across the street and walking over. "Do you need a jump?"

"Probably. I don't know."

"I have cables. I'll pull right over here," he says, moving back to his truck.

He brings it alongside mine, hooks it up, and tries to jump it, but it won't start. Seriously, I could use a vacation from my life.

"I mean, why not?" I say aloud. "Why not have one more thing today?"

"I'll call Tom, our mechanic in town, and he'll get it in to look at it. Didn't think to put him on the list," he jokes.

I shake my head. "Har har. Anyway, I can't be without a car. I have to get to work and then home. I…this is…ugh!"

"I'll take you to work, and pick you up to bring you home."

"I can't ask you to do that." *For so many reasons,* I don't add. He's already done so much for me and I've given almost nothing in return.

"That's what friends are for. Come on, get in the truck."

I blow out a long breath, knowing there's really not much of a choice when Everett wants something, and I get my things. I climb into the cab, thankful for the warm air, and put my hands in front of the heater. "I feel like it gets cold so fast here."

"Dad used to joke that fall only lasted two weeks, so don't blink or you'll miss it."

I smile, almost hearing his voice as Everett said it. "You sounded just like him."

"That's the nicest thing you've ever said to me," he jokes.

"I'm pretty sure I've said a lot of nice things to you."

"Name one?"

I laugh. "There are too many to recall."

"You can't even think of one."

"Yes, I can," I say, with a touch of petulance. "I've said you were a god in bed."

Really, Violet? That's the first thing you go to?

"Thinking about that night, are you?" Everett says, his voice low and husky.

I scoff. "Not for a second."

Liar, liar, Violet's pants are on fire.

How long is this car ride anyway? Shouldn't it be like five minutes to school?

"I think that's bullshit. I know you are."

I turn, my jaw falling slack in mock indignation. "You do, huh?"

He's right.

"I do. Your face is all flushed and you're remembering, just like I do every night. When I close my eyes, I can see your face as you come. I can hear the moans you make when I'm between your legs. When I grip my cock, I imagine it's your mouth sucking me deep in your throat. You think about it because it was, hands down, the best night of my life. It's impossible to forget."

My palms begin to sweat, and it's not from the heat. What is he playing at? We agreed to…you know…not keep up whatever we were starting.

To pump the brakes while I try to get my life situated.

It doesn't matter that I think about him all the fucking time.

That each night I find myself at my window, pushing the curtains to the side and staring out at his house.

It doesn't matter that when I lie in the bed he gave me, I remember his body against mine.

Or that I see his face when I close my eyes.

None of that is the point, because I might have to leave him.

It's better this way—better to hurt and ache for him than to keep having him and then be completely destroyed if Dylan decides he wants to be in our child's life.

While leaving Ember Falls is the absolute last thing I want to do, for my child, I'll do what's best, and that's for him or her to have a father.

Instead of confessing any of that, I shake my head. "I think you're delusional."

He laughs. "I bet you do."

Then the truck comes to a stop in front of the school. I look over to him, both grateful and sad that we're here already. I've missed him. "Well, thank you for the ride to work. I owe you—again."

"You owe me nothing, Violet. I'll text you and let you know what the mechanic says. I'll pick you up after school if the car isn't ready."

"I can get a ride with Miles," I say quickly.

"I'll be here."

"Don't you have work or Frisbee or something?" I ask, hoping to find an excuse not to be in such close proximity to him again.

He shakes his head. "I'll be here for you, anytime you need me."

His words send a flood of warmth through my body, and I want so badly to reach across the truck, take his face in my hands, and kiss him, but that would be stupid.

"Okay," I say, keeping my appendages on my side, and then I open the door. "Thank you, Ev."

He nods once as I exit the truck. Then as I'm halfway to the door, he calls out: "Violet? Romeo should've never let Juliet leave. He should've taken her off that balcony and run away with her.

Romeo should've stood and fought the world. I don't plan to make his mistakes for the girl I want."

Then he drives off, leaving me completely speechless.

Thankfully my car just needed a new battery, it was corroded, and they explained that it wouldn't jump-start for them either.

However, they said there was no cost, that a mysterious benefactor paid the bill and refused to disclose his name.

I have one guess and I know his name.

Not to mention, there was a note on the car windshield that said:

Violet,

We're going to add the mechanic and also a handyman named Mike to your list. Also, I got something that's in the car, it's for the baby. You can't name it so don't get too attached.

E

When I opened up the vehicle, ready to ride over and demand to know what the bill was, all my anger evaporated.

There, in the front seat, in the seatbelt was a goat stuffed animal.

When I got home, I went to see him but he wasn't there—he had a vet emergency.

The next day I saw him at Prose & Perk to which he said he was very busy and couldn't talk, but he'd stop by later.

Then two days after that, he was at the Ember Falls football game with Brutus. Who I was told wasn't feeling well.

It's been days of him avoiding me and I'm starting to wonder if this is all part of his master plan.

Now I'm pulling into the driveway, and he's walking around the side of my house.

What the hell is going on?

"Everett, what are you doing here?" I say as I get out, pulling my coat around me tightly and following him.

He doesn't reply.

"Everett?"

Again he ignores me.

Ugh, this man.

He turns around suddenly, and his eyes go wide, as though I surprised him. He pulls off his headphones and smiles. "Hello, Violet."

I go to sigh, but it comes out more of a laugh. "Hello, Everett. What are you doing?"

"Filling your woodpile."

I stare, managing only to blink. "What?"

"I saw that your woodpile was low, so I'm refilling it."

Yes, it is low, but how the hell did he see that or know that? "Are you stalking me?"

He grins. "Is it stalking if you see me?"

I laugh, remembering our first encounters when I came back. "Funny."

"I'd like to think so."

"Okay, but why are you filling my woodpile? I was going to do that this weekend."

He looks over at the very low stash. The heat in my house is fine, but it really doesn't warm me well enough. Having the fireplace going has helped keep the cost of the propane down, which is so expensive, and it's a nice ambiance when I'm working on lesson plans, or reading a book. It also provides light at night, as I often have to run to the bathroom because the nausea is so bad. I'm hoping the doctor tells me something when I go for my first checkup in two weeks.

"It was low, and I didn't have anything to do tonight, since practice was canceled," he says as though it makes all the sense in the world.

"You can't keep doing nice things for me," I say, needing to get some kind of higher ground.

"Why not?"

My muscles lock for a moment and I stare at him. "Because."

"Because why?"

Because I'm already more than halfway in love with you, and I need that to stop, damn it.

"You know why."

Everett's grin widens. "I don't think I do." He steps closer, pulling his work gloves off. "I don't know why you'd want me to stop doing things for you, being near you, when you said we were friends and all."

I hold my ground as he takes another step. "We *are* friends."

"Are we?" he asks, eyes narrowing a bit. "Because I promise, I don't get jealous when I find out my friends are having a baby with their ex-husband. I don't imagine them at night. I don't watch their windows, waiting for their curtains to move." I gasp and then he's in front of me, his chest against mine. "I don't remember their taste, their sounds, or the way their lips fit with mine. I don't worry every day and every night that they might need something and they're alone. I don't think about my friends' woodpiles. Those things, they don't keep me up at night regarding my *friends*, but they do when it comes to you. So I'm going to fill your woodpile, check on your propane levels, ensure your fire alarms work, weatherproof your doors or anything else I can think of until you realize, we're not friends. We were never friends and we're never going to be *just* friends." He leans in, and I think he's going to kiss me. I wait on bated breath, desperate for it, but he moves to my ear. "Call me whatever you want, Vi. Call me your lover, the man you want to forget, the man you pretend you don't wait at windows for. Just don't ever call me your fucking friend. We both know it's a lie. We're more, so much more."

Again, he leaves me before I can reply, going back to the woodpile and grabbing the ax.

Yeah, we are so not friends, but I don't know that we can be more without it destroying us both.

CHAPTER 24
VIOLET

I manage to stay away from the window for two days, pretty sure that Everett will make good on his promise.

But I miss him.

I know I shouldn't, but I want to see him, so before I can think about it twice, I move to my bedroom window, pull the curtain back, and wait.

And wait.

And wait.

And…nothing.

Well, that was anticlimactic and disappointing.

I let out a long sigh and go do my nighttime skin routine, layering all my serums and lotions. Once all that is done, I slip into my comfy satin pajamas and head downstairs to grab my book and make sure everything is ready for the night.

I clean up the kitchen and am shutting the lights off when there's a knock.

Oh God.

He came.

My stomach drops and my nerves are scattered.

I'm happy about this. Right? I should be. I mean, I stood at the window, and he said he would come over if I did.

I rush to the door and open it.

"Violet."

Everett.

My heart immediately starts to race with excitement, but the look in his eyes has me instantly concerned. Everett runs his hands through his dark-brown hair and sighs. "Hey, look, I hate to ask you for a favor."

"What is it?" I ask quickly.

"I have an emergency at the clinic and I really need to go, but my mother isn't...well, I need someone to sit with her."

That's not a favor I would ever say no to. "Of course, let me get changed real quick and grab my coat."

I step back inside, run up the stairs, change back into my leggings and sweatshirt, grab the jacket sitting on the edge of the couch, and return to him.

He sighs heavily and then he looks at me. "Are you sure?"

"Everett, I don't mind at all."

Relief washes over him. "Thank you. This only happens once in a blue moon, and today nothing is going right."

I reach my hand out, resting it on his arm. "Hey, that's what friends are for." Although I'm kidding myself thinking we're only friends. He's more. So much more.

He looks down at where I'm touching him, and then our eyes meet. "Right."

The flutter in my stomach has nothing to do with the warmth in his eyes. Nope. It must be the baby or something I ate.

I'm such a liar.

I quickly remove my hand and say, "Okay, so you need me to just sit with her?"

He gives me a tight-lipped smile. "Yes, usually one of her friends comes over and knits or something, but she's not feeling well."

"Oh no, okay. I mean, I don't know how to knit, but I'll hang out with her. I'm sure we can find something."

"Thanks, Vi."

"Again, no thanks needed. You've come to my aid more than once."

We walk into the barn, and I am absolutely blown away. When he said he built her a home, he wasn't kidding.

This place is absolutely stunning. The front entryway leads to a beautiful open floor plan with a vaulted ceiling in the living room area. There is a television mounted on the wall where Mrs. Finnegan's old recliner from when we were kids sits.

The kitchen boasts stunning two-tone cabinets, and there is a hallway toward the back.

"Her bedroom and the bathroom are back down there." He points to the hallway. "There is plenty of food in the fridge. The front door is automated to close if it's left open more than fifteen minutes, so don't be alarmed if you hear something shut."

"Anything else I should know?"

Everett nods. "She can't remember things. I know I told you that, but she won't know if she did something, and she may forget why you're here or that she saw you recently. I'm sorry, I really wouldn't ask this if—"

I lift my hand. "Stop, it's fine. I love your mom."

He's done so much for me. This is not even a favor.

"Okay," he says, the resignation causing my heart to ache. "Mom! Can you come to the living room?"

She comes shuffling out. "Everett." She smiles as though the sun has just risen. "Hi, sweetheart." Then Mrs. Finnegan smiles at me. "Hi, Violet."

"Hi, Mrs. F."

Everett steps forward. "Mom, I have to go to work for a little bit. I know I wrote down that we were going to spend time together, and I'm sorry."

Her eyes go to the board that's on the wall. "Now? You have to go now?"

"Yes, there's an emergency, so I need to go, but Violet is going to hang out with you for a little while." Everett walks over and wipes off the timing that he would be there now and writes that she's going to spend time with me.

I can see the concern in her eyes. "It's so late, Everett. You can't drive now."

"I promise I'll be okay, and I'll come right here when I'm done."

She shakes her head. "No, it's dark out."

Everett looks to me. "I have to go."

"Go, it's fine. I got this."

While Mrs. Finnegan is not the equivalent of a child, Everett said sometimes that's what it feels like, so I do what I would do if one of my students didn't want to do something.

Distraction.

"Mrs. Finnegan," I say quickly. "Everett said that you are really good at knitting? I've never done it before, and I would really love to learn. Do you think you'd…be willing?"

Her eyes light up. "I am very good at knitting, dear."

Everett winks at me and mouths, *Thank you.*

I smile at him and then turn back to Mrs. Finnegan.

We spend the first thirty minutes with her explaining all the different things about knitting. I had no idea there were different ways to hold the needles or loops or patterns.

Once she determines that I am now knowledgeable enough to attempt it, she starts me off with a row and hands it to me.

I thought that I was pretty crafty and smart.

I realize now—I am not.

Somehow almost half of the first row undoes itself and comes off, causing her to have to fix it. "It's okay, Violet. You're doing great."

I snort a laugh. "I am terrible."

"Well, you're not awful," she says with a smile.

"I'm a much better baker."

"Your grandmother used to make me the best carrot cake each Thanksgiving."

That was one of the first things she taught me to make. She said a carrot cake was the best cake for any occasion. If I could master it, I would be well on my way to being a good baker. I never understood it, but she said most people would justify eating a piece since it was a vegetable. Also, because she prepped every ingredient by hand, it gave us quality time in the kitchen.

I reach over, resting my hand on Mrs. Finnegan's. "Would you like to make one with me?"

"You know how to make her cake?"

I nod. "I do, and I have all the ingredients at my house."

I have enough baking items to make pretty much anything anyone can think of.

"That would be lovely," Mrs. Finnegan says. "But we'll have to do it in Everett's house, since my oven doesn't work."

"Okay, we can do that."

We both put the knitting supplies away, and I leave a note on the board for Everett, just in case he gets back before we do. I help her with her coat, and we head to my house to gather all the supplies we need.

Mrs. Finnegan walks around the first level, a wide smile across her face. "This place hasn't changed a bit."

"I didn't want to take my grandmother out of this home."

"Oh, honey, I don't think you could even if you knocked it to the ground."

I let a soft laugh out. "I bet she'd still find a way to be here."

"This home was as much a part of her as she was of it. Is that why you are here now?"

"Yes, I needed to be somewhere that felt like home."

She walks closer, her hand resting on my cheek. "Home is where you feel like yourself."

"It's why I'm here."

Her grin widens and then drops, her eyes looking out across the field. "It's why I can't be in Everett's house. I miss the other half of myself. When I'm there for too long, I get sad."

My chest grows tight as I think about the pain she must've felt returning to her home, only for it to no longer be that. I guess in some ways I know that it's why I had to leave California. It was too hard to see places where I thought my home was becoming a prison in so many ways.

The pain of seeing a bed I shared with someone who betrayed me.

The living room where we laughed, watching a movie before we'd end up in each other's arms.

Even if the last three or more years have been hard, it was my dream and it was taken from me.

"Do you like the barn apartment?" I ask her.

"Oh, yes, very much." She looks around and then her eyes widen. "Do you know where my phone is? I need my phone."

"I have it right here," I say, holding it up. She exhales and then reaches for it. "Are you ready to bake a cake?"

Mrs. Finnegan nods. "Yes, you know I used to love your grandmother's carrot cake."

I smile, grab the basket of supplies, and link my arm with hers. "Well, we should make that."

We head to Everett's house, which he left unlocked, and I shoot him a quick text.

Me: Hey, we're going to bake a cake at your house.
Everett: My house?
Me: Yes, your mother and I want to do something nice and she said her oven doesn't work.
Everett: Okay, have fun...I think...

I put the phone away, and we set up our workspace and then get to work on the cake. Together, Mrs. Finnegan and I prep all the ingredients. Throughout the entire process, we laugh and do a pretty good job. We have a few hiccups, like when she can't remember what ingredient we were looking for or what the measurements we need are. Regardless, we have a lot of fun.

She is still the sweet woman with a heart of gold I grew up with, and even though she seems frustrated at times, she pushes through.

"You want to actually crush the pineapple by hand?" she asks, almost horrified.

I chuckle. "We have to. Granny would never buy it from a can."

"Okay, then."

Pineapple juice sprays us in the face and pretty much the entire area around us. Once we get it assembled, we put the cake in the oven, and she gives me a high five.

"And what are you two doing other than making a mess?" Everett's voice breaks in as we laugh.

I turn my head to see him and instantly smile. "We're making a cake."

"Are you?" Everett looks around at the absolute mess of the kitchen and shakes his head. "I think the cake made you."

"Well, carrot cake is very labor intensive."

He shakes his head again. "Mom? You let her destroy the house?"

Mrs. Finnegan laughs. "I guess I did. Come and help us clean up."

He pulls off his coat, tosses it over the back of the chair, and enters the kitchen. "I leave for two hours and come back to a complete disaster," he says in mock affront.

"Do you want to eat some cake?" I ask.

"What kind of a question is that?"

"Then you have to help clean. The cook isn't supposed to be the one doing all the work," I inform him.

He laughs. "Then I guess I better get to work, since this mess will take hours to finish."

The three of us work together, and about halfway through, Mrs. Finnegan slows down and clutches her head.

"Mom, are you getting a headache?" Everett asks, clearly noticing it as well.

She nods. "I'm sorry."

"Here, sit." I pull a chair out for her.

Everett walks over and grabs a lockbox from the top of the refrigerator. He opens it and gives her some medication.

"It's going to be bad," she warns him. "I want to rest."

"Okay, let's get you home then."

"I'll grab her things," I say quickly.

The three of us walk over to her apartment. "Not to bed yet, Everett. Not yet."

He nods. "Okay."

We head into the living room and it's such a sweet moment, I could cry. He helps her into the recliner, drapes a blanket over her, lowers the lights, and then kisses her forehead.

She squeezes his hand and then looks to me. "Thank you, Violet. I can't wait to eat some cake."

I go to her and kiss her cheek. "Thank you for teaching me how to knit. Well, kind of. I had a great night."

Her head falls back against the chair. "I did too, dear."

"Let me just get her settled, and I'll come back to the house."

"Okay."

I walk back and go right to the disaster area that is the kitchen. There's flour, sugar, and carrot peels all over. I swear it wasn't this bad as we were doing it.

I'm picking up the peels when I hear his back door close and his footsteps as he approaches.

Slowly, I rise, trying hard to stop the erratic beating of my heart at being alone with him again.

"Thank you," he says as he stands across from me.

"I had an amazing night. Did everything go okay with the animals?"

He sighs heavily. "It should be okay. I'll know more tomorrow."

"I'm sorry tonight was hard."

Everett shrugs. "It's all part of the job. How was tonight with Mom?"

Tonight was everything I didn't know I needed.

I was able to relax and not think about my worries for a little while. Baking with his mother healed a part of me that felt broken. She reminded me of when I was a little girl and was learning new things with my granny.

"It was perfect," I tell him.

He looks at the kitchen and laughs. "I think she had too much fun."

"Is she going to be okay?"

"Yeah, her medicine will kick in, and she'll be fine. She doesn't get headaches as frequently anymore, and I think we caught this one early." Everett walks toward me. "Let me help."

"You don't have to."

"I want to."

"Okay."

I start to wipe the counter, where there is probably enough flour to make another cake, so I focus, but then I feel Everett behind me, his warm body brushing against my back. "You missed a spot."

I clear my throat as I feel the loss of his heat. "Thanks." I wipe the counter a little harder and then move to the other one.

Once that's cleaned up, I go to the mountain of dishes in the sink. As I start to wash, I do my absolute best not to notice where he is, but he's making it incredibly hard by occasionally grazing my arm or bumping into me lightly.

As I'm elbow deep in the soapy water, he comes up behind me, his chest against my back, and reaches his arm in front of me. I gasp softly when I feel his cheek against my neck.

"Sorry, I need the paper towels." His gravelly voice sends a shiver down my spine.

My heart is pounding as I force myself to breathe. "It's fine."

Although it's not. I'm burning up and it isn't from the hot water. I want him.

I want his arms around me. I want to feel his scruff against my neck and everywhere else.

"Is it?" he asks, still standing behind me, both arms now caging me in.

The air in the room is charged—one spark and we could explode, which might happen anyway.

The question feels loaded. As though he's not talking about the paper towels or the mess, but about this moment. I turn my head, looking at him from over my shoulder. The heat in his eyes confirms that we are not talking about anything else except each other.

"Everett..."

His eyes close, and he runs his nose along my neck. "Hmm."

"I want..." I stop. Not able to say the words. To kiss me. To take me. To claim me because dear God, I've never been anyone else's the way I am his.

That staying away from him is too much. It's impossible and I'm so tired of fighting.

His lip is against my ear, and the heat of his breath causes me to shiver. "I know what you want. Tell me, Violet, and I'll give it to you."

I can't say it. I gasp, my fingers gripping the edge of the sink. "Please," I beg.

"Do you want me to kiss you?"

I shut the water off and turn to face him, my desire winning out over my common sense. "Yes."

CHAPTER 25
EVERETT

Yes.

I don't hesitate. I move my lips to hers, pressing in the most tender kiss I can manage. It's been weeks without her. Weeks after having her, kissing her, making love to her that I've gone without.

I'm a starved man, and right now I'm being fed.

Violet's hands move to my face, and she deepens the kiss. My tongue slides against hers, the kiss becoming more and more heated.

She tastes like sugar, and her vanilla-and-cinnamon scent fills my senses. I've waited for her to come to me, to let me convince her that we can have a future, but she wasn't ready.

Now that I have her in my arms again, I'm going to do everything I can to keep her.

"Everett," she says and breaks the kiss, turning her head. "God, I'm sorry."

I clear my throat. "Sorry for what?"

"I...I shouldn't kiss you. I shouldn't do this to you."

"I promise, kissing you is not a hardship." Although it does make some things very, very hard.

She shakes her head, resting her hand on my chest. "It's not for me either. But my situation hasn't changed. My life is just so up in the air, and the last thing I want to do is hurt you."

"Why do you think you get to make the decision for me?"

Violet's eyes widen. "What?"

"You heard me. Isn't it also my decision? Don't I get a say in whether or not I'm willing to take the risk?"

She glances down at her hands and then back to me. "Of course you do."

"Then how about you ask me what I want, Vi?"

It takes a moment before she speaks again. "Okay. What do you want?" she asks, her eyes filled with hesitation.

"You," I say without pause. "All of you. The baby. A chance at a life together. I want our second chance."

Tears fill her eyes, but she holds them back. "And if I have to leave Ember Falls?"

"Then we come up with a solution—together."

I can see the wheels turning in her mind, and I take her chin between my thumb and pointer. "Look at me, Violet. I'm not afraid, even though my heart has always been yours to break, but I'm not afraid of it. I'm not running away. I'm standing here, willing to take whatever time we can have together. If it's a week, a month, or a lifetime. What are you afraid of?"

She drops her head to my chest before letting out a long breath. "I'm afraid that if I have to leave here, after falling back in love with you, it will absolutely destroy me."

"Do you think it won't if you don't give us a chance?"

Violet laughs and she pushes at my chest, starting to pace. "No, I know it will no matter what, but if we do this, and we have this relationship, then what?"

"Answer me this, do you think about me?"

"Ever?"

I grin. "Let me rephrase. Do you think about us, what we could be?"

She nods. "Every day."

"And would you rather live those days together or apart?"

Just then she grabs at her side, wincing. "God, that hurts."

Fear grips me as she doubles over.

"What's wrong?"

"I think I'm going to be sick!" Violet says and then runs to the bathroom.

"Violet?" I call after her, but she shuts the door.

"Don't come in here!"

Then I hear her getting sick. Yeah, that's not going to happen.

I push the door open and rush to her side, pulling her hair back behind her, as she gets sick again. Violet pants and I grab a towel, handing it to her.

"Does your stomach still hurt?" I ask as she dabs at her mouth.

"Yes, but…I really didn't want you to see that."

"You know I'm a doctor, right? I've seen my share of puke, poop, and blood. Nothing scares me."

Not to mention the things I have to do when I work with farmers and in vitro. Her pregnancy nausea is a walk in the park.

What I did hate was watching her suffer. I grab a cup by the sink, fill it, and then she takes a small sip. "I hate this part of pregnancy. I really thought it was starting to fade. Apparently it was just lying in wait."

I smile and brush her hair back. "Hopefully it was just this once."

"Your lips to God's ears." She gets up and winces. "I haven't had this constant cramping before, though."

"They say cramping is normal."

When I found out that Violet was pregnant, my doctor mode kicked in. The only thing was that I didn't know shit about human pregnancy. I can tell you all about a horse or a goat, but the gestational periods aren't the same.

So I spent hours researching so that I could at least be a little knowledgeable. Then I got on some blogs and online forums, now I know things I wish I could forget.

"Who says that?" she asks as I help her up off the floor.

"The Mommy blogs."

"The what?"

I clear my throat. "So, there are hundreds and hundreds of websites that are literally nothing but helpful women willing to offer their advice. I went on one, then they made me register to ask a question, to which I became a member and pay ten dollars a month for, and they sent me to another."

This is truly embarrassing, but it's the truth.

She blinks. "I'm sorry, what?"

"Blogs, chat rooms, forums, there are so many and the information is really conflicting. One woman was saying her milk didn't come in then another one said it was because she ate too much broccoli. I don't know, that became heated."

"Everett, you joined a forum?"

I scoff. "I joined thirty. I'm a favorite in there because they found out I was a soon-to-be father and they wanted to make sure I could get the information I need. When I was on the first, they recommended a few others, and I needed to have a large enough sample size to make an accurate conclusion. So, I joined them all."

"You're paying for these forums?"

I nod. "Some, but only like ten are paid."

"Oh, only ten."

"I also read a few books, talked to the pediatrician in town, but the online community is much more forthcoming."

"I…bet they are," she says looking at me as though I sprouted two heads.

"Wait, books? You read a few books about pregnancy in a couple of weeks and talked to a pediatrician?"

"I don't know why you're so shocked."

Violet shakes her head. "You're not? Why would you join groups and talk to doctors?"

"Because you're pregnant," I say, not sure where her confusion comes from. "You're pregnant and you're not alone. I'm right here and I'm going to learn anything and everything I can so I'm prepared to do whatever you need."

Again, not sure why she's shocked by this.

Her eyes go soft and she touches my cheek. "You know you really can be sweet."

I grin. "Good to know that reading really does it for you."

The laugh that falls from her lips goes right to my cock. Not that it takes much of anything to turn me on around her.

"Can you give me a minute to clean up and then head home?"

Only I don't want her to go home. I want her to stay here, to curl up on the couch. I want to hold her, like we did the night she found out she was pregnant. I want to be her comfort, her safe place, and tell her how much I want to make this work.

However, minutes pass and Violet doesn't come out. I head back to the door, hand ready to knock when her panicked voice screams. "Everett!" I push the door open to find her sitting on the toilet, tears in her eyes. "I'm bleeding."

I'm pacing outside of the hospital room. The doctor is in there with Violet now, and I'm just trying to keep myself calm.

When we got here, they didn't seem all that concerned. I didn't comprehend the fact that they weren't immediately wheeling her back and doing something.

One would think that I would understand, more than most, that if she's miscarrying, there's nothing they can do to stop it. She's still early into her pregnancy, and this would just be a sad reality.

All that knowledge went right out the fucking door because it's Violet.

She was scared and I was fucking terrified. I've never felt more helpless than I did as I was driving her to the hospital.

The doctor exits and I come to a halt. "You can come in."

"Is she…"

"I can't disclose anything, but Violet is waiting for you."

Right, privacy laws and all that shit. Hopefully this will be the last time this is an issue when it comes to Violet.

I open the door, steeling myself. No matter what she tells me, I will be stoic and be there for her.

Violet turns her head when I walk in. I don't speak, and then she gives me a soft smile. "It's just some spotting."

Relief floods me and I move to her bed, taking her hands in mine. "And she's okay?" I ask the doctor. She must have followed right behind me. "She's pregnant? The baby is fine? Everything is all right?"

"She's doing well. This is very normal. The cramping and the spotting can happen, and it's nothing to worry about."

Nothing to worry about? I don't think I've ever told anyone that regarding blood, but she seems confident in her assessment.

"What do we have to watch for? Does she need to stay in bed?" I ask.

"Nope, none of that."

Violet squeezes my hands. "It's really okay. Dr. Cowles said everything looks fine, but just to be sure, she'd like to do an ultrasound, and we can also hear the heartbeat. Do you want to…be in here?"

I stare down at her, my own heart rate accelerating. "Are you sure?"

I don't know why I ask that since she called me in here, but I can't help but feel like this is a monumental moment for her, and to share it together must mean something.

"Everett," she says on a soft sigh. "Of course I'm sure."

"Then, yes, I would love nothing more."

Dr. Cowles smiles. "Okay, let's hear your baby's heartbeat."

She heads out of the room and wheels in the ultrasound machine. Once it's set up, she explains where exactly the wand is going, puts some lube on the end, and then we start to see the screen.

Neither of us move, and I hold Violet's hands as we wait. Dr. Cowles points to the smallest speck on the screen. "This is your baby, and that right there is the sac. Everything looks perfectly normal."

I stare at the monitor, completely transfixed, and then the room is filled with a whomping noise.

The heartbeat.

Whomp. Whomp. Whomp. Whomp. It beats over and over, and I swear my chest expands so large I can't breathe.

It's the most beautiful sound in the world.

Violet looks to me, tears in her eyes. "That's the baby?"

I nod. "That's the baby."

She turns to the doctor. "It's so fast."

"It is, but this is actually a good heart rate for a baby. Your pregnancy looks normal and healthy."

Violet looks to me, and I lean in to kiss her. There aren't words for this moment. Nothing I can say to explain the myriad of emotions that are moving through me. Love for the woman lying in the bed. Joy for the strong heartbeat that echoes in the room. Fear of losing her or the baby at some point. All of it swirls inside me, warring on which will win.

Ultimately, it's joy.

Right now, in this moment, I'm with the woman I've always loved, and I'm hearing her baby's heartbeat.

I know that our future is unsure, but I am not willing to let her go. If she has to go back to California, then I'll follow. Somehow. Some way, I'll find a way to be with her and the baby.

"I'll let you get dressed, and I'll see you in a week for your next appointment, okay?" Dr. Cowles says, and then the room is back to quiet.

"Thank you, Dr. Cowles," Violet says.

"Anytime."

She heads out of the room, and Violet and I stare at each other for a second before she starts to cry. "I have never felt like this. The whole time on the way here, I kept thinking…maybe this is good. Maybe I shouldn't have this baby because it's…his. Then I hated myself for thinking it, and I was so afraid I would lose him or her. I was so conflicted until I looked into your eyes."

I brush her tears away. "Mine?"

Violet sniffles. "You were so worried. I watched you drive like a maniac to get me here, telling me it would be okay. Just now, when you heard the heartbeat, you were mesmerized, and I knew that my heart and my head found its meeting point. I want you, Everett. Whatever we can have for as long as we can have it. No more pushing you away, I don't want to do it anymore."

I kiss her nose. "Good, because I was done letting you, and just know that I'll do everything to keep you safe."

No matter the cost.

CHAPTER 26
VIOLET

I wake up, feeling like I've been hit by a bus. Although I'm not really sure what that feels like, I imagine it's like this.

I'm tired, achy, and dazed.

I stretch and climb out of bed. We got back late last night, and Everett carried me up to my bed and tucked me in like I was a child.

He unfortunately had to go back to his house, check on his mom, and be up super early this morning.

Last night was the scariest one I've ever had. I was so worried when I saw blood, so afraid that while this pregnancy wasn't planned, I was going to lose my baby. Thankfully, that didn't happen, and, instead, Everett and I got to share a beautiful moment together.

We heard the baby's heartbeat.

I take a quick shower, get dressed, and then look at the clock. Oh my God, it's noon.

I can't remember the last time I slept this late.

My stomach rumbles, and while the idea of eating isn't all that appealing, I know I need something.

"Violet?" I hear Everett's voice and then a pounding on the door. Quickly I head down the stairs and pull the door open, revealing a very sexy Everett, who is holding a bouquet of roses, leaning against the door with a grin. "What? I don't get any *Everett, Everett, wherefore art thou, Everett?*"

I snort a laugh. "Oh, *now* you want to be compared to Romeo?"

"Juliet did die for him."

"She faked it and then his dumb ass stabbed himself."

"Because one day on this earth without her was too much. I know the feeling."

Yes, it was. It hurts and I've felt that in the last few weeks while being away from him.

I hold on to the side of the door and let out a long breath. "It is the most tragic love story."

Everett takes a moment, his dark-brown eyes taking me in. "These are for you."

I take the flowers and inhale deeply. "Thank you. They're beautiful. Do you want to come in?"

He nods and I push the door open, then walk into the kitchen to put the flowers in water. Everett comes behind me, placing his hands on my hips. I close my eyes for a heartbeat and let him cocoon me.

All the things we said to each other in the hospital come back. The fact that we both confessed our desires, that he wants the baby and me, that he wants whatever time we can have together.

It warms me.

He presses his lips to my temple. "How are you feeling?"

"Tired, but good."

"How tired?"

"Well, I woke up about thirty minutes ago." I lean against his chest, and he moves his arms around my middle.

"Any spotting?" The concern in Everett's voice is enough to make me cry. The damn hormones and his sweetness.

I shake my head. "No, it stopped."

"Good. I have a proposition for you."

Oh, this will be good. I turn my head up to look at him. "And what might that be?"

"Tonight, we're going on a date. A real one where I come pick you up, we go out, and then maybe you'll get lucky, if you play your cards right."

I snort a laugh, and he lets me turn completely to face him. "I think you're a sure thing."

"Probably, but I might play hard to get, you never know."

It's amazing to me that some woman didn't come in here and claim his heart. He's so damn perfect. However, I'm grateful no one did.

"Okay, so a date tonight?" I ask, leaning in closer.

"Yes. I'll pick you up at seven."

"And what are you thinking for this date? Just so I know how to dress."

"We'll start with dinner." He kisses me. "And then dessert." Another kiss. "And plan for a sleepover."

I loop my arms around his neck, pulling him in for a kiss. "I'm not a sleepover kind of girl."

"I think that's a lie, but humor me anyway. Give me a chance to show you that there's a lot more to me than just my hot body and amazing cock."

I giggle and rub my nose against his. "Oh boy, now I'm intrigued. I didn't know you were holding out on me."

Just then my phone rings, breaking the moment, and I sigh. "Ugh! I always have the worst timing. I need to get that. Ana calls me every day at noon. She was late, it seems."

She was probably doing God knows what with her husband.

He laughs and releases me. "Make sure you get it or she might fly back out here."

He's not wrong. I rush over to grab it but miss the call. However, I see that I have six missed calls. I quickly scroll and find that three are from Dylan, two are from my lawyer, and the last one is from Ana.

As I'm looking at the call log, Ana sends a text.

Ana: I called. Are you alive?

Me: Yes, I'm doing great. Everett is here, so let me call you once he's gone.

Ana: Ohhh be sure to take your time and remember pregnant people can have sex too.

I don't reply to that one, as my mind is on the fact that Dylan and my lawyer called. I'm assuming he's made a decision.

"What's wrong?" Everett asks as he walks toward me.

"Dylan called," I explain, not sure what exactly the status of our relationship is, but I know that I want to be honest with him always.

"Oh? Did he leave a message?"

"I don't know."

"Do you want to check? I'm fully aware that Dylan will be a part of our lives if we have a relationship. It's okay, Violet."

His voice is even and encouraging. It's always going to be like this if he wants to be around the baby. He's right that this will be part of our lives, and Everett is going into this with both eyes open.

I have two voicemails—one is my lawyer and the other is Dylan. I play my lawyer's first. "Hi, Violet, this is Gail from Riez, Mitchells, and Linde. I wanted to let you know we have officially pulled the paperwork. We can refile as soon as you let us know how you want us to proceed."

Everett leans against the back of the chair, just watching me, and I feel a sick sense of dread. I need to explain why we pulled the paperwork and my divorce is not already final. "Because of the baby, it will be easier to get child support if we don't have the divorce finalized. Even though our marriage is more than over."

"That makes sense."

I try to read his emotions, but he's very calm and collected. I'm not sure if that's a good thing or not. While he isn't indicating that he's upset by it, I can feel the tension in the room rise. I move to stand in front of him. "I'm divorced, Everett. In every sense of the word, we are. I don't want him. I want you."

He pulls me between his legs, his right hand holding my cheek and brushing the skin there. "I don't doubt that."

"As soon as I can, I promise, I'm pushing the divorce through."

"Again, baby, I didn't say anything. Listen to the other message if you want."

Right. The thing is, I don't want to hear it. I don't want to know if this thing that Everett and I are starting already has an end date. It's better sometimes, the not knowing, the bliss that comes from ignorance.

Unfortunately, there isn't any room for that now.

I press play and Dylan's voice echoes. "Violet, I've talked to my team, and we've decided that at this point in time, a baby would be the absolute worst news to drop. My lawyer will send you paperwork tomorrow with the details of a temporary agreement regarding a plan. As for me, personally, I don't see any way this works out well for either of us. If you'd like to have the baby, I understand, but I won't be involved."

I'm not surprised, but I am slightly heartbroken, which is stupid because this is exactly what I wanted.

For him to not be around. Then I can stay here. I can be a single mom and have my own life.

Yet, he doesn't want his baby, and that makes me sad.

I look up at Everett, who is watching me. "Are you okay?"

"Can I say I don't know? I mean, I'm glad I can be done with him. So fucking glad, but also so confused how someone could just let go of a baby."

He stands a little taller and rests his head on mine. I hate myself for saying that when Everett has made it clear that he wants this baby. He wants me and whatever comes with that. I never should've told him how I felt regarding Dylan.

I quickly move to make it right. "Everett, I didn't mean...I know that you're probably happy and I shouldn't be sad."

Everett lifts his head, his eyes finding mine. "Violet, stop. I already told you that I can't possibly understand how he let you go. But any man, no, fuck that, I am the luckiest man in the world because I get to be beside you. I get to love this baby and when the day comes that he wakes up and sees the mistakes he made, it'll be too late. He can't have you back. I will fight with everything I am to show you that I am the right man for you."

"I don't want him. Ever."

I know it's not exactly what he wants to hear right now, but I'm trying.

"Do you want me?"

"Yes," I say softly, tears filling my eyes.

Everett smiles. "Then go do whatever it is that girls do before a date with the man who plans to give them a night they won't forget."

"You still want to go on a date?" I ask hesitantly.

"Don't you?"

I want that more than anything. I lean my head on his shoulder. "With you? Always."

"Why is getting an outfit ready so difficult?" I ask as Hazel sits on my bed, eating the cookies I baked.

"I don't know, but if this teaching thing doesn't work, please open a bakery."

I laugh and then pull the dress down, smoothing out the bottom. "What about this?" I ask as I enter the bedroom.

She scrunches up her face and shakes her head. "I was really hoping for a Hollywood-type fashion show. Didn't your husband buy you all kinds of designer stuff?"

I roll my eyes. "I wasn't that type of wife. Dylan only outfitted his girlfriend, most likely."

"You've got to have something fit for a first date with your first love!" she says as she hops off the bed. "Seriously, I am always the date friend. Always the bridesmaid, never the bride."

"Do you want to be the bride?" I ask.

She shrugs. "Maybe someday, but I feel like I married the store when I opened it." Hazel grabs a shirt out of my closet and holds it up. "No, not that."

"I really don't have much. When I moved here, I left anything that was cute behind."

"Well, that was dumb."

I laugh once. "Maybe, but I had no intentions on ever needing a pants outfit with heels."

I packed the basics and gave a lot of things to Eleanor. She promised to box them in case I ever wanted them and put them in storage where Dylan couldn't get to them if he felt like being spiteful.

"You know, I don't know why you're fretting about this. You could wear a sack and Everett will still think you're beautiful," she says as she grabs a dress out of the back. "Oh, this is cute. Try it."

As I return to the bathroom to change, she reclaims her spot and moans as she bites into another cookie. "Which one is that?" I ask as I shimmy the silky material down.

"The double chocolate chunk. Seriously, this is so good."

"I'm glad you like it." I turn in the mirror side to side and watch as the dress catches the light. It's really pretty. The eggplant color doesn't wash me out and makes my eyes look brighter. "What do you think of this one?"

Hazel grins. "That's the one!"

She's right. It's the best I've got. "Why am I nervous? It's Everett and we've already..."

"Because you like him."

Yes, I really do. He sent me a bunch of text messages today that were so sweet. He was thinking of me, couldn't wait for our date, and the one he sent ten minutes ago was him reciting some of my favorite lines from different romance books.

I really thought I might cry as I read them.

The dress is back on the hanger, and I sit next to her, grabbing a cookie. "I wish I could explain it, though. He and I are different, have been through so much, and yet it's like time didn't pass. I trust him, but I worry that it's going so fast," I confess.

That's where my mind went all day today. Are we relying solely on old feelings? I don't think so, because even back then, I didn't feel this way. I was infatuated, yes, but it wasn't like this. The deep trust, the comfort, the honesty that we have.

Also, the sex was not that good before. The last time we were together, it was absolutely mind blowing.

"You guys always went full speed. I'll never forget the first time he introduced you to me. He was like fourteen or whatever, and he came to the house and was like, 'I'm going to marry her,'" Hazel says with a laugh as she tries to impersonate him. "I thought he was so stupid, but as the years went on, I saw that you guys had this really intense love. Everett loves with his whole heart. He's an amazing friend and son, so I can only imagine that transfers to how he cares for you."

He takes care of everyone he loves. "We're supposed to talk tonight."

Hazel rubs her forehead and then sighs. "I hate to ask this and it's really not my business, but are you still planning to leave Ember Falls?"

I shake my head. "No, I have no plans to leave here."

"This place is adorable," I tell Everett as we take our seats in the back area.

"It is *and* you'll recognize the owner."

I glance around, taking in the rustic cabin feel. Everything here reminds me of an old Italian restaurant we used to go to in LA. It had wood paneling and the lights on the table. I have no idea who could own this and why I would know her.

"Everett Finnegan, as I live and breathe!" an older woman with a full head of gray hair and glasses says as she approaches. Then she stops and looks at me, and I leap out of my seat. "Violet!"

"Marge!" I say her name and she wraps her arms around me. "Oh, Auntie Marge. He didn't tell me it was you."

She rocks me in her arms and then pulls back and takes my face in her hands. "My little Violet. Look at you, all grown up. You look beautiful. Doesn't she look beautiful, Everett?" she asks and ignores his answer. "He should tell you that every day."

I smile. "He has."

She eyes him suspiciously. "Hmm, that one was a lost cause. Almost as bad as Miles, but he at least found that lovely girl. Thank heavens, because I was worried about him, but I set him straight."

Everett rolls his eyes. "Yes, you're so good at that."

Marge points her finger at him. "You watch it. I'm serving your food."

"I apologize, Aunt Marge."

She takes my hands, leads me to the table, and pulls out the chair next to me. "Tell me everything. You're back? For how long? Are you happy? Did you let this idiot back in your life?" She jerks her thumb toward Everett. "If so, he's not that stupid. I just like to give the boys hell. They deserve it."

Everett clears his throat. "This *is* my date, you know?"

Marge ignores him. "I've missed you, love. Your grandma talked about you all the time. She was so proud of you."

Hearing that causes another pang to my chest. Each time someone talks about her, I feel so much guilt. I should've come back to visit. I knew how old she was and that she wouldn't be around forever, and I was just too afraid.

It's something I'll never forgive myself for.

"You have no idea how much I wish she were here."

"If she were, she'd remind you that Everett is a bit of a loose cannon."

I laugh. "He is, but I think he's a good one."

Her smile is warm. "If he's what keeps you here, then I would agree."

Everett sighs loudly. "Aunt Marge, if you don't mind, I'd really like to…you know…be on my date."

She grins and then turns to him. "You bring Violet Stewart in here after fifteen years and this is what you get. You should've brought her here sooner."

"Well, this was the first time I could get her to agree to a date," he defends.

"To be fair, he didn't ask me before today," I say with a mischievous smile.

"He didn't, huh? Not surprised. The brains in these boys are lacking, but they make up for it in their hearts. Now I'm going to go in the back and make you your favorite meal."

Oh, no. I have no idea what she thinks my favorite meal is. "Aunt Marge, you don't have to do that. I can order off the menu."

"Good luck with that. The menu is whatever she decides we should eat," Everett says with his arms crossed.

"If you were able to make good decisions, I wouldn't have to step in." Aunt Marge mirrors his posture and tilts her head. "I bet you don't even know what her favorite dish is, do you?"

"Anything with sugar."

I huff at that. "I like other things."

"You bake. A lot. You like sugar and sweet things, and for some reason you like me."

"Liked. Right now, it's past tense."

Everett tilts his head. "Doubtful."

"See, no brains," Marge cuts in. "I'll be back with some wine."

Before I can refute the alcohol, Everett cuts in. "No wine for us."

Marge looks affronted. "No wine? On a date? Look, I know you haven't had one in a long time, but…" She leans in, although she doesn't moderate her voice enough and I can hear it. "You have to wine her and dine her before you can…"

He coughs. "Please don't finish that. I might have to throw myself off a cliff. Neither of us are drinking, if you can bring us each some water to start."

She shrugs, muttering as she walks away. "You can lead the man to wine…"

Once she's out of earshot, Everett groans. "Miles warned me about coming here for our first date. I figured she wouldn't be bad, since she loves me."

"Marge loved Miles most, if I remember correctly."

"Seems she loved you most," he retorts.

Marge was my favorite friend that Granny had. She was funny, never hid her feelings around us, always thought that kids needed exposure to things so we were prepared. Analeigh reminds me so much of her. Devoid of a filter and utterly lovable.

"I'm sure she would've felt different if I lived here."

Before we can say anything else, Marge reappears with two waters and eyes Everett. "Are you *sure* you don't want wine?"

Poor Everett is going to get the heat for this, so I step in to save him from further ridicule from Marge. I reach out, resting my hand on her forearm. "I can't have wine or anything like that. I'm getting over an illness, and with the medication I took, it's for the best."

Her eyes widen. "Oh, my heavens. I didn't know you were sick." She turns to Everett. "Lead with that next time."

"I was trying to spare her the embarrassment," he says with a sheepish grin.

Then she yells back to the kitchen. "Ignore that order. Way too heavy for them. I'll come up with something else!"

"What were you making?" Everett asks. "We didn't even order."

"After the wine, I wasn't trusting you to decide what to eat."

He shakes his head. "I was warned and I didn't listen."

"Warned by who? Miles? I think that worked out rather well."

Marge turns to me. "He brought his sweet Penelope here on their first date. He needed a lot of guidance as well, but at least he listens. Anyway, I had a beautiful menu all set for him, but they had to leave early, something about her son."

"I'm sure whatever you make us will be fantastic."

She brings her hand to my cheek. "You haven't changed a bit. Still the sweetest girl with the biggest heart." Her eyes move to Everett. "You better hold on to this girl this time."

"I plan to," he replies without a pause.

My heart begins to race, and she laughs softly before walking away.

I want to say something, to start the conversation we need to have. Things with us were always full steam ahead, and we never talked. Then, if we did, I was never brave enough to say what I really wanted.

This time, I don't want the mistakes of the past to interfere with whatever future we might have.

"Everett…"

He leans forward. "I wanted tonight to be just a fun date, a chance to smile a little, but I can see you're not relaxed and you want to say something, and I do too."

I nod. "I just don't want to leave things unsaid."

"Do you want to go first?" he asks.

It's really the last thing I want, but if I'm going to step into this new world I'm creating, then I need to be brave enough to actually speak up.

"Yes."

"All right."

"I have so many worries about all of it. The fact that we'd be starting a relationship again, that there's a baby involved, that you'll feel trapped by it all. Everything is just so daunting. How do we navigate it?"

Everett leans forward, reaching for my hand. "Trapped? That's…

not even possible. I've been living in this version of purgatory since the day you left me. I've never moved on from you, Violet. Having you back in my life has made me feel free again. I waited for you, without even knowing I was doing it. As for the baby, I'm aware of what it all means. We're going to have hard times together. There will be good days and some bad ones, but sweetheart, I will take a million bad days if it means I'm by your side. There is nothing I fear about this relationship other than not being in it. So, let me shoulder the hard times and be by your side for the good. Let me have whatever days we can have together because I can't go back to a world where I don't have any."

Tears form, spilling down my cheeks and dropping. Each word he said puts a piece of me that was broken back in place. I'm not healed, not by any means, but I'm mending—because of Everett.

"I don't want to complicate your life," I say, my voice barely a whisper.

"Violet, you're the only complication I need." He releases my hand and comes around the table. Everett sits beside me and cradles my face. "I love you. I always have. I made you a million promises when we were young, but I never forgot the one where I said I would fight for you until my last breath."

The memory comes back when someone was being mean to me and Everett got in a fight because of it. I begged him to stop, not to fight for me because he would get in trouble. He wasn't hearing any of it, and he stood in front of me, breathing heavy, promising that he would never stop fighting for me.

"You don't have to fight alone, I'll fight for you. I don't ever want to lose you again," I say and then lean forward and kiss him. "Ever."

"Then let's stop making excuses and just be fucking happy together."

"I like that plan."

I like it a lot.

CHAPTER 27
EVERETT

OUR LIPS COME TOGETHER AND I FEEL IT EVERYWHERE.

After the most incredible date, she's here, in my home, and I'm going to take her to bed tonight with promises and every string I can possibly find.

To have had her, to have remembered, brought everything back with a vengeance. The long-ago heartache was new again. Violet was my other half, and even though we were kids, I knew it then and it's still true today.

The mess of her life is nothing compared to what it was like when she left me.

I groan and kiss down her neck, then up to her mouth.

Violet sucks in a deep breath, and I move my hands up her back, pulling her against me. I slow the kiss, taking my time and savoring every second of it.

She fits against me so perfectly, and everything feels like a damn dream.

Violet pulls back and our eyes lock, both of us questioning a million things, but not her.

I never question us.

I push my hand into her hair, gripping the silky brunette tresses. "Do you want me to stop?"

She shakes her head. "No, not ever." I pull her mouth back to mine, and she moans. I let her lead, giving her the control I know she's searching for. Everything in life has been happening to her—she needs to determine this.

To decide what she wants.

"Everett." Violet's voice drifts over my name.

I grip her hips, and her hands move to my chest. Her head drops back, giving me access to her neck. I kiss the skin there, then run my tongue down the smooth column of her neck.

"Anything you want, I'll give you," I promise.

"You, I want you. I have always wanted you."

I am hers, and I always have been.

I bring my mouth back to her ear. "Then come with me upstairs. Let me love you."

This pause is going to determine whether we do this or she pulls away again.

When her lashes fluttered and then closed, I tense, awaiting her rebuke, but then her hands slide down and she laces our fingers together.

She climbs the stairs, and I allow her to lead me to my room without a word. When we're inside, I quietly close the door.

Violet turns and walks to me. Her hand goes back to my chest. "This is going to change everything."

I want to tell her that happened a long time ago. "Why?"

Her amber eyes bore into mine. "Because I won't be able to lie to myself after this."

"I think we've been lying to ourselves from the first minute we saw each other in the coffee shop." I move my hand to her cheek. "I think we've been lying to ourselves for years that we didn't feel anything, that this was over, that we were happy. But I haven't been happy for a long time."

Tears well in those beautiful eyes and then slide down her cheeks. "I've tried to forget you."

"So have I."

"When I close my eyes, it's you I see."

Her confession breaks me, so I give her one of my own.

"I've tried to forget you, to erase you from my mind so I could love another, but no one has ever come close to you, Violet. You stole my goddamn heart when I was fourteen."

She tightens her fingers into my shirt. "Now what? How do we do this?"

That's the easiest question she's ever asked. "We stop fighting."

Her eyes find mine, and we move toward each other slowly, my hand cupping her face, guiding her back to me.

When our lips meet this time, it's soft, gentle, and unhurried. It builds like a song, the tempo moving to the chorus, and then the bridge hits. I kiss her deeper, my hands moving down her body, and grip the edge of her dress.

She steps back, giving me the space to remove it, and her hands rest on my shoulders as she steps out of it.

Violet is the most stunning woman in the world. As she stands in my bedroom in just her bra and underwear, it almost breaks me. It doesn't matter that we've made love dozens of times—and even just a few weeks ago—because, right now, it's almost like the first time all over again.

I push her hair behind her ear. "Are you afraid?" I ask.

She shakes her head with her lower lip between her teeth. "Never with you."

"Good, baby. I would cut my arm off before I ever hurt you." Her hands move to my shirt, pulling it off, and then she undoes my jeans, letting them fall. I kick them off and turn her to face the window. My fingers unhook her bra, and I slowly slide it down her arms, my mouth moving to the curve of her neck. "I know you're scared," I say against her skin. "I know you worry about what might come, but know this, Violet, I want all of you. Every part of you."

Her breath hitches. "Every part?"

I move my hands down her sides, then around to rest on her

stomach, acknowledging the child that grows there. She's been hurt, lied to, and betrayed by so many people. I understand her need for reassurance, and I'll say it until she believes it. "Every part of you. I have lived years without you. I've felt that hole in my heart, and I'm going to cherish every minute we have together."

She turns back to me, her beautiful eyes shimmering from the light of the lamp. "I don't want to go back to what life is like without you."

My chest grows tight just thinking about what that would be like. The daily pain of going through life without her. The way my heart didn't feel like it was even there. No, I'm not going there right now, because she's right here with me.

Practically naked.

Time to rectify that.

"There is only now, and right now I want you naked, baby." I squat down and run my thumb up her calf until I reach the band of her underwear. I don't take my eyes from her as I pull them down, leaving her bare to me. "I have thought of you in my bed for months," I confess. "I've imagined you here, waiting for me, wanting me."

"I do want you."

"Good. Climb up on the bed," I command. Violet obeys and moves to the center. I slide my boxers off and crawl to her. "I want you to watch me take you with my mouth. Sit up higher."

Her chest rises and falls, but she does it. I grin as I push her knees apart.

"Everett."

"Eyes on me, Violet. Don't look away while I get exactly what I've been starved for."

I kiss her ankle, then the inside of her calf, and then her inner thigh. I wait, listening to the labored sound of her breathing before I lift my eyes to hers. She is staring down at me, and I move incredibly slowly, wanting to draw this out for as long as I can.

She's panting, and I kiss above where she wants me most.

"Please," she croaks.

"Since you asked so nicely." I lick slowly, flicking her clit with the very tip of my tongue. Her hands move to the sides of her legs, clenching the bedding. I keep doing that, tasting her, loving her, listening to her noises.

Each one drives me wild.

She moans my name, sliding her fingers in my hair. When I increase the pressure against her clit, her legs clench around my head, and I don't relent.

I lick, suck, and vary the pressure over and over. I lift my eyes back to hers and see she's still watching. That's my good *girl*.

For that, I slide my finger into her cunt, then another, loving the way she clenches around me.

I can't wait for it to be my cock.

I move my tongue side to side, licking and sucking, circling her clit until she starts to shake slightly.

That's it.

Come for me.

"I can't stop it," she says, her breath ragged. "I can't. I can't."

"Let go. I'll be here to hold you together," I mutter against her pussy.

"Everett, oh God!" she yells, and then I feel her come apart. I keep sucking and fingering her, wanting to draw every ounce of pleasure out.

When her spasms stop, I lift my head, and the sight of her in my bed, sated, is nothing I ever imagined. "You are so beautiful when you come."

"I'll have to take your word for it," she says with a laugh.

"Trust me, baby, I wouldn't lie to you."

That is the one promise I will always keep.

Her fingers move to my hair, sliding her nails through. "Make love to me, Everett. Please."

"With all that I am."

I reach over into the bedside table and grab a condom, but she stops my arm. "We don't have to…if you…I mean, you can if you don't want to…"

My God, the idea of taking her bare is almost enough to make me lose it right there.

"You're sure?"

She nods. "I'm sure. I got tested after I found out he cheated."

"I got tested about a year ago, but I haven't been with anyone since," I tell her.

"Please, I need you," she says.

This time feels different. There's something a lot more than sex transpiring between us. I adjust myself and slide in with one deep thrust.

We both gasp and I am fully seated, unable to move or breathe or fucking do anything. I just stare down at Violet, and she rubs her thumb against my lips.

I rest my forehead on hers, feeling way too many emotions, and right now I can't sort them out. "Violet." I say her name like a prayer, a promise, a hope for what can be. "This feels like I'm…"

"Whole."

Instead of responding, I take her mouth in a searing kiss. I kiss her for the past, the present, and the future. It's a promise and a vow that I will do this for as long as I can. I'll protect her, the baby, the life we can have.

I'll do whatever I have to.

"Please," she pants. "Please, I need you to move."

Slowly I slide back and forth. Together we rock, and her hands rake down my back as she arches her body.

"You're close again, aren't you, baby? I can feel your tight, hot pussy clenching around my cock. Do you want to come again, Vi?"

"Yes," she moans loudly.

I edge myself to the side a little and move my hand between us. I rub her clit and she pants.

"Everett!"

"That's it, Violet," I say, holding back my own orgasm.

I want her to come again.

"It's too much," she says, her head thrashing side to side.

"No, you can do it. Feel how much I want you. Feel me deep inside of you, wanting you, giving you all of me. Fuck, Violet, it's so good. You are perfect."

That does her in. She screams as her orgasm rocks through her. I pump my hips harder as tension goes from my neck through my spine, and then I follow her over the edge.

I move her hair to the side and kiss her nose when we both come down from our high. "Are you okay?"

She looks up at me. "More than okay."

Good, because I plan to wake up like this every day.

CHAPTER 28
VIOLET

THE NEXT FEW WEEKS PASS IN A BLUR.

We went to my doctor's appointment, where they once again confirmed that I am indeed pregnant and three weeks into my second trimester.

Now I'm just waiting for this morning sickness to freaking end. They said for most people, it stops by the second trimester. I'm looking at my calendar and would like to inform the child that we're way past it and they can stop making me sick.

The gremlin doesn't seem to care about my wishes, because once again, I'm in the faculty room, trying to keep my breakfast down.

"Violet, hey," Miles says as he enters the room.

"Hi there."

"How are you feeling?" he asks, probably noticing the green tinge to my skin. "Still hurling every day and pretending it's a stomach bug?"

I'm surprised it's taken him this long to comment. Two weeks ago he was starting to eye me suspiciously.

"For a few more weeks," I say, confirming his suspicions. "Then maybe I'll tell the truth."

He grins. "I see. And how is Everett regarding your…bug?"

"He's happy," I say.

"Then we are all sure to be happy when you're ready to explain the vomiting that lasts for months. Does anyone else know or suspect?"

We haven't told anyone. After we had that scare, I was hesitant to say anything, only to then have to explain if we did lose the baby. Besides, the fewer people who know, the better. I don't want or need anyone digging around and putting two and two together about how far along I actually am.

Right now I'm not showing, and it'll be easy to just say I popped early, but as we get further along, those milestones will start not adding up.

"I don't think so."

"Then let me be the first to congratulate you." Miles opens his arms, and I stand to give him a hug. "I'm happy for you, Vi. Everett will be a great dad."

He already has stepped in and keeps talking about all the things he wants to do. I'm not sure what I did in this world to deserve him.

"I know, I'm very lucky."

He pulls back. "I think you're both lucky to have each other. I've known you both a long time, and I'm really happy you guys are back together."

I am too. It's been a rough road, with a lot of surprises, but I'm genuinely at ease now. He makes me smile, he takes care of me, and he never makes me question his feelings. The two of us fit so well together—it's more than I could have ever imagined.

"Thank you, Miles. I actually wanted to talk to you about next year."

He extends his hand, indicating for me to sit. "Are you still thinking about leaving?"

Now that Dylan doesn't want the baby, I don't have to leave. There are a million reasons to stay and the biggest one is the man I love.

"No, and I love my job here. If you're open to it, and there's still a spot left, I'd really like to stay."

Miles grins. "Violet, you can stay here for as long as you want. The idea of having to interview again is terrifying. If you want a job, you have it."

And one more piece of my life clicks together perfectly.

"Of course he gave you the job," Everett says as he's messing with the fire that's going out. "He knows I'd kill him if he didn't, and he still owes me for hiring you."

I roll my eyes as I put my book down. "Or, you know, it could be because I'm an amazing teacher."

"That is absolutely the reason, babe. I'm just saying I'm an extra incentive."

Yes, I'm sure that's what he was saying. "Sure that's what you meant. I'm getting tired. Are we staying at your house or mine?" I yawn as an added mark to the question.

He ended up staying later at the clinic today, which normally wouldn't faze me in the least, but I cooked—and baked—so he came over to grab a plate, which led to him eating it, which then had us curled up on the couch together.

"Do you mind coming to my house?" he asks after finishing whatever he was doing with the fire. "Mom wants us to come for breakfast."

I smile. "I'd love that."

A few times a week we go to his mom's for either breakfast or dinner. She came here yesterday, and Everett was planning to tell her about the baby, but we both decided to wait, as she had a few really bad days over the last week.

Everett shifts so we are both sitting. "Might as well go now before you pass out on the couch and I have to carry you over there."

The sad part is that is definitely a possibility. I swear, I can fall asleep anywhere.

"Oh, I almost forgot," I say, as we both stand and I stretch. "I was sick again in the teachers' lounge, and Miles guessed I was pregnant."

"Did you tell him that it's...?"

That it's Dylan's baby. I hear him finish the thought. I walk to him, resting my hands over his solid chest. "No. Dylan doesn't want anything to do with him or her. His lawyer sent over paperwork asking to agree to dissolve his paternal rights, which means I'll proceed with the divorce. All of this will be over soon. We're still trying to figure all this out, and I don't know what we tell people."

He wraps his hand around mine. "What do you want to tell people?"

"I don't know what to say. I don't want to lie to our friends and family. I'm pretty sure everyone will assume the baby is yours. Everyone knows we're together, and if you're by my side, that makes it appear that way."

"Other than the feeling of lying, is there something else that holds you back from telling people?" Everett asks, his eyes not moving from mine.

Sometimes it's as though he can see right through to my soul. That he knows all my fears and insecurities, and it's his job to ferret them out so he can fix them.

I have a lot of other things that hold me back in small ways. While I know that Everett is absolutely nothing like my ex, the fear of him finding me lacking is still there. It's a lifetime of never feeling like anyone's first choice.

It's being made to be small, to fit in the box that others wanted me in.

But being scared and feeling it, working through it, is what's going to make this work.

And, God, I want it to.

"I'm afraid that one day you're going to leave. It's not your problem, it's mine, and I worry that this fear is always going to live inside of me. I hate that this is a part of me, and I promise I'm working on it. So to answer your question, I think I'm scared to tell everyone and then we don't work out and…then what? Do you tell everyone that the baby was never yours? Do I have any choice but to leave Ember Falls? This is your home. It's your family and friends and…"

He squeezes my hand, and I take two deep breaths before looking up at him. "There is no world where we just break up. I know what commitment looks like and it doesn't scare me. You are the woman I've loved for the better part of my life, and if for some reason we choose to end our relationship, this baby will forever be mine."

No one has intentions of their relationship ending.

I sure as hell didn't enter my marriage thinking I'd get a few years out of it and we'd walk away. I watched a man go from being this sweet, loving, and attentive guy to the most egotistical asshole you can imagine.

People change, but I can't hold the sins of someone else against Everett.

It's not his fault, and he's done absolutely nothing to warrant my mistrust.

"I know."

Everett gives me a sweet kiss. "Time will prove that I'm not going anywhere. So, for now, we don't say anything about who the baby's biological father is. We can let people guess or make their own assumptions."

He needs to know how I feel about him. That even with my fear, in my heart, I know who he is to me and this child.

I reach my hand up and brush his hair back. "From the day I found out I was pregnant, you've been the father in every way that matters. You've been the man I've needed, and I love you, Everett. I love you."

He smiles, and the joy in his eyes sends a wash of warmth through me. His voice is thick as he speaks. "I love you so much I worry you'll drown in it."

"I don't think love drowns, I think it makes you fly because right now I'm not weighed down. I feel like I can breathe."

CHAPTER 29
EVERETT

"Good morning, beautiful," I say as I enter my mother's house with Violet.

Her smile widens. "Everett, hi, sweetheart. You brought someone."

"I did. I brought Violet. She wanted to see you again."

Mom reaches her hands out to Vi, and she takes them, pulling her to the chair beside her. "Oh, Violet, hello. I…know…we saw each other. I just, you looked different."

Violet smiles widely. "I changed my hair," she tries to explain.

God, I love this woman. She always makes my mother feel comfortable. If she says something or doesn't remember, Violet never puts her down. She just gives an excuse.

"You are positively glowing, darling."

"Thank you," Violet says.

I'd like to think I had a part in that. I did give her two orgasms this morning. Sure, it could be the pregnancy, but I'm going to take the credit where I can.

I sit beside Violet, taking her hand in mine. Mom has had two good days in a row, and so far it looks as though we might be going for a three-peat. Last night Violet and I agreed if she looked good today, we'd tell her about the baby.

Violet is starting to show. Her stomach has the most beautiful bump, and we'll find out the sex of the baby soon, so we thought it was time.

"Mom, Violet and I wanted to tell you something, and we'll come all the time and tell you again, so if you forget, it's okay," I say carefully. She tends to get pissed off when she can't recall things, but my hope is that if we tell her enough, and she continues to see Violet, it will become part of her memories.

"Are you okay? Is everything okay?" She starts to panic, and before I can react, Violet moves to her, taking her hands.

"Everything is fine. This is good news," Violet says quickly.

"Oh, okay," Mom breathes. "What is it?"

In the millions of ways I dreamed of telling my mother big news, I didn't picture it this way, where I don't know if she'll remember any of it tomorrow. If she'll ever really know Violet or the baby when she sees them.

I don't even know if, at my wedding, she'll have a clue who half the people are.

It really fucking sucks, and this will be a big test for her.

Violet squeezes my hand. Right, I need to tell her. "Violet and I are together again, and we're going to have a baby."

Mom looks to Violet and then me. "A baby?"

"Yes, Violet is pregnant."

Her eyes mist over, and she gets out of her seat. "You're going to have a baby together?" she asks again.

Violet and I both rise. "Yes, are you happy?"

She rushes toward us, wrapping her arms around both of our necks. "I'm going to be a nana." Mom steps back, tears now coming down. "Oh, I'm so happy. So happy for you both. I just wish...oh, I wish your father was here, Everett. He would be so proud. He would be such a good poppy."

My throat grows tight. I've been trying so hard not to think about him and the fact that he will never meet our child and that they won't know the man he was.

So many things we'll miss out on.

"He would've," I agree, choking on the words.

Violet rubs my back, and my mother clasps her hands together. "Oh, no tears today. This is happy news." Then she glances down at my hand. "Everett, are you married yet?"

I didn't think about that one. "No, Mom."

Her big blue eyes widen. "You're not? Are you sure?"

"I'm pretty sure I would know that," I say with a laugh. "We're not married—yet."

Then her gaze goes to Violet's hand. "Where is her ring?"

I'm just stepping in holes everywhere I go. "I didn't…we…didn't…you know."

Mom huffs and shakes her head. "Do you love her?"

"Of course I do."

"Then why aren't you married or engaged?"

My parents were really old-fashioned. To them there's a clear order on how this would go, and I'm in violation of that precedence.

I'm pretty sure Violet's parents are going to be just as bad with it.

The only saving grace I have is that my mother will probably forget about all of this by the end of the day.

The bad part about that is I'm going to have to tell her again and again.

Fuck my life.

"We're taking things slow. There's no rush to get married."

Also, Violet is still technically married to Dylan…so, there's that.

"I'm not sure how you getting her pregnant is slow, Everett Michael Finnegan." She turns to Violet. "I'm very sorry, honey. He knows better."

Violet fights back a smile and then nods, pulling her lips between her teeth. Once she has it together, she takes her hands. "He is doing everything right, Mrs. Finnegan. I promise this is what we both want. I don't need to be married to Everett to know he will be by my side."

Her words cut me to the core. It's been hard for her to trust me, I get it. She's been fucked over by her dickface of a husband. He left her for another woman and then left her again when he found out she was pregnant—well, in a way. All that she's seen is abandonment.

Not to mention her parents basically have done it to her since she was born.

They'd take her on those damn expeditions, leave her to pretty much raise herself, then drop her off at her grandma's house for the summers.

Mom doesn't say anything. She just gets up and heads back to her room. Violet looks to me. "Is she upset?"

I sigh. "I have no idea. I'm assuming this is hard for her. There are a lot of questions that she probably can't answer." I get to my feet. "I'll be right back."

There is nothing I hate more in this world than the women I love being hurt or upset. My mother has been through enough hell in her life, and I don't want to cause her more. As I'm getting ready to head there, she comes barreling out.

"Now, I know that I have memory issues and that sometimes, my brain doesn't work right, but I know this." The tone in her voice sets me back to when I was six and was about to get punished. "I know love. I have lived it, breathed it, mourned it, and I see it when I look at you." She takes my hand, flips it over, and places something in my palm. "Don't waste it."

When I look down, there is my mother's engagement ring. The one she hasn't worn since my father died, because it was too hard.

"Mom..."

"For when you're ready, which I hope is soon, because like I said before, Everett, you can't ever get back time, no matter how hard you try. Now I need to lie down." She looks to Violet and smiles. "If I forget, please remind me, because I would like to feel this happiness again."

Violet nods. "I'll remind you every day."

Mom taps my cheek. "Marry her before she gets away again."

"Are you going to propose then?" Killian asks as we're making our way back to check on his horse. It's been a few weeks, and while I was pretty clear that the horse needed rest, his trainer is a fucking prick and ran him out, which caused further injury—like I said it would.

When we got here, Killian asked how I was, and I told him everything. Like an idiot, I just blurted it all out.

"I don't think she's ready for that."

"Did you talk about it after?"

I run my fingers through my hair and shake my head. "No, we sort of pretended that entire part of the conversation didn't happen."

What the hell was I going to say? Do you want to get married while you're still married? How about engaged? You can wear my mother's engagement ring to the divorce hearing. Sound good?

No, none of that sounded good, and I don't know that she would say yes. As much as I want forever with her, I want to do it right and on our terms.

"All right, I can't help you there, but you know, marriage is just a piece of paper. I know your mom has her feelings, and I get it. We all know marriages end, so a ring and a license doesn't secure your relationship any more than it is."

"Wise words, old man," I joke, but he's right.

He snorts. "I'm just telling you how I see it."

"No, I know that. I appreciate your honesty."

Killian is quiet for a few minutes and then clears his throat. "I think being a good dad has nothing to do with a ring on her finger. It's more about showing up, which is where I've failed my daughter, but I'm trying to make amends."

He never talks much about his personal life. Killian has always been more private, and he doesn't live in Ember Falls full-time, so it's hard to know him well, but he's a great guy. He is always there for us, and he walked away from a professional football career to try to form a relationship with his daughter.

"I just want to do right by them both. I want to be a good dad but also a good man. Violet needs someone to show up for her, no matter what."

He clasps my shoulder. "Then she's lucky she found you to show her how it should be."

CHAPTER 30
VIOLET

"Have a good night, Ms. Stewart," my last student out the door says.

"You too."

It was a long day, but thankfully I felt great, as though maybe this pregnancy isn't trying to kill me.

So there's a plus.

I grab my bag, ready to get the hell out of here, and head home.

My life has finally fallen into a pretty amazing cadence. I usually wake up with Everett, we have breakfast with his mom before both of us go to work, then we come home, eat together, and most nights we end up naked.

He brought over his Doppler last night, and we sat, listening to the baby's heartbeat for an hour. It was…magical.

We've started trying to guess the sex of the baby too. I'm pretty sure it's a boy. I don't know why, but it just feels—male.

Everett warned me that if he is a boy, baseball will absolutely be introduced.

Great.

I'm smiling, thinking about a little boy throwing catch with his superstar athlete father when I pull down my driveway and my entire body freezes.

There are cars and people everywhere.

Immediately I see cameras, and they're running toward me, taking photos.

No. I left all of this behind.

Why the hell are the paparazzi here, and how the hell did they get my address?

I quickly get out of my car and push forward, knowing I need to get in the house and out of view. I get to my front door, hearing the familiar clicks over and over and them yelling at me. "Violet, how do you feel? Violet! Over here. Violet, are you taking him back? What about the baby?"

My heart sinks at that last one, and I rush inside, closing the door and panting with my back to it.

They're knocking on the windows, surely taking pictures of the inside of my sanctuary.

Fuck this. I've been done with Dylan, why are they here?

I move through the house, closing curtains and pulling down the shades where I can.

The kitchen windows don't have anything, so I grab a box, covering as best as I can. Once I'm done barricading my home, the tears I fought back are streaming down my face.

They know about the baby.

How? How can they? How is this happening?

I hear my phone ring and I grab it from my purse. It's Ana.

"Ana, what the fuck? How do they know?" I ask quickly.

"Your fucking husband is a piece of shit."

"I know this, but…oh, God, he told them?" I slide down to the floor, out of view of any window. "Why would he do that?"

Dylan was sent the paternity-resolution papers this week, and he was supposed to sign them.

None of this makes sense.

"About fifteen minutes ago, news of their split came. Whitney went on television stating that it was over, and she wanted time to handle this separation. Dylan isn't the man she thought he was, and it's best for her to step away while they work on themselves. She said he's selfish and his ego couldn't handle her success since he lost another role." Ana huffs a laugh. "Yes, poor mistress, upset because he's a dickhead."

"Analeigh, please," I say, my stomach churning as I wait for the rest.

She sighs. "I guess Dylan's team was prepared and…"

"He leaked it?" The silence is the answer. "He fucking leaked that I was pregnant? Why? What could he possibly have to gain? I wasn't asking for anything! I just wanted him to be done like he said he was!" My voice goes higher as my devastation grows.

"He released a statement that he and Whitney ended their relationship due to the fact that she wasn't supportive and wanted him to abandon the child he's expecting with his estranged wife."

I laugh once, but it's more of a sob. "He did it for PR. He ruined my life, my child's life, my fucking home, and the goddamn safety I had here, for himself!"

My hands are shaking, and the rage that fills me is unlike anything I've ever felt before. He's so selfish. So fucking horrible.

"I'll kill him or have him killed, don't worry," Ana says matter-of-factly.

I love my friend, but she would never make it in prison.

"Ana, they don't let you get your nails done in jail. I just…" I sniff. "I can't believe this. He had a chance to do the right thing. To sign away his rights, to walk away without anyone knowing, and he used this baby to further his agenda."

Analeigh makes a noise that tells me she's crying. "I'm so sorry, Vi. I sent a message to Catherine Cole. I know you think she was wrong for how she treated you while working with Dylan, but she's really, really good at her job. She's been my dad's crisis manager for a long time. Since she no longer works with Dylan, she would like to speak to you, if you're open to it. I know you hate PR, but you need to protect yourself, okay?"

"I can't think about this. I can't even think at all. What do I do about Everett? We've never told anyone that it isn't his." Two weeks ago we started telling people. Hazel was overjoyed, and Penny already knew thanks to Miles. It was all coming together perfectly.

"I don't know, which is why I think you need to talk to Cat. Let her make the decisions on how to handle this."

There's a loud banging on the back door.

God, now they're trying to come in other ways.

"Violet! Open the door!" It's Everett.

"I have to go," I say to Ana. "Text me her number."

"I love you," Ana says back.

"Love you too."

I rush to the back door and pull it open, and immediately he engulfs me in his arms. I grip the sides of his jacket, burying my head in his chest.

Safe.

I'm safe.

Everett won't let anyone hurt me.

I look up, tears streaming down my face, and he's shaking. "Hazel called me. I...came right away. Are you okay? Are you hurt?"

"Not physically."

"What the fuck is going on? He put out a statement about his unborn child?"

I nod. "I guess so. I just heard about it. I pulled up and there were a dozen photographers outside the house."

"I saw. That's why I came around the back. I walked through the field so no one saw. How did they find you?"

"I have one guess," I say, knowing he's the only asshole who would gain from this.

Everett rubs my back. "I'll kill him."

"You'll have to get in line behind me and Analeigh."

"I don't want you here. Not with these fucking people camped outside your house. Let's pack a bag, and you'll stay with me."

I know he's worried, but I don't want to leave my home. "Everett…"

He stares down at me. "Please don't fight me on this, Vi. I need to do what I promised you, and that's to protect you. I don't want you here, where they could hurt you. I don't want you here, where I can't be sure you're safe and the baby is okay. I sure as hell can't go back to my house, knowing that you're alone, maybe crying, maybe plotting homicide, and I can't be there for you."

I close my eyes and lean into him. "All right."

His body relaxes, and he kisses the top of my head. "Thank you."

I turn my gaze to his, and I can see the distress there. "I love you."

"I love you."

My phone rings nonstop—my parents, my friends, Dylan, my lawyer, everyone who knows me leaving messages asking what's going on, what baby, why I lied. It's continuous.

Dylan did not leave a message, and I had to pretty much restrain Everett to keep him from answering. The only call I answered was Ana, who once again reminded me that I needed to call Catherine, and after a small argument with Everett—he was on Analeigh's side—I finally caved.

Catherine answers on the second ring, and I put the phone on speaker. "Violet, I'm so sorry."

I wish I could believe her, but for years she would urge me to do things I didn't want to do, in service to Dylan. I would ask her for another way, and while I could see she was uncomfortable, she was doing her job.

My nerves are frayed, and I honestly don't have the patience to weigh my words. "I want to be honest, Cat. I really struggled to call you."

"I understand that. I'd like to say that I no longer represent your ex-husband, and while he will undoubtedly state that he let me go, I want to be clear that isn't the case. Once I heard the news of what he'd done, I released him from my client list. I was unwilling to do what he was asking and felt it was in my company's best interest to part ways. While I can't take you on as a client, I *can*, as a friend, hopefully, offer guidance and suggestions."

Everett looks to me and nods, but I have one major worry. "I can't afford—"

"Violet, friends don't charge friends," Catherine says quickly. "Hypothetically, if you asked me what I would do, I could…offer some advice."

The feelings I had about Catherine start to dim. "You're sure?"

She's quiet for a heartbeat. "I know that I wasn't your favorite person. I could see how hard the adjustment to Hollywood was, and I hated that. You were thrown to the wolves, and I was part of the pack. My job was to help him always, and I knew that would sometimes make you uncomfortable, which was not my favorite thing. I'd always thought that maybe, after a while, you'd find your footing. Please know there are some parts of my job that I hate, and this is one. Ana can tell you, I will do anything to help my clients and their families, and in this case, I'd like to help you."

The sincerity in her voice is what causes me to cave. I don't know what to do. Everything feels like the wrong step. My lawyer has been on the phone with Dylan's, demanding answers on how we went from one extreme to another. It seems his lawyer is also trying to get those same questions answered.

Right now, all I can do is stay hunkered in the safe harbor that Everett offers.

"Thank you for that. It never felt like you enjoyed asking me to push outside my comfort zone. This, though, it's not even in the same orbit as what I wanted or thought. I honestly don't know what to do."

"Let's start from the top," Cat says softly.

I go through it all, from when I left California, to coming here. I go through all the ways I found out about each new layer of hurt Dylan inflicted. She has me give dates, times, tiny details that I can remember about what was said and when paperwork was exchanged. After I'm done with the story, I'm surprised I can even talk. It feels as though I've been through a war, and I'm so battered that it's a miracle I'm here to tell it.

Catherine sighs heavily. "I hate that you've been through all of that and that you're pregnant, which I remember all too well how freaking emotional that makes you. Okay, well, the good thing is that I can help."

"You can?" I ask.

"Yes, but I'm afraid you're not going to love the options."

I laugh once. "I'm pretty used to that."

"You're going to have to come back to California, without your boyfriend."

I look at Everett, seeing the pain in his eyes, and now I really know what heartbreak truly feels like.

CHAPTER 31
VIOLET

I'M STANDING AT A PRIVATE AIRPORT AS ANALEIGH'S PLANE IS being readied to take me back to hell.

"You'll be back in my arms in a week or two," Everett says, and I'm not sure whether he's trying to tell me or himself.

The reality is, we don't know that.

We have absolutely no fucking idea what Dylan's intentions with all of this are. Catherine and my lawyer agreed I needed to say nothing and return to California to handle this. With him across the country, I'm being painted as the villain who is trying to keep his child from him.

Never mind that he cheated, got engaged, and drew up dissolution of paternal rights paperwork. Of course no one looked into any of that.

"I'll be back as soon as I can," I promise. I fix the collar on his shirt and leave my hands there, trying to keep my voice steady and fighting tears. "We meet with the lawyers in a few days. After that, I'll know more."

This is everything I worried about. That if Dylan wanted the baby, I'd have to be semi-close to him so he can have a place in the baby's life. When he walked away, it was easy for me to let my heart release what it was holding back, to let myself love Everett. That against all odds, we could be together again.

Seems I was counting my chickens before they hatched.

I should've waited until I had the paperwork signed.

"Don't look like that," he says with a stern tone. "Don't look like you're giving up on us."

"I'm not."

"You are. You're going to be there, alone, and able to convince yourself that all hope is lost, but I won't give up on us, Violet. Things may look dark and as though there's no chance of this working, but those are lies. We didn't go through fifteen years apart to find each other and then end up alone again."

He reaches into his pocket and takes my hand. I look down as he places a ring in my palm. My chest grows so tight I can't breathe. Tears prick my eyelids, and I try to fight them back. "Please don't..."

I can't handle a proposal. I would want to say yes even if it seems too fast, and I can't do that until this part of my life is resolved.

I won't be able to handle it.

"I'm not asking you to marry me. I'm asking you to take this, hold it, know that it has every part of me with you. My father gave his heart to my mother, and I'm giving mine to you. This is a symbol of it. It's one of the most valuable items in my possession, and I'm asking you to bring it back to me. Bring *you* back to me." He cups my face and brings his lips to mine. "Come back to me, Violet."

Our foreheads touch as the tears I'd been holding on to stream freely down my face, and I close my hand around the ring.

I love him so much.

I don't want to leave.

However, it's my time to do what I have to for the people I love. For my child. I know I'm strong enough, and I have the people in my corner now who give me the power to do what I must.

I kiss him softly before looking deep into his eyes, using all my strength. "You are my home," I say through the thickness in my throat. "You are where I want to be. I love you with everything that I am." I lift my head, staring into his beautiful eyes that are glossy with unshed tears. "You promised to fight for me. Now I need to fight for myself, the baby, and you. For our family we were building. I'll bring this back to you the moment I can."

Someone clears their throat. "Excuse me, Miss Leone? We're ready and need you to board now," the pilot says.

I nod. "Thank you. I'll be right there." When I look back at Everett, there's so much pain and worry in his eyes. I reach my hand to his cheek. "I'll be okay."

His jaw clenches, and I feel the turmoil coming off him in waves. "I should be there with you. I should be on that plane."

"No, your mother needs you here, and we agreed that photos of you and me in the press would only hurt my case."

Even if Catherine hadn't suggested that I keep Everett here, I wouldn't have asked it of him. He needs to be in Ember Falls, and I need to go handle my life.

"Call me, okay?"

I nod. "I will."

"I love you, Violet." He moves his hand to my belly. "I love him or her too."

In two weeks we have an appointment scheduled where we will have another ultrasound and get to see the sex of the baby. We've been looking forward to it, and now I might be stuck across the country.

No, I can't think like that. Even if things with Dylan aren't figured out, I'm coming back for that. I want to share that moment with Everett. He's the only one I want to share every moment with.

"We love you and I'll be back for my appointment." I lift up on my toes, kiss him softly, and turn to grab my bag, leaving Everett again and my heart in Ember Falls.

"Violet!" Ana yells as she rushes toward me the moment I'm off the plane. "I've missed you."

I force a smile, feeling so fucking heartsick. "I've missed you too."

Her face falls, and she pulls me into her arms. "Don't worry, babe. We're going to fix this and get you back to your man."

I laugh once. "I just can't believe this is my life. That now I have to come out here because he couldn't do what's right. He needed to, what? Save himself again and at my expense. I just…I can't fucking believe this."

"I really can't, either, but alas, it's what it is, and I have people ready to do whatever we need to."

Whatever that means. "I'm pretty sure I don't want to know."

"You don't." She loops her arm in mine. "Come on, let's get to my house and put the plan in motion."

Ana does most of the talking, filling me in on whatever gossip has been going on in her inner circle. She has always confused me regarding the people she spends time with. I'm not sure she even likes any of them, but I sit there, letting her fill the silence as I look at the busy streets and palm trees, wishing they were evergreens.

My phone buzzes and it's a text from Everett.

Everett: I miss you.
Me: I miss you more.
Everett: Kick ass, my love.

I grin.

Me: I plan to.

Ana clears her throat. "Everett?"

"Yeah, he misses me."

She pouts. "Aww, that's so cute. I know how you're missing him, too, but just remember that the sooner you handle this, the sooner you can get back to Lumber Falls."

I laugh. "I swear you're just doing it to be stupid now."

"Maybe, but it made you smile."

It did. "Thanks, Ana. For letting me stay with you and the help with Catherine."

Ana takes my hand. "That's what family is for."

"I'm glad you're on my side."

"You should be. I'll fuck someone up if they come after the people I love. If it weren't for Cat, I probably would've done something to Dylan, but she reminded me that this is a game and I have to play the right move. So I'll behave—for now."

There are so few people in my life that I can truly count on, and if I have to be back in this den of vipers, at least I have the most vicious snake on my side. "I'm guessing you guys came up with some ideas?"

"Yes, she'll be at my house, and we'll go over the possibilities." She squeezes. "Don't worry, I'm not going to let him screw things up for you."

I really hope not.

We pull up to the gate that opens when she scans the card, and we go down the windy drive. I know it hasn't been all that long, but I genuinely forgot what it's like to pull up to her home.

The house is absolutely massive. It has eight bedrooms, ten bathrooms, three living rooms—it's stunning, but you honestly can get lost in it. The double doors open, and her assistant is there and…Eleanor.

I jump out of the car, and we both practically run to each other. She gives me a huge hug, and I rock back and forth with her. She cut her hair into an adorable bob, and the outfit she's wearing is unlike anything I've seen her in. I step back, looking at her again. "You look amazing," I tell her.

"You do too! You are adorable!" She grins as her gaze moves to my stomach, where you can see the bump.

"Thank you. I didn't know you were going to be here."

Ana chuckles as she comes up behind me. "You needed your army, girl. It's all-hands-on-deck."

As alone as I felt out here, I did have good people around me. Eleanor and Ana always had my back. I guess I forgot that in a way.

The two of them flank me, and we enter the house. Catherine rises from her chair. Her dark-brown hair falls in soft waves down her back, and she's wearing a navy-blue pantsuit with heels. She's formidable, but she smiles warmly at me.

"Hi, Violet."

"Catherine, thank you for being here," I say, trying to hide my nerves.

She steps forward. "You're very welcome. Are you ready to fight fire with fire and change the narrative?"

I've never been more ready for anything in my life. "Yes, let's do it."

My hands are shaking, and I feel that familiar nausea like I had during the first trimester. I'm sitting in the conference room with my lawyer as we wait for Dylan and his team to arrive. I wore a green dress with a blazer to try to hide some of my pregnancy. Obviously, he knows, but I don't want to draw any attention to it so we can discuss the issue at hand.

"Let me do most of the talking," Gail says as she fills my water. "If you want a break, just clear your throat and ask to use the restroom."

"What would I need a break for?" I ask.

"Trust me, divorce and family law are not for the weak. His team is going to try to paint you as the bad guy, even though it's the furthest thing from the truth. Just stay calm, smile when you can, and let him make an ass of himself."

That shouldn't be too hard, since he's become a master at it.

Ten minutes later, they are escorted in and Dylan takes the seat across from me. He looks tired. That's the first thing I can think of.

His hair is longer than it normally is, there are dark circles under his eyes, and although he always had swagger, it's not there anymore. I'm not sure if he was told to look this way or not, but I know he's not that good of an actor and it'll slip after long enough.

He lifts his blue eyes to meet mine, and he quirks his lips into a half smile, not villainous, more of a gesture of hello.

I look away. Fuck him.

His lawyer speaks first. "We're here because—"

Gail cuts in. "We're all aware of why we're here. Your client went public with a pregnancy that he decided he didn't want to be part of. He was signing his rights away until it no longer served him due to his own actions."

Get him, Gail!

"A father has every right to be involved in his child's life. Mr. Leone was made aware of the child and was forced to make a decision immediately."

My eyes widen, but my lawyer slides the water toward me, an indication I need to stay quiet and calm.

Right.

I take a sip and drop my hands to my lap. I wanted a piece of Everett with me. A sort of talisman to hold on to him and his strength. So I wore his mother's ring on my right hand, diamond down so it looks like a gold band to anyone else.

I spin the ring slowly, trying to feel his presence. Just the thought of Everett calms me, and I return to my stoic demeanor.

"There was absolutely no pressure from my client. In fact, you sent the dissolution paperwork to us. So where exactly do you claim to be getting such...urgency from?"

Dylan shifts and I stay statue still. "I didn't have a choice." He looks to me. "I want this baby. It's my child. You know I've always wanted children."

It takes every ounce of strength I have not to scream at him. He did want kids, when we were first starting off. He wanted to get a job at an accounting firm, work his way up, start a family while I was teaching. That was the plan.

Until he decided otherwise.

Once he started acting, there was never talk of kids or any of the life he'd promised.

It was what was best for him. His acting. His fandom. The roles he could get and the money he could make. Him, him, him.

Which still seems to be the case.

I turn my head to Gail, who nods once. "We never disputed his rights as a father, but it was made abundantly clear he was uninterested in any parenting."

"He is now."

Of course he is. "As you know, my client no longer resides in California. Upon the birth of the child and confirmation from a DNA test that it is, in fact, Mr. Leone's child, we can discuss options for co-parenting."

His lawyer speaks immediately. "Unfortunately, Mrs. Leone would be considered a flight risk in our assessment. She disappeared after their separation and has abandoned the marriage. It's clear she has the means to do so with the child. We're going to request that she remain in California, and we'll be requesting fifty-fifty custody where they can split time each week."

My eyes instantly fill with tears. They can't do this. I can't stay here. This is absolutely unfair. I fight back the tears, the pain that fills my heart at the idea of having to stay here.

"Absolutely not. She's not a flight risk," Gail says. "If anything, we can show that Mr. Leone has wavered this entire time. He hasn't even seen his wife once since they separated or shown any interest in his child."

"She cut me off!" Dylan says. "She left and then just filed for divorce."

I know I'm supposed to stay quiet, but I can't hold back anymore. The fact that he is asking me to leave Ember Falls is too much. I can't spend the next five months here while Everett is in Virginia. Not when I can be with him. Not when I know he can't be here.

"You cheated on me! It was literally all over the television. I didn't leave. You pushed me out."

"And now you're punishing *me*," he growls. "I'm being dragged through the mud and called all kinds of names."

Here's the opening that Catherine talked about. My chance to show him the way out, which I hoped would show itself.

Image and his work are his sole focus. It's not the baby or me—it's what will serve him.

Whereas my goals are what's best for my child, which isn't Dylan, and it isn't me being stuck here because of co-parenting demands.

"Can you give us a minute alone to talk?" I ask the room.

Gail shakes her head. "I would strongly advise against it."

I ignore her and look at Dylan. "We used to be able to talk. I'd like to think we loved each other once. Surely we can discuss things."

Dylan looks to his lawyer. "Leave."

"Mr. Leone."

Dylan's arrogance is above his sense. "Give us ten minutes."

Gail's pleading eyes tell me how much of a bad idea she thinks this is. I nod once. "Please."

She leans in, whispering in my ear. "You have the upper hand in this. Don't give that up and agree to anything you don't want."

"Thank you."

Gail hesitantly rises, extending her hand toward the door to show his legal team out, and she follows, closing the door behind her with a click.

The two of us sit here, and Dylan's mask drops, revealing the man I knew a long time ago.

Please let him be the man I once knew, if even for just ten minutes.

"Dylan," I say softly. "Why are you doing this?"

He looks over at the wall, shaking his head slightly. "You're with him?"

"Who?"

His gaze moves back to mine. "Him. Everett. The guy that you loved before me."

I blink, confused and a little unsure why the hell that is the first thing he's talking about. "What does that matter? You cheated on me," I say slowly, keeping my voice even and without censure. I need him to be relaxed through this. "You were happy without me. I don't understand why you would do this."

"Do you know why she left me?" Dylan asks with a huff.

"Well, I know what the press and your statements have said, which is what has me back here now."

Dylan shifts in his seat and turns to me. "She said I wasn't over you. That I clearly still loved you, which is why we went on that trip together, why she had to force my hand for me to make a decision. She leaked those photos of me and her so that you'd leave, which you did. So I officially got with her, and for a while it was great. It was everything that we didn't have. Whitney loves the spotlight, she thrives in it, where you wanted no part of it. When she sees the cameras, she turns to get a better angle, kisses me so that they'll capture it, where you hid behind me or refused to even be seen with me. I wanted to be in the light, Violet. You didn't."

As I listen to him, I don't feel sadness for myself, considering he's talking about all the things wrong with me. I just don't…care.

"No, I didn't."

"And I resented you."

"Yes, you did," I agree.

"So, after the paperwork was drawn up, I…couldn't stop talking about it. That we were going to have a baby, that I wasn't going to be around, that I wondered if you were okay, and I guess I did it all the time."

"And she left you," I finish.

He huffs. "Then she painted me as the villain."

I sigh heavily. "So you used the baby? Don't you see how...unfair that is? If you really cared about me, if you...were so worried if I was okay, then how could you do that to me—to us?" My hand moves to my belly.

He doesn't miss the movement, and his eyes go to where it would be. "I think that being a father...it will fix things."

"Fix what?" I ask.

"Whatever I need it to fix. I lost roles, Violet. They're talking about killing my character off on the last movie so I can't be in the sequel. Do you know what all this is going to do to my career?"

I truly loathe him. The fact that his entire concern is around himself is the entire reason we're here. He doesn't care about me or the baby. He cares about his job.

"And what about the child you so want? What about their life?"

Dylan rubs his forehead. "I'll share custody with you, and we'll figure it out."

"Okay, let's talk it through." Now is when I'm using the things Catherine suggested. To point out all the ways it won't work and where it'll be inconvenient to him. "You want shared custody?"

"Yes, I want the baby with me during the week. We can split time," he demands.

"All right, then you can have them Thursday through Sunday? Or even Wednesday, if that works better?"

Immediately I'm hitting him with the fact that he will have the child on the weekends.

"I can't do that. I have to work."

"I see, well, if I have to be back here, then I'll have to work as well. I think it's only fair we split up the weekdays, and since you make more, you can afford to pay more in childcare, don't you agree?"

"You can keep the baby during the weekends, and I'll do...the childcare part. I'll hire a nanny."

Another opening. "I don't want a nanny raising our child. You'll need to spend the weekends with him or her without someone else taking them."

"I have to film sometimes."

"You'll have to figure that out. Now, what about during the summer? I'll have off from school, and since your schedule is flexible, I think maybe we should do like every other week. So you can get ample time, and I can have a chance to travel."

His eyes widen. "This summer I'm filming in France. I can't come back and forth every week."

"Dylan, this is your child. The one you said you wanted."

I can see the frustration mounting. "Yes, but I thought that you'd be more helpful."

"I am going to help when it's my time with them."

"I meant that you can keep the baby when I have to film or travel for premieres," he says with exasperation. "I'll pay you so you don't have to work."

My voice returns to its original softness. "I can't rely on that. I'll need the income on my own, plus benefits. So back to my original point: You'll have to keep the baby every other week during the summer and then half of the week during school."

"I can't."

I know he can't. Well, more like he won't.

I stare at him, my face as docile as I can make it. "Do you really want the baby, or do you just need a way to help get back the roles you've lost?"

"I want my life back. I don't have…time…I can't give up my life for a kid. I'm sorry, Vi. I just can't."

It's what I thought. He really doesn't want the child. He just wants the good PR that would come with it.

I have never hated him as much as I do right now.

His blue eyes find mine, and I continue to do what I have to in order to protect my child. If Dylan doesn't walk away, signing his rights away, he will be a deadbeat father. He'll abandon the baby anytime it suits him, and it'll break their heart each time he doesn't show up.

He should know better than most.

I lean forward, resting my palm on the cool table. "Please don't do what your father did. Don't come around, asking for things, and not wanting a relationship. I'm asking you, for once in this entire situation, to put me or even the baby first. To think about what you're asking and willing to do. This baby will need a father. One who will do anything for them. One who will love them, give them attention, and whatever they need. If you can't be that father, then please, don't do this."

"Violet, I can't…fuck, I can't walk this back."

"We can."

Hope flares in his gaze. "What?"

"You can put out a statement. You can do what you wanted from the beginning, but do it so it's what's best for the baby."

CHAPTER 32
EVERETT

I'M SITTING IN THE COFFEE SHOP, WATCHING THE PHONE, WILLING for it to ring.

This has been the most agonizing two hours of my life.

Violet has a plan, but it hangs on her ex being a decent human being or being selfish enough to take the offer to better himself.

Either way, it's out of all of our control.

I look up, watching the people pass by, talking, laughing, earbuds in as they listen to music, all while I stare at the building.

The door opens, and I see Dylan first. He puts his glasses on and is ushered into a black SUV. Then I see Violet.

Her beautiful brown hair is pin straight. She's wearing a light-green dress and a blazer over it.

She looks radiant.

I get up, walking out the door, ready to cross the street when my phone rings and her name appears.

"Hi, how did it go?" I ask, standing fifty feet from her.

Fifty feet too many.

"Good, he…agreed. He signed the paperwork, and the divorce papers are being refiled now. It's over. He…" I see her shoulders slump from relief. "God, he agreed."

"Oh, baby, I'm so happy. Are you happy?"

I can hear her choking back the tears, and I cross the street this time, needing to pull her into my arms, to hold her so she doesn't fall apart.

"I'm more than that. I'm coming home. I'm coming back to you, and we can put this all behind us."

Fifteen feet.

She looks up at the sky, wiping at her cheek.

"I can't wait to hold you."

Ten feet.

Five feet.

"I wish you were here now," Violet says, sniffling a little. "God, I would do anything to have you here with me."

I can't wait to have her in my arms.

"Anything?" I ask, as I come to a stop.

"Anything."

I smile. "Then turn around."

She does and her jaw drops. "Everett!"

I open my arms and she doesn't hesitate. Violet closes the remaining distance between us and practically launches herself against me.

"Hi, baby," I say against her ear as I hold her tight.

"You're here?"

"I am."

"How?"

I chuckle. "I took a plane."

Violet shakes her head, pulling back a little. "I know that, but how are you here? When did you get here? Who is with your mom?"

I love that her initial response is worry for everyone else but her. "My mother is fine. She's spending a few days with Hazel, Donna, and Marge. I got here very late last night and Ana found me a hotel room, since I wanted to surprise you."

She touches my cheeks. "You're here."

"You needed me."

"I did, but…I told you not to come."

"I will always come for you if you need me. I will always show up," I vow.

Violet has learned to live with disappointment and people not being there, but that ended the day she walked into that coffee shop. She will never have to walk alone. I'll always be beside her.

Someone clears their throat, and I turn to see Ana. "As much as this has truly been the most romantic and touching thing I've seen, we should get off the street."

Violet laughs and then pulls out of my embrace. "She's right. Dylan is going to release a statement, and it's better if we don't have any photos prior."

"Okay."

"Come on, in the car," Ana says and ushers us toward a large SUV with tinted windows.

We get in, and as soon as she's next to me, I take her face in my hands and kiss her. She does the same. It's been six days, but it's felt like six years.

I missed her so much, worried nonstop, and when my mother asked why Violet was gone and I explained, I knew I had to be here. So I asked for help for the first time in my life. Violet was worth risking my fears for.

The kiss gentles and Violet leans back, looking at me again as though she can't believe it.

Something scrapes my cheek and I pull her hand down, and that's when I see it. She's wearing the ring.

Her breath catches as I stare at it. "I needed you with me."

I meet her amber gaze. "Did it help?"

She nods. "I swear, I could feel you near me. I could sense you and…well, you're here."

I spin the ring so it sits with the diamond up. "I can't wait until this ring sits on the right hand and it's after I've proposed to you."

"Six days was too long to not be able to see your face."

Violet pulls back, giving me a good look. "Let's not do it again, then."

I grin. "Let's go home."

CHAPTER 33
VIOLET

We're on the plane back to Ember Falls. I couldn't get out of California quickly enough. I definitely didn't want to be around when Dylan's statement dropped. I'd like to be safely ensconced in my little town with the man I love.

"You know, flying like this is really spoiling me," Everett says as he comes out of the bathroom. "Do we have to give this back to Ana and Nick?"

I laugh and sigh. "I don't think either of us can afford this plane's maintenance and staff."

"That's true." He chuckles and lies beside me on the queen bed.

Yes, the entire back end of the plane is a bedroom.

The sky is an inky black with a splattering of light from the stars, and we informed the flight attendant that we would be sleeping and we'd call if we needed something.

The two of us are exhausted and desperate for rest.

However, seeing him beside me, the last thing I'm thinking about is sleep.

It's been days since I've felt his touch, and I want it so much right now.

I roll over, straddling him, and his eyes widen. "I thought you were tired."

"Call it a second wind."

His hand moves up my thigh and to my back, pulling my T-shirt up, leaving me bare. "And what do you want to do with this extra energy?"

"I want to make love to you."

"Good answer."

My mouth moves to his, and his kiss infuses me with life. Our tongues tangle in the most passionate kiss we've ever shared. It's raw and intense, the weight of our worries drained once and for all, and we can just have each other.

"You came for me," I say as I move my mouth to his neck. "Now I want you to come for me."

He groans and his fingers dig into my ass. "With you, that's not even a question. I could come just thinking about you. Imagining you in front of me is enough to make me hard."

I drop my hips, rubbing against his hard cock. "I can feel that you're ready for me now."

He chuckles low in my ear. "Always ready for you, baby."

Well, I wouldn't want to keep him waiting then.

I kiss down his neck, pushing his shirt up so I can slide my hands down his chest, over his stomach, and to where his shorts are tented. I scoot back and pull his shorts and boxers off. Once he's bare for me, I wrap my hand around his cock and pump.

Then I drop my head down, taking him in my mouth.

"Violet," he moans, his hand moving to the back of my head. I run my tongue along him as I hollow out my cheeks and start to bob my head.

Everett makes incoherent noises, and each one sends a jolt to my core. I'm so turned on by making him feel good.

"That's it, sweetheart. Take me deeper."

I do. I take his cock back as far as I can, and he groans even louder. I lift my head to see the pleasure on his features, the way his face scrunches when he's trying to keep himself in check. His fingers tense in my hair, and then he looks down at me.

I take that as my cue to go even deeper. "Fuck, Violet. God, I'm going to make you come so hard," he promises. "I can't wait until I can taste you, love you, have you ride my cock until you fall apart. Do you want that, baby?"

I moan, knowing the vibrations will give him more pleasure.

Everett drops his head, and I keep going, pumping my hand along with my mouth, wanting him to lose it while he's at my mercy. "No. Shit. Violet. Please…" Each word comes out in a gasp.

I pull back, running my tongue along the head of his dick, giving him my best innocent look. "Do you like that?"

"Yes," he says with his jaw tensed.

"Do you want me to do it again?"

"Don't make me come yet. I want to do it inside of you," he practically begs.

I want the same thing. I'm aching for him. "So you don't want me to do this?" I lick around the head again.

He makes an incoherent noise.

"What about when I do this?" I lick the underside of his cock and then his balls.

"That's it." He moves so fast, grabbing my arms, moving me so that I'm on my back and he's on top.

He struggles for breath and then crushes his lips to mine. At first the kiss is powerful and out of control, but he slows it as he regains his senses. Our lips break apart, and I'm ready for him. I need him inside me.

"Please," I pant.

He looks down at me. "What do you want, Vi?"

"I need you. Please, take me."

"Oh, I'm going to take you," Everett promises. "I'm going to take you, keep you, love you, and I'm going to make you mine in every way." My eyes flutter as he nips at the sensitive spot on my neck. "But first I'm going to make you ready."

My pulse is racing as he moves his hands from the backs of my thighs to my pussy, only he doesn't touch me. He just feathers his touch, keeping it so light it's barely there.

"I promise, I'm ready. Touch me and you'll see."

"I am touching you." I hear the smile in his voice. "Don't you feel it? Don't you feel my fingers?"

Each breath is labored, my heart pounding as my desire pulses through me. "More," I beg.

"More what?"

"You."

He rolls us again so I'm on top, and I'm going to take advantage of this.

As I go to move myself to where I can rub myself on his cock, he grips my hips, holding me still. "Not yet."

Can someone die from desire? If so, I'm nearing that tipping point. "Everett," I moan, and he chuckles.

Then he pushes me so I'm even farther from him. Right when my lips part so I can complain, he moves his one hand to my clit, rubbing circles, sending fire through my veins.

God, I'm so ready.

He has to feel how ready I am.

"So wet," he praises. "Now, we aren't alone on this plane. So you're going to need to be very quiet. Can you do that for me?"

Right now I'd do anything he asked.

I nod. "Yes, I can be quiet."

Everett's grin is full of mischief. "Hands on the wall." I sit up, placing them there, and he slides down the bed. Oh God. "Keep them there."

"Everett," I pant.

He rips my underwear in one sharp tug, exposing me to him. Then he slips a finger inside me and I moan, my head falling back. But he doesn't stay inside long. Instead he removes it and I look down, desperate to see why he stopped when suddenly he grabs my hips.

"Sit on my face and let me taste you."

Yup. I'm dead.

Everett positions me exactly where he wants. When his tongue flicks my clit, I almost lose it. I bite down on my lip, trying to hold in the moans as he does it over and over again. My hips begin to move as I'm desperate for my release.

It's building higher and higher, and my heart is pounding, my palm sliding down the wall, my muscles trembling.

"I can't hold on," I say, and Everett redoubles his effort.

He pushes a finger in, fucking me with his mouth and hand. Then his other hand slides up my round stomach, and he rolls my nipple. My muscles tighten before I shatter to pieces.

I'm able to keep from screaming, but I'm definitely not quiet.

At some point Everett put me on my back, and he's leaning back on his heels, and I turn my head to the side to gather myself.

"Look at me," he commands. The deep timbre of his voice causes me to obey. "I love you. I want your eyes, baby. I want you to watch me as I make love to you."

His palm cups my cheek, and I hold the back of his neck. He kisses my eyes, my cheeks, my nose, my forehead, and then my lips.

"Make love to me, Everett. I need you," I say when he pulls back from the gentle kiss he pressed to my lips.

I feel him push inside me, inch by inch while we stare deep into each other's eyes. "You're the most beautiful woman in the world. My heart. My soul. The breath in my lungs. Everything I am is for you."

I gasp as he thrusts deeper. "I love you. God, I love you so much it hurts."

"No, baby, it never hurts. Feel how good this is?" He rocks his hips again. "We fit together because you were made for me."

"Yes," I moan, arching my back to meet him. "For you. I need you."

"I'm yours."

We make love like this. Slowly, sensually, as though we are the only people in the world, and right now, it feels like we are.

Tens of thousands of feet in the air, in the sky—alone.

Every part of me is now his. Not that I wasn't before, but this is so different, so intense.

It's more than the incredible pleasure—it's two souls connecting. All the fears, questions, and pain I've endured are being erased by his touch.

"I'm close," Everett warns. "It feels too good to hold back."

I run my fingers through his thick, dark hair. "Don't hold back. Please, just love me."

"Always," he says as he falls apart in my arms. He moans against my neck, jerking his hips.

Somehow he manages to hold himself up to keep from crushing me, and he moves to the side, pulling me with him. The two of us work to even our breaths out. After a few minutes, Everett kisses my temple. "Stay here."

I don't move and he returns with a wet rag. We clean up and climb back into bed, my arm draped across his middle. Everett makes patterns against my spine, and neither of us speak—honestly, we don't need to.

We've said everything we could ever need to with our bodies and our hearts.

As my eyelids start to grow heavy, he huffs a laugh and I lift my head to look at him. "Why are you laughing?"

"Three things, really."

"Oh?"

He lets out a yawn and then taps my nose. "One, we are now a part of the mile-high club."

I snort a laugh. "Let me guess, you're proud."

"Fuck yeah I am. None of my other friends can ever say this."

"You're such a man," I joke.

"Good observation."

Ignoring that, knowing where this will end, I forge ahead. "And what are the other things?"

He grins and rolls to his side to face me. "Second is that you were not quiet, my love."

Ugh. I know I wasn't. "Maybe they didn't hear."

"Violet, it's a nice-size jet, but I'm going to bet they heard."

The heat from my cheeks is hot enough to burn. "I can't think about that."

"Just think, when we get off in Ember Falls, they'll know why there's a little more color in your face."

I slap his chest. "Everett! Stop, I'm going to die of embarrassment."

He chuckles and then pulls me tight to his chest. "Don't worry, babe, I'll hide you so you don't have to see them."

Like that's any better.

Still, right now, in the aftermath of the bliss we shared, the fact that we don't have my divorce, the custody battle, or the uncertainty of where I'm going to live hanging over me, I just don't care about anyone else outside of this room.

"And what's the last thing?"

Everett kisses the top of my head. "I love you and we're going home."

CHAPTER 34
EVERETT

"It's a girl," the doctor says as she moves the ultrasound wand.

"A girl?" Violet asks, her voice full of love and excitement. "We're having a girl?"

Dr. Cowles nods. "You are."

A girl. A little girl with potentially Violet's amber eyes and dark-brown hair. One that I'm going to have to chase boys away from because she'll be so beautiful, so smart, and so much freaking trouble.

Violet looks to me, and I lean down to kiss her.

"God, I love you so much," I say, my voice thick with emotion.

The last week has been pretty fucking perfect, and this is the cherry on top. We were told yesterday that the judge signed the paperwork for Dylan's paternal rights, Violet agreed to move in with me instead of us going back and forth each morning, and now this.

"I love you too." Her hand rests on my cheek before she returns her attention to the doctor. "The baby is healthy, right? You said everything looks okay?"

Dr. Cowles smiles. "Yes, the heart looks good, as does everything else we can see. You're progressing along really well, and I don't see anything out of the ordinary."

Violet lets out a long sigh. "Okay. Thank you. I'm just so relieved."

I am too. Violet has been under a ridiculous amount of stress, and hopefully this will ease her mind and allow her to relax. Things in our lives are settling, and I honestly didn't think she could endure another setback.

The doctor wipes her stomach and moves the blanket back to cover her. "You're welcome. I'll see you in a few weeks, okay?"

Violet nods, and once the doctor leaves the room, she takes my face in her hands. "We're having a little girl."

"Yes, I'm in a world of trouble, aren't I?"

She laughs and nods. "I think you are."

"There will be boys."

"Oh yeah?"

I sigh. "There are always boys, and they want the girls."

Violet snorts a laugh. "I seem to remember you being one of those boys."

"Exactly."

Yeah, I'm so screwed. If they're anything like me, I'm going to have to invest in some kind of repellant, or maybe I'll just follow her around. I can retire and make sure no one approaches her. That sounds reasonable.

"I think I did okay with the boy I found," Violet says, bringing her lips to mine. "You turned into an amazing man."

"After a lot of stupid," I say before kissing her again. "It's the stupid I worry about."

Violet shakes her head. "We have a few years before we have to worry about any of that."

"If she looks anything like you, I'm going to be swatting them away like flies."

I remember back when she was young, I wasn't the only boy who liked her. Miles had a crush on her too. I could see it in his eyes. Then there was that other kid who ended up moving here when we were sixteen. He wanted her too.

Violet laughs and gets off the table. "You're ridiculous."

"I'm not wrong, though."

She gets dressed and we head out. On the ride back to Ember Falls, she calls her mother, which goes exactly as I thought it would—very…odd. Instead of overwhelming joy about having a granddaughter, she only said she was happy and then proceeded to talk about the new find they had yesterday with so much enthusiasm.

It made me sad for Violet.

"I promise, my mother will be over the moon," I say once they hang up, taking her hand to comfort her.

"I know she will."

My mother may not remember everything, but she sees Violet every morning when we go over there, and if she's working late or can't make it there at night, Mom always asks where she is. She doesn't always recall that there's a baby, but I do my best to talk about it each time I see her.

"How about we stop and get some coffee?" I suggest with an ulterior motive, but hoping she won't catch on.

"You know, you really need some help with this addiction," Violet says with a laugh.

"And you need help with your baking, but I don't complain."

"No, because you reap the rewards."

She's not wrong. When we got back from California, she baked a lot. It soothes her, and both my staff in the office and the teachers at school beam with joy when they see a wrapped basket in either of our hands.

"That I do, love, that I do."

Violet laughs. "All right, let's get some coffee. Besides, I want to see Hazel and tell her it's a girl."

That is the plan.

Plus a surprise.

We get to Prose & Perk after driving way slower than I ever have, to which I explained that I didn't want to chance anything since the temperature has dropped into freezing levels, which means ice.

Even though the roads are fine.

I help Violet out of the car, and she clutches my arm with a huge smile. I love this woman so much. Seeing her happy fills me in a way I never thought possible.

She's sunshine and stars and comets and heaven. All the brightness that illuminates the dark that used to surround me is inside her, and I'm blessed to bask in it.

When we get inside, Violet stops short as she sees the assembly of people who yell, "Surprise!"

Her eyes come to me and I grin. "They wanted to celebrate your official address change."

"And baby shower!" Ainsley yells.

"And joining the Ultimate Frisbee Significant Other Club!" Penny adds.

"You guys! This is too much." Violet slaps my chest. "And you knew?"

"Of course I knew. Now, where's my coffee?" I ask, looking at my best friend, who rolls her eyes but brings a cup to me.

"You're such a pain in the ass," Hazel complains.

"Yes, but you love me anyway."

She snorts. "Only because I get to have Violet back do you get to stay in my good graces."

I laugh. She's so full of shit.

Violet pulls Hazel in for a hug. "Thank you for this. I seriously can't believe you're all here for me."

When I was in California, I got to witness firsthand all the people who love her. They were there, like an army behind her, ready for battle. Ana she never questioned, knowing there is nothing Ana wouldn't do for her. But Eleanor was paid to be with her all the time, and while I believe their friendship was real, it was also transactional.

Here, there's none of that.

We don't care about what you have, just what we can give.

Violet walks through the crowd, hugging Miles, Lachlan, and

Killian, then all the girls. I walk over to the guys, giving them a handshake and a pat on the back. "Thanks for being here, guys."

"We wouldn't miss it for the world," Lachlan says with a smile.

"For all the shit we give you, you know that we'd do anything for you."

I do know that. Miles has been my friend since I can remember, and Killian and Lachlan are there for me anytime I need them.

"I'm glad everything worked out this way," Killian says.

I watch as Violet is swarmed by the girls, all of them laughing and smiling as they talk. My chest aches at the sight. She's happy, and I'd like to think I have something to do with it.

"I am too."

Lachlan claps me on the back. "So do we have to wait to find out what the sex is?"

I chuckle. "Yup, you sure do."

"Such a prick."

Killian laughs. "You know, I thought we might be celebrating another thing."

"Did you?"

"I did."

I've thought about it every day since we left. When we got back, she handed me the ring and asked me to hold on to it and allow us to settle in a little more. She explained that until all her problems are settled—meaning Dylan—she wants to wait.

Me being impatient, I wanted to argue, but that's unfair to her and also acting like her dickbag ex.

So I'll wait. Being with her is all I've ever wanted. I don't need a ring or a piece of paper to tell me that she's mine. And that I'll always be hers.

"Not yet, Violet and I are in no rush. Well, Violet isn't. I'd marry her tomorrow."

Miles laughs. "Been there."

"How did you handle it?" I ask.

"If you ask Penny, she'd say like a petulant child, but I think it was more of a manly stance."

Lachlan snorts. "Yeah, you were so manly as you pouted."

He shrugs. "Just give her time, Ev. She's been through hell."

"Did her piece-of-shit ex release his statement yet?" Killian asks.

"No, we keep waiting."

Lachlan shakes his head. He dealt with this with his ex as well. She wasn't as vile or public about it, but he worried for a while that she was going to want custody back of his daughter. She decided she didn't in the end, but I remember how stressed he was, thinking he could lose Rose. "I hope he does right by Violet."

"Me too. Speaking of Violet, I'm going to see when she wants to announce our big news."

I head over and wrap my arm around her. "Hi, baby."

"Hello, love. Are you having fun?"

"That's what I was going to ask you."

She looks around at all our friends. "The best time ever."

"The guys want to know."

Violet laughs through her nose. "The girls too."

Just then Hazel comes over. "We have some food in the back and a cake. I'd like to decorate it with the right color…"

"Nice try," I say.

Hazel lets out a very long sigh. "You're annoying, that's what you are."

I shrug. "What can I say? I am who I am."

Violet grins. "I happen to love who you are."

Hazel makes a gagging noise. "Ugh, I forgot how much I hate being around you two when you're all googly-eyed."

"After the last few weeks we've had, I think we should get a pass."

"Fine, but you get two days. After that, no more of it," Hazel jokes. "We wouldn't want to let you get a big head. Besides, I think you owe me."

I owe her for so much. She's been there for me through it all, but most recently, it was Hazel who came to my rescue when Violet was in California. I was a fucking mess. All I did was worry about her, and when I came to Hazel, told her that I needed to go, she didn't hesitate. She packed a bag and came to stay at my house.

I clear my throat. "I wanted to thank you again for staying with Mom."

Hazel snorts. "Everett, shut up. Of course I was going to stay with her. She's like my second mother, but more than that, Violet needed you. I would do anything for you guys."

Violet steps forward. "We know, and you're an amazing friend."

"I would agree with that," Hazel tries to joke.

She hates compliments. She almost runs solely off sarcasm and the need to cause me stress. I just won't stop telling her how much I appreciate her.

"And you truly are. I wouldn't be here without you," I say in all honesty.

Hazel blinks and then practically chokes on a laugh. "Everett Finnegan, who are you? You had the perfect opening to give me shit and you didn't?"

"I'm turning over a new leaf."

She rolls her eyes. "Anyway, can you please tell us what you're having now?"

Violet shares a look with me and I nod. "It's a girl!"

The room erupts, and the rest of the day we're surrounded by the people we love.

I'm standing at my father's grave, a place I haven't visited since we laid him to rest in the back corner of our family lot. I just couldn't find the strength to stand before the man I would never measure up to.

This morning I woke before Violet and looked at the fresh snowfall out the window, immediately remembering this day when I was a child. This was my father's favorite time of the year, the first snow. He would say it was like a fresh start to a whole year. The ground was new and you could use that time to change things so when it melted, it went down to the roots.

I kissed Violet's forehead, rolled out of bed, and got dressed to come here and say some things I needed to say.

I brush the snow off the top of his headstone and sink down, resting on my heels. "Hi, Dad," I say, my throat thick with emotion. "Been a while."

As if he doesn't know that.

My fingers slide over his name, and I continue talking. "After you died, things sort of just existed. Mom, me, the world—it was as though while we were here, we were lost, which I think caused me to stay away. I didn't want to tell you any of it. I didn't want to tell you that I was failing you," I admit, hating the words and the truth in them. "You always told me it was my job, as a man, to take care of the women. I didn't really understand it until you were gone."

That was when my life went from one extreme to another. My mother needed me to be strong, to take care of her and make sure she was happy. I've tried, and I think I've done a good job at it so far, but it's been a struggle.

"I'm doing my best, Dad." I sigh heavily, closing my eyes as my hand sits on the cold stone. "My life is mirroring yours in so many ways, and I'm afraid," I admit. "I know I'm not half the man you were, but I want to be. I'm back with Violet, sort of like you and Mom. You guys fell in love when you were kids and were together until death did you part. She's pregnant with a little girl. While the baby isn't biologically mine, I'll raise her as my own, the same as you did with me. I pray the similarities in our life events end there," I say, speaking the worry into existence. "If you could keep an eye on us, that would be great."

I can almost hear his laugh, telling me that each man makes his own destiny, but he'll definitely watch out because that's what dads do.

He was always good with the one-liners, always quick to offer advice that never sounded like it. Sometimes I find myself quoting him, and I can't help but smile.

I exhale, my breath coming out heavy, causing a cloud to form from the heat and cold mixing. "I should get back to her so she doesn't wake up alone. I'll come again soon, Dad. I'll bring Violet and the baby. Maybe someday Mom will want to come, too, but I hope you know that we love you and miss you." I rise, resting my hand over his name.

"Thank you for everything."

CHAPTER 35
VIOLET

My phone buzzes, and I see it's from Dylan.

I get up, moving quickly upstairs to find Everett. He was shoveling all morning as we got another dumping of snow—something I did not miss—and hopped in the shower right after.

"Ev?" I say, stepping into the bathroom.

"Are you coming to join me?" he asks from behind the curtain with a chuckle.

I wish that were the case. "Not this time. I got a text from Dylan."

He pulls the curtain back. "What did he say?"

"I don't know. I haven't opened it."

I've been waiting, and waiting, and waiting for him to make his statement. I don't know what the hell the holdup is. Catherine and Ana suspect he's making sure his story is bulletproof, or he's just a chickenshit.

I'm going with option two.

"Open it. No matter what, you're going to be fine."

My stomach is tight, and it has nothing to do with the baby this time. Anytime Dylan's name is anywhere near me, it's never good.

Dylan: Vi, I'll be releasing the statement tomorrow. Here is a copy of it. I was also informed the divorce will be finalized within the week. I hope you and the baby are well. ~D

AGAINST ALL ODDS 297

"It's the statement," I tell Everett.

He shuts the water off and exits, wrapping the towel around his hips as the water runs in rivulets down his hard chest. Yeah, I really do wish I was joining him now.

We walk into the bedroom, and I sit on the bed, him beside me.

"Do you want to read it?"

"Not really," I confess.

"You don't have to."

Yeah, that's not going to work either. Whether I read it now or when it's sent to me a hundred times, I'm going to end up seeing it and having to deal with whatever it says. My only hope is that it doesn't cause more attention to fall on me and the baby.

I've had enough press bullshit to last me a lifetime.

Everett places his hand on my back, and I look up into his warm brown eyes filled with encouragement and unrelenting love. I can do this. I can read and know that no matter what it says, I have the love and support of a man who loves me.

"I don't have to, but I'm going to because it changes nothing for us," I tell him.

"Absolutely nothing."

I nod and then read aloud.

> After much thought and consideration, I have come to the difficult conclusion that it is within the best interest of my child and ex-wife to relinquish any paternal rights. I am not ready to be a father, and I fear my continual absence and inability to provide a stable environment will inflict more harm than my presence will help. Because of that, I have chosen to take some time to enter a therapeutic rehabilitation center to become a better man, as my recent actions have proven my selfishness and immaturity. My goal is to come out of this period of self-reflection changed for the better. I want to profoundly apologize to my ex-wife for the pain my actions

have caused her, and I hope that by doing the right thing, she can find peace. I ask that she and I be given privacy during this time.

I have no idea how many times I read it, probably ten, before looking up at Everett.

"How do you feel?"

I shrug. "I'm not sure."

"He apologized."

"He's playing to the sympathy of people, but…yes, I guess he did."

And maybe that's the best I'm ever going to get. A press release apology that could or could not be false.

But I find myself not caring. I can put him and this entire thing in my past. I'll have the baby, Everett, and the ability to build a life with someone who loves and wants us both.

"If any of what he said is real, then…he did the right thing."

"He did the right thing when he signed the papers. Regardless of the reasons, he did what was right for her and for me."

"He's allowing you to heal."

That's where Everett is wrong. He didn't allow me anything. Dylan's actions didn't give me confidence or the strength to face any situation.

I reach out, resting my hand on his cheek. "I think I was already healing."

He smiles. "You were?"

"I still am, and do you know why?"

"I'm going to guess it's because of a very sexy, very smart, very capable, and very good-in-bed man that happens to love you beyond measure." He shrugs. "But that's just my guess."

I laugh, and my heart is so full it could burst. "I think…your guess is pretty accurate. I mean, I'm not sure, but I'm going to go out on a limb and say it's part of it."

Everett turns, rolling me to my back, holding his weight above me, and that towel that was tucked around him is loose.

"I've got a piece of wood that's growing," he teases.

I reach my hand down, finding his cock and wrapping my fingers around it. I stroke up and down. "Hmm, now let's see how hard we can get it."

Then he shows me. Oh, how he shows me.

"Why am I blindfolded?" I ask as I move down the hallway.

"Because I don't want you to see."

"I figured that much. Does this have anything to do with the fact that you sent me shopping with Hazel for six hours yesterday?"

I love shopping, don't get me wrong, but after a while, I just wanted to lie down. This week we officially moved all my belongings in. Well, when I say *we*, I mean Everett, Killian, Lachlan, and Miles.

I was instructed to sit and relax.

Which I didn't really do because I couldn't handle it.

"You really aren't great at surprises." He chuckles.

After the last six months of my life, it's no wonder why. Each surprise was more like getting hit on the head with a baseball bat.

"Give me a hint," I say as he shuffles me down the hallway.

Everett sighs. "Just…go with it."

"That's not really my thing."

"I'm aware."

I don't love the hint of exasperation there, but I keep that part to myself.

"I swear, Everett, if you took your dumbass friends' advice and put an Ultimate Frisbee simulator in that bedroom upstairs, I might kill you."

Yes, that was the debate during the move, which room he could dedicate to some simulator that Killian is working with a company to create. Since we have extra bedrooms, they thought we should knock down a few walls to really give it a chance.

I threatened homicide.

The conversation stopped.

Until Miles suggested that we use my grandmother's house, since it's vacant until we decide what to do with it. Since, you know, the sport is ever growing, we could turn the entire house into a game park.

That was when Everett made up some bullshit about his mother and asked me to check on her.

"I mean, it isn't fully that."

I groan. "Everett."

"Just a few more steps. And stop." He grabs my shoulders, maneuvering me this way and that. "Okay, come forward."

I take two steps and inhale. The smell is faint, but instantly recognizable. "Paint?"

"Yes, there is paint." He chuckles. "All right, I'm going to take the blindfold off, but only if you promise not to kill me."

Ugh. He did make that damn room.

I feel him behind me, his hand moving up to the tie around my head. Slowly it loosens, and then I gasp. "Oh my God. What? When?" I look around at the room, cream colored with soft hints of pink and purple. There is a crib in the center with a sheer curtain cocooning it. It literally looks like the dream nursery I showed Hazel. "How? How did you do this?"

There is a changing table against the far back wall and the plush, incredibly expensive rocker that I had to be removed from just yesterday.

This makes no sense.

"Do you like it?"

Tears fill my eyes and I blink them away, not wanting to miss a single detail. "Everett...you...this is incredible."

He smiles and pulls me deeper into the room. "Hazel said you weren't sure on the bedding, so I don't have that. You can decide when you're ready."

"This is exactly like I pictured, but how? I just told her yesterday." Everett wraps his arms around me from behind, his head resting on my shoulder. "I was at the store and the guys were here. I had painted this room when you were in California. I got the crib and the dresser. I just didn't know what you'd want for a theme or whatever. When you showed Hazel that photo, I was able to buy it all and get to work."

I shake my head, amazement running through me. "You...I don't even know what to say."

He kisses my neck. "Do you like it?"

"I love it," I say immediately. "This stuff is so expensive."

Everett chuckles. "Violet, I'm a doctor who does well and saved a shit ton of money because I live in a house that's paid for. But all the money I have or don't have doesn't matter when it comes to us. I wanted you to have the nursery you wanted. Besides, little Brunhilda will need a pretty place to come and hide."

I snort a laugh. "We are not naming her that."

"I'm really partial to it."

"Well, you can visit your cat whenever you need to say it."

He turns me, taking my hands in his. "All right, what name do you have in mind?"

This is something I've been thinking a lot about. My name has deep meaning to my parents. My mother's favorite color and flower are violets, but it's a derivative of nature and the earth, which they loved. As much as my parents aren't the models I want to mirror for parenting, I do like that a name has something deeper.

"I've been trying to find something that represents us."

"And you think Brunhilda is a bad choice?"

I roll my eyes. "Be serious."

He laughs. "All right, I'll put it on the back burner. Tell me, what do you think represents us?"

My hand rests over his beating heart. "Hope, love, second chances, a phoenix who is reborn."

Everett leans closer and kisses me softly. "Do you want to name her Hope?"

I shake my head. "No, I want the meaning of her name to be more specific."

"Why am I now worried?" he jokes.

"Well, there was no way I could pick the name I loved thanks to your last name."

"My last name?"

He looks confused, as though the baby wouldn't…oh, he didn't think the baby would take his last name.

It looks like I'm not the only one getting a surprise, it seems. "Of course, it's our baby."

"But we're not married."

I smile, moving my hands up his chest to loop around his neck. "We're not, but that doesn't diminish the fact that I want to spend my life with you. A ring or a marriage license isn't what makes a marriage."

He laughs again. "Actually, I think it does."

"As someone who has been married, I can promise, it doesn't. Love is what does. Commitment, trust, and compromise are the marriage part. The rest of it is just stuff."

I had the stuff before and it did nothing to keep my marriage together. I'd much rather what we have than a ring and a man who doesn't honor it.

Everett pulls me tight against him—well, as tight as we can get with my ever-growing belly.

"And what name do you want our daughter to have?"

"I loved the name Imogen—it means second chance—but Imogen Finnegan was…cruel."

He shakes his head. "Yeah, could you imagine her in school?"

"God forbid she has even the slightest ginger hair to her—it would be a disaster. Trust me, kids are the worst. I see it daily."

Even in high school there are some nicknames that these kids can't recover from. I'd like to make sure I don't give them any ammunition. "No Imogen, then."

"I loved the name Brynn, too, but again, if they shorten her last name to Finn—nope."

"Please tell me we have a possibility here," Everett implores.

I smile and nod. "I have one, and if you like it, I really would like to put it on the short list."

"Okay."

"Courtney."

Everett tilts his head to the right a little, almost as though he's testing it out. "Courtney Finnegan."

"It's cute, right? It's Irish, which is a bonus with your last name, and I think it's so pretty. We can call her Court or Courtney if we don't shorten it," I explain quickly, hoping he doesn't hate it.

"I love it."

"You do?"

"I do. You know, I love you and Courtney with everything I am." He releases me and takes two steps back. "I have known a lot of things. For example, I knew, deep in my heart, that you were coming back after you left for California. I knew that I loved you from the first time I saw you." Everett sinks to his knee in front of me, removing something from his pocket.

"Oh God," I whisper as he reveals a beautiful diamond ring. A different one than his mother's, which I have been wearing daily since he gave it to me.

"I knew as I stood at my father's grave that I had everything I could ever need. I know this feels fast, but at the same time, it's taken forever. We've wasted fifteen years not being together, and I don't want to waste another minute. I love you. I want to marry you, have children with you, wake up beside you, and fall asleep with you in my arms. I've loved you for as long as I can remember, and I will love you until the day I die. Will you marry me?"

I sink to my knees with him, my hands holding his face. I didn't expect this. I didn't need to be engaged, but I need him. Everett is the other half of my heart and soul. He's the reason that I know love exists, and there is no one else in the world I want to spend my life with. I nod, tears streaming down my face, and I say the single word he's waiting for.

"Yes."

EPILOGUE
EVERETT

I'VE SEEN ALL THE MOVIES AND SHOWS OF A FATHER FREAKING OUT when the woman says, *It's time*.

I always thought they were freaking idiots.

That was until it was my woman.

It's not just because I was elbow deep in a cow as I was trying to get her to birth her calf, but because Violet apparently didn't want to bother me while I had an emergency call.

Yes, because my fiancée thought it was better to let her become an emergency.

Now I'm driving balls to the wall to get to the hospital before she has the baby.

"Relax, Everett. It's fine. Violet is doing great and I'm here," Hazel tries to reassure me.

"I should be there."

"Well, you're not and it's fine. Again. She's not pushing. She's like, seven centimeters, and you have time."

That does nothing to reassure me. I've seen a birthing animal go from one to one hundred in minutes.

Almost to punctuate my worries, Violet screams in the background. "Ohhhh shiiitttttt, I can't do this!"

Hazel makes a noise. "Gotta go. Hurry up."

The rest of the drive, Hazel does not answer the goddamn phone, and I'm losing my ever-loving mind.

I finally get to the hospital, tear my sweatshirt off, throw on a new one that doesn't smell like a barn, and rush inside.

As I pass by the front desk, I toss my keys to the security guy. "If they come to tow it, just move it for me."

The guard gives me a weird look. "Sir, this isn't valet!"

I shrug. "Can't talk, I'm having a baby!"

This place is a maze, and I spend five minutes trying to find the labor and delivery wing, and when I finally get there, I can hear her.

"Where is he?" Violet screams. "I can't stop this!"

"It's okay, Violet. He'll be here," Hazel says reassuringly.

"Sir!" the nurse yells.

"Violet Stewart, she's the one yelling."

The nurse nods and I rush toward the sound.

When I open the door, Violet's eyes widen and the amber color brightens. "You made it!"

"I'm here. I'm so sorry, baby. I'm here." I enter the room, shooting a scathing look at my best friend, who did not call me immediately when my girl's water broke, and I rush to Violet's bedside.

Dr. Cowles clears her throat. "Violet, you're now ten centimeters, and the baby is coming. You're going to need to push."

I lean in, kissing Violet's head. "She's coming, baby. You're doing it."

She makes a face. "You stink."

"I didn't have time to shower, love," I say a little defensively.

"I know, but you smell and I'm in pain and I need you. Come here," she implores. "I need to kiss you."

I'm not sure what to think at this point, but this has been her mood the last five weeks. We go from one extreme to another in a nanosecond. I move toward her and kiss her softly.

When I pull back, there are tears in her eyes. "Hey, no tears."

"We're going to have a baby."

"I know."

"I'm not ready. What if I'm not a good mom? What if I'm like my mom? What if she doesn't like me?" Violet fires off her fears, and I brush her sweat-dampened hair back.

"We are ready. You're already an amazing mom who is nothing like your own, and no one who has ever met you doesn't love you. Courtney will be no different."

She sniffles and then a contraction hits, her hand gripping mine so tight she might break bones. My jaw drops and I want to say something, but dear God, I really need my hand to work.

It ends quickly and I pull it back, shaking it out. "Jesus, that hurt."

That causes every pair of eyes to turn to me, all three women, and I realize I am probably going to get hit with something. "I realize now that was stupid."

The doctor raises a brow. "Yes, very." Then she looks back at Violet. "Next contraction, push."

Violet's head rests to the side, staring at me. "What if I don't know what she needs? What if she hates me as a teenager?"

I smile. "What if you're her best friend?"

She scoffs. "No teenager loves their mother."

Hazel raises her hand. "Umm, I did. My mom is the best."

"See, Hazel loves her mom and Hazel is…normal?"

Hazel flips me off and looks to Violet. "Look, if she's a hellion, we'll blame Everett, okay?"

Violet laughs. "That sounds good."

"Yes, let's all blame Everett," I joke.

Violet sucks in a breath, and I take her hand in mine again. "You can do it, Vi. Push."

She does that, and the doctor keeps encouraging her. "Good job, a little more."

The contraction ends, and Violet looks run-down. She's panting, her hair is matted to the side of her head, and she closes her eyes. "This is terrible. Zero out of ten stars. Do not recommend."

I laugh softly. "It'll be worth it," I promise.

"Says you."

"I know, I have no idea what I'm talking about, but just think—all of this is for Courtney."

Saying her name causes Violet to go all soft. The anger and frustration disappear, and I see a woman prepared to battle.

"Here comes the next one. The baby is close to crowning, push hard," Dr. Cowles instructs.

We keep on this way, Violet pushing, taking a break when she can and going right back to it. After another ten minutes, her breathing is labored and she looks close to tears.

"I can't do it, Everett."

This woman still doesn't know her own strength. "You can."

She shakes her head. "No, I can't. She's not coming."

"She is, baby. She's coming, but she needs you to be strong for just a little more." If I could bear this for her, I would. Holding both her hands in mine, I bring them to my lips and kiss them. "You are the strongest, most amazing woman I know. You have conquered so much, and nothing can stop you."

"I hate you," she says. "I really do. I want to give up and you're not letting me."

I smile. "No, I'm not."

She looks down at Dr. Cowles. "Please tell me she's closer."

Dr. Cowles nods. "She's right there. Just push through this next contraction."

"You said that last time," she grumbles. As it hits, she grabs my hands as tight as she can, puts her chin to her chest, and pushes.

"That's it. That's it, Violet. The head is out. Breathe."

"It's out?" Her eyes widen and she looks to me.

"Yes, just a few more pushes. You can do this."

The contraction comes on faster than the last, and the love of my life gives it all she has. "She's out!" I tell her as I see the doctor twist and pull the shoulders.

She wipes at her, and then the most beautiful wail I've ever heard fills the room. Violet is pushing herself up a little, her eyes misting, and Dr. Cowles places Courtney on her chest.

Violet holds her as the nurse wipes the baby, and I stare down at them.

"Everett," Violet calls. "Meet your daughter."

My God.

My heart.

My world will never be the same again.

I'm holding Courtney in my arms, wrapped up in her blanket, shielding her from the wind. Violet is holding my arm as we move slowly, since she's still a little sore from giving birth five days ago.

All of us are quiet as we make the walk to the grave.

This will be my Violet's first time out here and only my second since his death.

There is a lot of emotion, but also a sense of peace. I'll introduce my father to his granddaughter, like I promised him I would.

"Are you okay?" Violet asks me.

I look down at her with a soft smile. "I'm sad, but okay."

We talked a lot about this moment, coming here together, and Violet was really who encouraged it. She wanted my father to meet Courtney and for me to get to talk to him about her.

We approach the clearing where the headstone sits. She places flowers and the plant we decided to put in the ground near him. Something that will represent Courtney as she grows.

After doing that, she returns to me and wraps her arms around my waist, adjusting the blanket over Courtney as she fusses. "I think someone is excited."

"Or hungry," I say.

"Or that, but let's pretend it's my version," Violet says under her breath.

I walk forward, crouching like I did the first time I came here. "Hi, Dad. I wanted to introduce you to your granddaughter. This is Courtney Ivy Finnegan."

The last word comes out almost choked. I thought I could get through this without crying, but it fucking sucks. It shouldn't be like this. My father would've loved her, doted on her, and spoiled her rotten. A rush of sadness overwhelms me.

Violet's hand rests on my shoulder, and I keep it together. "She's beautiful, Dad. She looks like Violet, so of course she is. While you may never meet in this life, I promise to tell her all about you, and I know you'll be checking in on her. Thanks for helping me throughout my life and showing me what real love is like."

I kiss Violet's temple and the top of Courtney's head.

This is more than I ever imagined, and I'm going to hold on with both hands.

Next is Killian and Tessa!
What happens when a one-night stand turns into a lot more?
Preorder: *Come What May*

———————

I wasn't ready to let Everett and Violet go just yet.
Turn to the next page for access to an EXCLUSIVE bonus scene!

———————

Have you met the other residents of Ember Falls?
All Too Well (Lachlan and Ainsley)
Here and Now (Miles and Penelope)

BONUS SCENE
EVERETT

"Courtney, don't touch that!" I say as my four-year-old daughter is reaching for the three-tiered wedding cake.

Dear Lord, if she knocks this over, Violet is going to kill me.

"Daddy, it's pretty!"

I nod, taking her hands in mine. "It is, and Mommy loves it very much."

"Mommy loves me and you," Courtney declares with all the confidence in the world.

"She does. She also made me promise you wouldn't get into trouble before the wedding."

Which is comedy in and of itself.

Our daughter is…well, me at her age.

I was wild, unwilling to compromise, and trouble.

Which is Courtney.

"I love my dress, Daddy." Courtney spins and the skirt flows around her.

I smile, loving how carefree she is in this moment. "I'm glad. You look very beautiful."

She stops, coming to me and putting her hands on my stomach. "You look beautiful too."

I squat down, coming face-to-face with one of the loves of my life. "Do I?"

Courtney nods. "Yup."

"Good. Are you almost ready to do your very important job?"

Courtney is the flower girl who takes her job very seriously. Last night, before bed, she spent a good thirty minutes explaining how she was going to walk, put petals down, and then stand like a big girl next to her mommy and daddy.

I'm pretty sure it was all a part of her master plan to avoid going to bed. She's very smart and manages to bend me to her whim when she's got a goal, which is always avoiding sleep.

"Yes, and I can hold your hand?" Courtney asks.

"After you walk down the aisle with Colston," I tell her. Lachlan and Ainsley's little boy is our ring bearer and only six months younger than her, and they are best friends.

Well, as much as four-year-olds can be or until he takes her toy, then forget it.

"But then I can hold your hand?"

I smile. "Yes, honey, then you can hold my hand and Mommy's."

That last part doesn't seem to excite her since she's a Daddy's girl through and through, which suits me just fine.

Courtney has brought more love and warmth into our lives than we could've imagined. She's smart, playful, a handful, but she's my heart and soul. I can't imagine this world without her and I'm grateful I never have to.

"And who is this little girl?" My mother's soft voice calls from the open door. She's dressed in a soft blue dress and her hair is curled, the majority of it is now gray, but she looks beautiful.

"Hi, Mom, this is Courtney, my daughter."

Courtney walks over to her grandmother and smiles. "You know me, Nana!"

My mother nods slowly. "Oh, yes, Courtney, hello, my sweet girl."

We've done our best to make Courtney a daily part of my mother's life and some days, she knows who she is immediately.

Other days we have to gently remind her and wait for her to remember a piece of the past.

Courtney, even not fully comprehending the scope of the situation, knows that sometimes, Nana has a hard time remembering things and we always have to be kind when that happens.

"I'm going to walk down the aisle to Daddy and I have to walk with Colston and drop flowers."

My mother smiles. "That's a very important job."

Courtney straightens her head with a grin. "I know."

I chuckle. "All right, monster, why don't we bring you to where Aunt Hazel is and you can wait with her until it's time."

"Can I go with Auntie Ana? She said she would do my makeup."

Absolutely not.

"Of course she did," I grumble. "No, Aunt Hazel is waiting for you since she's going to walk in front of you."

Courtney sighs heavily. "Okay, fine."

On any other day, Hazel is Courtney's most favorite person in the world. She spoils her rotten, gives her anything we say no to, and loves to take her to the park or anywhere she wants. There is no one in Ember Falls—other than me and Violet—who compares to Hazel.

Until Analeigh shows up.

Then, it's hats off and we all rank below her absolutely unhinged aunt who has zero discipline when it comes to Courtney.

I knock on the door where all the bridesmaids are hanging out and the door opens a peek, Hazel's green eye poking out. "What's the password?"

Courtney giggles. "Boogers."

"Boogers?" Hazel asks. "Yours or mine?"

"Yours!" Courtney says.

I huff. "Really, Hazel?"

Hazel opens the door a smidge more. "I think we should change the password to Daddy's boogers."

Dear God. "Don't encourage her."

She smiles and pulls the door open enough to grab Courtney and pull her close. "Says the man who would've done the same thing. Now, give me the girl and you go get to the front of the church."

"Bye, Daddy!" Courtney says with a grin and then she's gone.

I need new friends.

I walk to the front of the church where Miles, my best man, Lachlan, and Killian are standing in a circle.

"There's the groom," Killian says with a clap on my shoulder.

"Cold feet?" Miles ask.

"More like a lunatic best friend and a menacing daughter."

Lachlan laughs. "I know that all too well."

Yeah, he would. Rose is in that horrible teenage phase where she hates everyone and everything. I'm really not looking forward to that time in the future.

"I have to admit," Miles says as he rests an arm on my shoulder, "I didn't think you'd be the last of us to get married."

I really didn't either, but it wasn't something Violet and I were in a rush to do. We've been honestly just happy and living our lives as though we already were married. It wasn't until Courtney asked that we felt like maybe it would be a good time.

Violet had one shit-ass marriage and it was kind of a feeling of if it wasn't broken, there was no need to fix it.

We were committed, happy, and raising our daughter.

"Well, we're here now," I say, slapping Miles in the stomach. "Is everything set?"

Lachlan nods. "The girls are with Violet, her parents—yeah—they're settled over there. How the hell did someone so warm and wonderful like Violet come from them?"

I snort. "You would've loved her gran. She was the best."

Miles bobs his head slowly. "She was."

"Well, I think it's time to get your wagon hitched," Killian says as he's looking toward the door.

Sure enough, the wedding planner, aka Tessa, is waving and tapping her wrist.

About fucking time.

I'm so ready for her to be my wife. Not that we haven't spoken a form of vows in one way or another since we found our way back to each other a hundred times, but this is—official.

We line up, Miles turns to me, brushing my jacket, and then gives me one curt nod. "Make her happy."

"I already do."

He grins. "Make her happier."

I roll my eyes. "Thanks."

"You're welcome."

I turn around and watch the procession of the bridal party. First is Ainsley who smiles at me as she turns in. Then comes Penny, who winks. Then Hazel who flips me off under the bouquet so only I see it.

Classic.

Then comes Ana who blows me a kiss.

After that, is the most important people in my life.

Courtney, in her white dress with lavender flowers, comes, dropping petals one at a time and actually placing them down where she wants them, and takes her time approaching.

The assembly laughs as Courtney puts a petal down and then goes back to it, adjusting where she wanted it, and Colston grabs her, now almost dragging her down the aisle.

Courtney, who does not do well with being told what to do, yanks her arm out and goes back to her task.

I squat down. "Courtney?"

Her soft, amber-colored eyes find mine. "Daddy, I have to fix it."

I smile. "It's perfect, come on."

This doesn't seem to make her happy considering the pout on her face, but she takes Colston's hand and now pulls him down and stops at me.

"You did great," I tell her and she beams.

The music changes and the double doors open, revealing the most beautiful woman in the world.

Violet is there, in an ivory-colored silk dress that drapes around her chest. She didn't want to be given away, since she isn't anyone's possession, she's her own woman and she's coming to me freely.

She stands there, like a fucking queen, holding court over everyone here. Her long brown hair is half up with a veil that's longer than her dress behind her. She smiles at me and I return it.

Then she slowly makes her way to me.

My heart is pounding with each step she takes, a mix of excitement and desire thrumming through my veins.

Courtney glances up at me, her hand reaching for mine. "Don't cry, Daddy."

I didn't even realize I was, but sure enough, there are tears leaking from the corner of my eyes.

She's just so perfect. Everything about Violet is made for me. Her smile, her eyes, her soft heart, the way she loves without hesitation. She's the sun and the stars and everything that makes up the world I exist in—for her.

I would die for her happiness and comfort.

After what feels like the longest walk ever, she's in front of me.

"Hello, husband to be."

I grin. "Hello, wife to be."

She looks down at Courtney. "Your flowers are the best ones I've ever seen."

Courtney shakes a little with glee. "Daddy made me hurry, but I wanted them perfect for you."

Violet nods. "They were."

I reach my hand to Violet and she clasps it, Courtney holding our entwined ones.

The reverend speaks and then we recite our vows, the ones that thousands of couples have said, and in what feels like an instant, we're married.

"I now pronounce you husband and wife," he says. "You may kiss your bride."

Violet eyes me, knowing that she didn't want a spectacle, but also well aware I don't give a shit.

She's my wife. She's the star of today and everyone is going to see just how much her husband loves her.

I reach for her, taking her in my arms and dipping her back. Her hands fly to my chest and she laughs. "I knew it."

I grin. "Kiss me, wife."

She moves her arms around my neck and laughs before we kiss each other.

After the catcalls die out, I put her back on her feet and we make our way out of the church.

When we get to the end, I kiss her again. "You have made me the happiest I've ever been, Violet."

"More than when we had Courtney?"

"Not more, just even more, if that makes sense."

It's not that I'm happier than then, just that my scale for happiness has grown even more. I didn't realize things could get better and then they just keep going.

"It does, I just wonder…what could top this?" Violet asks, her hands gripping my lapels.

I look around at my daughter who is running around outside in the sun, the church filled with our friends and family are starting to file out, and I have the woman I love in my arms.

"Honestly, not a damn thing."

Violet smiles. "Nothing?"

I shake my head. "No, this…this is everything."

"Well, I think I have one thing and it'll be here in about seven months."

My eyes widen. We've been trying for about two years now for another baby. It's been hard watching her month after month not conceive. Dr. Cowles assured us that everything was fine after a battery of tests.

Finally, about four months ago, we decided to stop trying to try and just let our life be whatever it is.

"You're serious?" I ask, the joy I didn't think could become any greater builds.

Violet grins. "I am. I wanted to tell you a few weeks ago, but wanted to be sure."

"You're pregnant?" I require the words.

"I'm pregnant."

I lift her up, kissing her and turning her around. I hear Courtney yell, "Me too, Daddy!"

I laugh, setting my wife down and hoisting Courtney up, wrapping my arms around them both.

I kiss each of their cheeks. "I love you so much."

Violet rests her hand on my cheek. "We love you, more than you'll ever know."

ACKNOWLEDGMENTS

My husband and children. I love you all so much. Your love and support are why I get to even have an acknowledgment section.

My assistant, Christy Peckham, you always have my back and I can't imagine working with anyone else. I love your face.

Melanie Harlow, you have no idea how much I cherish our friendship. You are truly one of my best friends in the world and I don't know what I would do without you.

My beta and editing team: Salma, Nina, and Catherine. Thank you for loving me and these characters. You all made this book better and pushed me hard. Thank you.

My daily writing loves: Lauren Blakely, Laura Pavlov, and Natasha Madison. This little group of misfits is my favorite thing in the world. You have no idea how much I love you guys.

My agent, Kimberly Brower, thank you for having my back and always being on my side.

The team at Sourcebooks, my editor Christa, thank you for believing in this story and my work. I am beyond grateful.

The entire team—Maddy, Meagan, Tori, and Kayla—who support me, rally behind me, and keep me actually functioning.

James, my editor, for taking such great care with my story. My cover designer, Sommer Stein, who deals with my craziness. My proofreaders: Julia, Michele, and ReGina.

To my author friends who are truly the best support system I could ever wish for. Thank you for showing what women uplifting women looks like. Catherine, Elsie, Lena, Amy, Willow, Laura, Kandi, Rebecca, Samantha, Amber, Kennedy, and so many more.

Every influencer who picked this book up, made a post, video, phoned a friend…whatever it was. Thank you for making the book world a better place.

ABOUT THE AUTHOR

Corinne Michaels is a *New York Times*, *USA Today*, and *Wall Street Journal* bestselling author of romance novels. Her stories are chockfull of emotion, humor, and unrelenting love, and she enjoys putting her characters through intense heartbreak before finding a way to heal them through their struggles.

Corinne is a former Navy wife and happily married to the man of her dreams. She began her writing career after spending months away from her husband while he was deployed—reading and writing were her escape from the loneliness. Corinne now lives in Virginia with her husband and is the emotional, witty, sarcastic, and fun-loving mom of two beautiful children.